READERS TALK ABOUT RICHARD EVANS

Richard Evans' first book, *Deceit*, is a five-star thriller that brings the Australian political process to life. — *GOODREADS*

I absolutely loved it, couldn't put it down. I would love to see your book become a movie. — *IAN S., MELBOURNE*

Richard Evans first book in the Democracy trilogy was compelling. — *GOODREADS.*

Rich in ideas and provokes much thought about our parliamentary process, abuses of power, corruption, and the need, at times, for ordinary people to step up and take a stand in the name of honour and professional integrity. — *NADINE D., EDITOR*

This is an outstanding debut from Evans, and this terrific read comes highly recommended.' — *GOODREADS*

From former Federal MP Richard Evans comes this exceptional political thriller debut, which serves as the first part of his Democracy trilogy.' — *CANBERRA WEEKLY*

I adored Gordon O'Brien. Straight as an arrow amongst those who are only in things for themselves, I couldn't help but cheer him on as he was like a dog with a bone, searching out the truth' — *BJ'S BOOK BLOG*

Just finished reading *Deceit* and it was gripping; I could not put it down. It was brilliant. I just loved the book and can't wait to read *Duplicity*.' — *FORMER CLERK OF VICTORIAN LEGISLATIVE COUNCIL*

I thoroughly enjoyed the book and did not want to put the book down, but neither did I want the story to end! Congratulations! — *TRINITY MARKETING*

ALSO BY RICHARD EVANS

Democracy Trilogy
Deceit
Duplicity
Doomed

Non-Fiction
The Australian Franchising Handbook

FIRST NATIONS NEVER CEDED SOVEREIGNTY

FORGOTTEN PEOPLE

IS CULTURE WORTHY OF REVOLUTION?

RICHARD EVANS

852
PRESS

First published in 2020 by 852 Press,
an imprint of Corven Pty. Limited
Suite 208, 5-11 Cole Street, Williamstown Victoria 3016 Australia
www.852Press.com

10 9 8 7 6 5 4 3 2 1

National Library of Australia Cataloguing-in-Publication entry:

Author: Evans, Richard
Title: Forgotten People / by Richard Evans
ISBN: 978-0-6489328-0-2 (paperback)
ISBN: 978-0-6489328-2-6 (ebook)
ISBN: 978-0-6489328-1-9 (hardcover)

 A catalogue record for this book is available from the National Library of Australia

Australian fiction.
Cover Design: Working Type, www.workingtype.com.au
Internal design: Working Type
Cover Image: Photo by Warren Wong on Unsplash, https://www.facebook.com/wflwong/

I am not an indigenous person and this work of fiction does not, and could not, replace an Indigenous voice.

I would like to acknowledge the Traditional Custodians of the land now called Australia and pay my respects to Elders past, present and emerging. I extend my respect to all Aboriginal and Torres Strait Islander peoples.

My friends inspire me.
One friend inspired this story — I share her passion for justice.

PROLOGUE

No one heard a thing.

No bracken rustled, no stick cracked, no gravel shifted. There was nothing. They lazed about the fire, some under blankets, others sitting on plastic chairs or boxes, a few snoozing in meagre humpies. The night was crisp, and most dozed, weary after another long day defending ancestral lands. Miller noticed Aunty Mary's head jolt back driving her off the stool, upending it.

'Aunty Mary? Are you okay? What happened?' Miller shoved up from her bedroll and hurried over to check on the woman everyone called Aunty. As she bent over, she felt a sharp bite on her calf, and slapped the bug away, checking her hand for its remains but seeing blood, lots of blood.

'RUN.'

Silence no longer mattered, the men hidden at the edge of the clearing opened up with rapid-fire weapons, smashing the mob's signs, smashing lean-tos, smashing tents, smashing bones. Miller heard the rolling echo cross the valley as she crashed uphill, barbs tearing at her. She kept running until she reached the ridge, stumbling down the other side, breath rasping.

The destruction stopped at a command and then from the silence someone asked, 'Did we get 'em all?'

'I think so, Commander.' A large man stood and entered the clearing, dressed in black, a balaclava obscuring his face. 'Shall we burn them or bury them?'

More black-clad men entered the camp site, weapons at the ready.

'Burn the equipment. Throw the kaffirs in the river. Give the crocs a feed.'

The men combed the killing field for evidence of failing life, finding none. Like any elite military unit, they organised themselves, some dragging bodies to the nearby river bank while others tossed junk onto the fire, the flames and wafting embers reaching high into the overhanging trees.

'Pity there's no wind, we could start a bush fire,' joked the big mercenary. 'Nothing left of their precious land then.' A few comrades chuckled.

'We're here to do a job, McGuiness,' snapped the commander. 'Let's get it done and start back to the rendezvous point. It's a long way, so remain focused. Plenty of time for jokes later.'

'Yes, sir. Sorry, sir.'

§

Miller couldn't run anymore. She crashed over a log and lay there, panting, then wriggled under the fallen giant, caring little what might be sharing the small, damp space. She listened and waited for the sound of heavy footsteps, but the only thing she could hear was a pulse pounding in her ear. In time, when her breathing slowed, and anxiety weakened, the lair became a bed.

Warmth roused her. The sun was high, ants scurrying across her face searching for food and anything else she offered. The buzz of frenzied flies nearby was the first sound she heard. Miller crawled from her hideaway, brushing and flicking insects, grubs and dirt from herself, as she left her burrow stopping to listen and checking about.

Nothing.

She was stiff and sore as she stretched to stand, then collapsing as a sharp pain in her calf crippled her for a moment. An ugly gash along her calf had congealed with bugs wriggling in it, a blowfly extending its stay until she flicked it away. After testing the leg a few times, she assessed it was sturdy enough to walk, albeit little by little. She wanted to bathe and dress it, but options were limited.

Miller twisted onto the log to survey the landscape, searching for familiar markers. She figured what was left of the camp site must be back over the hill behind her; the stench of acrid smoke meant it was close. She gazed out over the valley, over a stand of forest and rough terrain, squeezing a smile, feeling good about what she could see. The land of her ancestors provided a deep sense of spiritual wellbeing.

Cautiously, slowly, painfully, she crept back up the hill, alert for unusual shapes or sounds, thanking her father for the skills he had taught her. 'Stay low, blend in, become one with the land.' She collected as much spider web as she could on her way back to camp, just in case.

She reached the edge of the clearing late in the day and waited. She studied what was left of the family's camp but could hear or see nothing other than the charred remains of equipment in the smouldering ash-laden fire, a trail of smoke filtering high into the trees.

Miller took a deep breath and stepped out into the clearing, tense, rigid, listening for any sound of aggression. She circled the clearing, watching, searching for any sign of her family.

Nothing.

Her mob had been at the site for a week, working and playing together. Their plan had been to stop the wrecking machines consigned to build essential services for a mine that would scar the landscape and drive away ancestors' spirits. They intended to take as long as was needed to prevent the works. Diamond deposits had been found years earlier and now the prospectors wanted a mine to extract the rich vein of valuable diamonds. First the government, then the courts denied the traditional owners' rights to stop exploratory mining that had been undertaken to assess potential yield of the deposits, and now the miners were coming.

Traditional owners demanded sacred sites be protected; they explained sites were used for ceremonies and spiritual connection, but the government rejected their submissions. The courts dismissed claims of native title, determining the almost extinct language and diminishing cultural links to the land meant there was no authentic connection to qualify their claim, so the sole action left for the Umbakarta people was to fight to protect ancestral lands. Their strategy was simple enough: deny access to the excavators. To them, no access road would mean no mining. They hoped any delay would convince the government to rethink its policy and support them. Now, Miller stood alone; she was all that remained of her people.

She walked to the river's edge and dribbled water onto her wound, keeping an eye out for crocodiles, then sat cross-legged, back straight, facing the streaming water, humming and reciting a spiritual chant to her forefathers. Once the wound was dry, she packed the spider web she'd collected into the wound, resuming her chant until the sun set.

'Miller? Is that you? Where is everyone?'

She jumped. 'Who is it?'

'It's me, Jimmy. What the hell happened? Where is everyone?' Miller's cousin hurried from the clearing down to the river.

'Where have you been?' asked Miller, scrambling to her feet. 'Why weren't you here?' She stepped back, moving away, heading toward a clear escape path.

'What's wrong? Where are the others?'

Miller sucked in a breath, filling her lungs to calm emotions, then another. She was trembling, unable to say what she thought might have happened. 'You said you would be here; where were you?'

'I was in town buying supplies . . . you know that.'

'Dave always manages supplies,' Miller said, circling back into the camp site. 'You never like handling food supplies, you hate it. You administer the money, so why now?'

'Miller, don't be like that, come here. I had nothing to do with this tragedy.'

'Yeah?' Miller cocked her head. 'So, what tragedy are you talking about?

1

FIVE YEARS LATER

The scratching whirl of the overhead fan slinked into Miller's consciousness as she roused from sleep. It was already hot, her cotton sheet was damp. She rolled over to gaze out across the balcony onto the empty beach. It called to her, so she jumped up, grabbed her sarong and skipped along the thin sandy trail until it opened out onto the cove. The waves were gentle, so she dropped her wrap and ran in until she met a wave, diving through it, flipping onto her back and spouting water.

This was the unsullied life she cherished, untouched by Europeans and seldom shared with the peoples from nearby islands. A life as it should be with little care for economies and markets. The worries of the warring countries to the north were of little interest. She didn't know them; their disputes were of no concern to her. She was in country and that was the most important thing to her.

She stood her ground, looking back to shore, letting the small waves break over her. Her father must have been a visionary to have built their shack so close to the beach, and although she now lived by herself, she was happy with the simple, yet sturdy building. Unless you knew where it was, nobody stumbling onto the beach would be able to find it.

The tide was out, exposing a fringing reef, so Miller went fossicking for a meal. She had left a piece of metal wedged between rocks, to

5

prise shells from the reef whenever she needed a feed. The reef was overrun with breakfast and soon Miller had heaped enough onto a rocky outcrop. She collected her sarong gathering the shells into a ball then strolled back, picking up a sea cucumber she noticed on the way.

Once back at the shack she unhooked a pot dangling from the ceiling, half filled it with water from the overflowing rainwater tank before putting it on a gas burner. She rinsed the shells in a bucket before tossing them, with the cucumber, into the pot to boil for five minutes. While she waited, she stepped outside to the rudimentary latrine, turning on the shower, sluicing salt from her skin and soaping her hair, before rinsing in the warm water. As she patted herself dry she felt the scar on her calf. It had taken a long time to heal and still looked nasty, the pale gash contrasting with the dark honey colour of her skin.

She came to visit her father's house whenever she needed to re-energise her spirit, which happened more often over the last five years. The loss of her family was like a heavy sludge upon her soul, dragging down her thinking. Sometimes, she spontaneously wailed when she thought about them, distressing those about her. It was still raw for her, often feeling answerable for what happened and uncaring. She had a duty to avenge what had been done; she just didn't know how, or what she could do, until a few months back concocting a plan.

After breakfast, Miller relaxed in a chair with a glass of her special mix iced tea, enjoying the noises of country. Always a perfect moment for her.

The peace was cracked when she heard a male voice call from near the end of the dirt track. 'Hello.'

Miller kicked out of her seat and crept to the edge of the verandah to try identifying who was calling.

'Hello, Nellie?' The call came again — then there was a pause before the call was repeated. 'Hello?'

'Wooy,' Miller called back, hoping to catch a glimpse of who it might be.

'Hello?' The man was tramping closer.

'Wooy.' Miller couldn't yet see any movement through the bush. 'Yes — I'm here,' she called. 'Come through, follow the trail.'

It wasn't long before Neesham appeared. 'I thought you might have been here. Don't you ever answer your phone?'

'No reception out here. Well, at least that's my excuse.' Miller stood with hands on her hips inspecting Neesham walking toward her. 'What do you want?'

'Yeah, nice to see you to, cuz,' Neesham said, sauntering to the steps. 'Do you want to, maybe, put some clothes on?'

'Hasn't bothered you in the past.'

'You were a kid back then.'

'Don't tell me a naked woman frightens you,' Miller laughed as she retreated to wrap the sarong around herself. 'I sometimes had my suspicions about you.'

'You don't scare me . . . but I'm here on business.'

'Do you want anything to drink?'

'A tea would be nice.'

'A tea?' Miller laughed. 'Now I definitely have my suspicions.'

'Get stuffed will you and put the kettle on.'

'I have iced tea; will that do?'

'If you made it, and it's not processed crap, then that'll be great. Do you want a hand?'

'No. Relax and I'll be right back.'

Neesham stepped up onto the verandah, placing his bag beside a wicker chair collapsing into the cushions as Miller moved off into the kitchen. 'I have serious business to talk to you about.'

'Oh yes?' Miller called from the kitchen as she prepared the chilled tea. 'It must be important for you to come all this way on the off-chance I might be here.'

'It is.'

'Sounds ominous,' said Miller as she returned, handing Neesham a glass, plonking herself on the cushioned lounge. 'What's troubling you?'

'I've been approached by the government about a couple of things,' Neesham said, before taking a long draught of tea.

'What do those flakes want?'

'Well, it seems they're concerned about you.'

'What have I done that should concern them?'

'You do and say things that concern Homeland Security.'

'What a joke. We don't have a homeland.'

'They reckon that's their issue,' said Neesham as he took another mouthful, placing his glass on a wooden crate beside him. 'They reckon you're stirring up trouble talking about wanting to create a homeland.'

'The Congress have had the idea as part of their strategy for yonks, but they never act on it.' Miller swung out of the lounge and sauntered back into the kitchen as Neesham's eyes followed her, switching to the ugly scar on her leg. She picked up a bowl of chopped vegetables and nuts and brought it back, offering it to Neesham to select a nibble, before resting it on her lap as she lay back on the lounge.

Neesham bit into his carrot stick. 'We have been debating the idea for years, but Congress is yet to agree on anything. We can't seem to get past what it means and where we should claim — too many traditional owners want to have a say. They want to stay close to their land and don't want others sharing Country.'

'A homeland wouldn't override native title claims; it would complement it.' Miller crunched on some nuts. 'A recognised homeland gives us identity and place. It shouldn't matter who the traditional owners are, we should be able to work with them. Claims in other parts of the country can remain as valid as they are today. I don't see a problem.'

'The government sees a problem.'

'They want our land to extract riches from it; to rip it open and feast on it. They never give anything back. They are killing us and our culture, and it's been like that for years.'

'That's ridiculous, the government is not killing us.'

'Time is killing us, Jimmy,' Miller shoved the bowl away, sitting forward, 'they stole our land — no problem, they did that in other countries they conquered — the trouble is, they've forgotten us. We didn't resist them tough enough when they arrived, and we've been paying the price ever since.'

'We resisted, we still do — I do.'

'You know something, Jimmy, if I was at Warrane all those years ago, fucking Phillip would never have come ashore.'

Neesham avoided her gaze. 'Yeah, maybe,' he smirked, 'fact is, they did come ashore.'

'We have been done over by every government ever since. It's even worse now with their false promises of reconciliation and closing the gap.'

'We are making significant steps getting what we want; it just takes time.'

'While you blokes talk, talk, talk and fucking talk, our culture dies, and we just become the dregs of the country as every other immigrant group that comes here generates greater benefits and acknowledgement from the government. Squatters, the lot of them.'

'That may be so, but we have to work with what they've given us.'

'That's the point, Jimmy,' Miller perched on the edge of the lounge, 'we accept their handouts and get nothing more from them. Why not fight and take our country back?'

'This is the type of language they have a problem with. They reckon you are stirring up trouble amongst the community and want you to stop pushing this idea of revolution.'

'I'll stop when we get action from the government.'

'No — you'll stop now. The Council of Elders has withdrawn your membership.'

'They can't do that; I represent my mob.'

'Your family no longer exists. The Elders have insisted you need to wait until you are of age to take your place at Congress.'

'That's bullshit. Why?' Miller stood creeping to the edge of the verandah, squinting out to the beach.

'The elders believe you are speaking the language of hate, on social media especially. We hear you're recruiting some sort of secret mob.

They believe you are stirring up too many spirits from the past — they say we have come too far to fight the battles of the past.' Neesham also stood and faced her. 'They see the young listening to you and rejecting the elders' proposals for reconciliation and building respect through dialogue and negotiation.'

'Gee, hasn't that worked well for the first three hundred years.'

'We now have the Congress, which is arbitrating well, and our needs are being acknowledged by the government. We influence laws affecting us and elders are treated with the respect they deserve before the commonwealth parliament.'

'You don't think they treat the elders' days in the parliament as anything but tokenism, do you? They sit with the senate for a few days? So, what? They meet with us, we have members sitting in the parliament, so what? It hasn't solved a damn thing.'

'It's been an important step to recognition — it's what we agreed to do when we were proclaimed acknowledgment in the constitution.'

Miller stepped away, shaking her head.

'We are close to getting a treaty signed.'

'Then what?' Miller snorted, turning back to glare at Neesham, arms crossed. 'All our troubles will be over?'

'This idea of a homeland may have merit, but it will never be sanctioned by the government.'

'Of course, it will never be approved by the government — they would lose credibility and respect if they did,' Miller barked. 'We have to take it from them.' A bird screeched, others fluttered away at the sound of her voice.

'We'll get it. It just needs time.' Neesham tried appeasing her.

'Talk, talk, fucking talk — that's all you ever do.' Miller wished he would leave.

Neesham was cautious, 'Nellie, they know you are asking around about weapons.'

She dropped her head shaking it then squinted out to the beach again.

'They want me to satisfy myself you're not dangerous.'

'Dangerous?' Miller shook her head and brushed a tear from her cheek. 'Was Mandela dangerous? Was Gandhi dangerous? Was Pancho fucking Villa dangerous?'

'Just assure me you are not planning anything crazy.'

'Why don't you go back to your cosy nest of thieves and continue to get fat and lazy while your brothers and sisters remain forgotten by you and your mates. Our people are struggling, and you lot do nothing but appease.'

'I work hard for them.'

'You know that's crap.' Miller turned and ripped her sarong away, tossing it on the lounge. 'You have done nothing, and our culture continues to be the loser. Now, fuck off.' She skipped from the verandah, heading for the beach.

⁋

A few hours later, as night darkened the waters, a fishing boat puttered into the cove. Miller, waiting on the beach, flashed her torch a couple of times and the vessel changed direction, navigating toward her. As it neared the shore an athletic man jumped off the bow with rope in hand, heading for the shore, searching for a solid mooring. The skipper shut down the engine and waddled from the wheelhouse to the bow.

'Ahoy there,' he growled.

'Are you from Moresby?' Miller stood at the water's edge.

'Where else would I be from, lady? I've got a load for you — where do you want it?'

'On the beach is fine.'

'Try not to leave it out too long; the salt and sand won't do the mechanisms any good.'

'I'm leaving first thing, it'll be okay.'

'Do you have me money?'

'Come ashore and we can settle up.'

'Not that I don't trust you, lady, but I'd prefer you come aboard.'

The young man had waded back to the boat and was passed a large grey plastic chest, which he hoisted onto his shoulder, striding back to shore, dumping it near the tree line. He returned and lifted Miller onto the boat as if she weighed no more than a child.

'Strong boy. Where did you get him?'

'He's from the mountains. He got sick of eating his neighbours, so he came to work with me,' laughed the skipper. 'Now he's a vegetarian. Go figure.'

'Yes, yes — very funny,' Miller dismissed him. 'I have your money; I suppose you want to count it.' She tossed a plastic-wrapped wad of notes to him.

'Lady, if it's not all there then I'll be back for it, and you.' The skipper snatched at the wad and waved her to sit as he walked back to the wheelhouse, tugging a bottle of dark rum and two glasses from a shelf. 'Fancy a drink, love?' He filled the glasses and offered one to Miller. Not a shot, but a half glass. 'Here's to international business.'

The skipper held out his glass and Miller clinked hers before following the skipper's lead, swallowing the load. She coughed as it burned, but it felt good. The old man poured another.

'If I need you again, I'll be in touch,' Miller said, tossing back the glass before slipping over the side.

'You don't want to stay for a bit of fun? Maybe a quickie?' The skipper squeezed the front of his trousers, a scheming grin on his grimy face. 'You look as if you could do with one, and it's been a while ...'

'I don't screw dirty, old white, fat bastards, but thanks anyway.'

The skipper cackled as he resumed his position in the wheelhouse, restarting the engine. Miller loosened the mooring and the trawler headed out to sea as the deck hand hauled in the rope. She didn't bother waving and turned to the chest, dragging it up the beach to the hut, where she unfastened the clips, lifting the lid.

The greasy smell of stiff waxed paper thrilled her as she tugged apart the wrapping. Her first discovery was a body armour unit, which she dragged from the chest, tossing it onto the lid, eager to get to the foam-encased lethal weapons below. She hauled a handgun from its mould, toyed with it gingerly, then gripped it in a firing position before placing it on the body armour. Next, she dragged the entire foam casting from the chest, placing it beside her pulling aside more greased paper, revealing an encased M4 carbine, the preferred weapon of most military special forces. It was lighter than an M16 and she had no trouble pulling it from the chest.

Miller stood and held the weapon up to see it better in the fading light. She chuckled as she put it aside and dug deeper into the chest. There she found 240 rounds of green tipped bullets, two 30 round magazines, eight M61 hand grenades, twelve blocks of Semtex plastic explosives and three remote detonators.

Miller stood and admired her cache then did a little animated dance on the spot.

'Let the revolution begin.'

2

The Umbakarta people had never given up their demand for the recognition of their traditional rights and resisted every attempt to include them in the project; it wasn't about money and ignored the government's requests to kow-tow. No offers of money, entreaties or special programs could switch the thinking of the elders. When the United Aboriginal Congress directed them to acquiesce under threat of disqualification and banishment from the Karrakatta, even this heavy-handed approach did not convince the traditional owners to conform.

They wanted their Country protected.

Then a week before the scheduled start of site works the group disappeared. No one was able to explain what happened — they just disappeared. The Congress continued to be perplexed by the government's lack of action and failure to investigate the disappearance of fourteen people. There were theories, rumours and conjectures, but no substantial evidence other than Nellie Millergoorra's claim of a massacre, with her leg wound the solitary evidence of the lethal gunfire used to rid the site of whining natives.

The campaign to stop the mine was abandoned and with the Karrakatta acting as trustees for the traditional owners, approving the mine in return for a substantial annual contribution toward its operating costs. The mine went into full production two years after construction commenced, and the economic yield improved as the mine began producing quality gems; Koning Mining's share price improved with every new batch of quality stones released to the market.

The second shift of the day was due to start when Miller pulled her Colorado into a gap on a hill overlooking the mine. She had left the access road a few kilometres back and brought her arsenal as close as she dared. The sun was blazing low in the sky causing a bead of sweat to trickle to the small of her back; the heat would dissipate as darkness swept across the land. Miller estimated she had forty-five minutes of daylight left to reconnoitre the area.

She hopped from the cab and sat on the metal bull bar to scout the site with military binoculars, identifying points of access and security checks. The workers' accommodation was sited by the East Alligator river some kilometre from the mine's underground cage portal. Staff in offices positioned closer to the site were finishing up for the day and strolling back to their hub. Vehicles were scattered throughout the site and she couldn't see any sign of the 120 listed miners.

Her plan was simple enough — blow the crap out of it.

Years earlier Miller travelled to Papua New Guinea for training at a mining school in the highlands, which didn't ask too many questions. Now she was ready for the retribution she needed to cleanse her soul. She felt little empathy for the workers who might be injured by her impending attack — her family hadn't had a say in their demise either.

Once the sun was gone she organised and prepared her equipment, beginning with the explosives. She stowed the three devices into a knapsack, checked her carbine and armed the handguns.

She was ready, and in six hours she would go to war.

¶

The dull soft shrill of her wrist timer snapped her up, scanning for unfamiliar shapes outside the vehicle. Satisfied, she stretched and forced a yawn before stepping from the cab. The air sent a shake through her as she dressed in a black drill shirt followed by the armour vest and webbing. Next, the holsters from the back of the truck, clipping the belt before checking the handguns, loading a round into each breech, snapping on safety and securing them in each holster. She then slung her pack of explosives and other equipment onto her back, checked her carbine, loading the breech before heading off over the ridge. She had an hour before the second ten-hour shift ended, allowing a four-hour window of opportunity before the scheduled start of day shift.

The sky was cloudless with the half-moon brightening the terrain. Avoiding movement across the horizon Miller crawled, edged and clambered down the hill toward the mine. As she reached the clear graded site the cranking mechanical noise of the elevator engaging startled her. She ducked for refuge behind a mound of soil and before too long voices were heard and she counted off heads as they began their stroll back to the accommodation hub. The elevator returned for another three trips and she watched, counting the miners as they placed their tags onto the shift board confirming they had ended their shift and were out of the mine.

Thirty minutes after the last miner logged off, the floodlights and the ventilation compressor switched off and the mine fell silent. Miller waited another thirty minutes before stalking to the elevator shaft. She slid open the railing and stepped into the cage, prodding the down arrow; the machine engaged. It was the longest two minutes she could remember before the cage bumped to a stop. She pushed at the railing, opened the cage and stepped out into total darkness, her breathing rapid and sweat now dampening her fatigues.

Miller tugged out a LED head torch from her webbing, settling it on her head, switching on the power. The beam was bright, lighting up the tunnel, casting dramatic shadows against the walls. She knew from her training what she needed to do and loped off to secure the charges. Her first, the farthest from the mine entrance, a hundred metres along the tunnel. As she counted off her paces she squeezed past equipment and warm machinery. The air was thin and mixed with gaseous smells. She struggled for breath by the time she reached her designated point of detonation. Dropping the knapsack from her back, Miller dragged out the first charge and pressed it against a ragged edge of the tunnel, setting the detonator to activate in sixty minutes. She checked her watch and scooted back fifty metres to lay the next charge.

Miller surveyed the area noticing a transporter ten metres further along the tunnel. She clambered onto it, reaching up toward the roof. She was just too short so dropped back to the floor searching for something she could stand on. A wooden truss was leaning against the machine and she figured she could use it to push the charge onto the ceiling. It would be difficult, but the explosion would be more effective if the second charge was attached to the roof of the tunnel.

She scrambled back on top of the transporter and stood on the highest point before setting the detonator for forty minutes. She balanced the charge on the truss and raised it to the roof, prodding the malleable plastic explosives into the rock. Once it took hold she patted the truss into the bomb to make sure it would stay in place. Satisfied, she dropped to the ground and trotted off to the cage where she would place the last charge. She had twenty minutes to get to safe ground before her fireworks kicked off.

The damage to the mine would be disastrous, but she knew Koning would be back to recover the mine and recommence production. They would not give up, but she needed to send a message and enjoy her retribution.

9

Security at a mine site relied upon its remote location and the risk factors associated with production. Australia had a secure economy, was free from insurgencies, unlike Africa and South America. Apart from the weird environmentalists who chained themselves to machinery or climbed trees, there was little to concern companies extracting minerals. Diamonds and gold were a different matter. Security teams were often engaged to protect workers from anyone with criminal ambitions.

Koning Mining, a South African company, shipped in their own security — former special services personnel — to provide a safe worksite and protect the company's assets.

Conan Messaris was fading in and out of sleep when he caught the faint sound of the cage machinery being activated. He strained to listen, tossing a pillow to his colleague, Terry McGuiness, snoring on the other side of the room.

Messaris stumbled out of bed, turning off the air-conditioning unit as McGuiness struggled up to an elbow, grumbling. 'What's going on?'

'I can hear a machine.' Conan stepped out into the night to listen and establish if there was movement amongst the sheds. 'Get dressed and let's explore the hub. We'd better arm up.'

'Yes, sir.'

Hurriedly dressing in fatigues, they went to a more solid structure at the back of their quarters, heaving open a heavy door, unlocking a cage and stepping into an armoury. They stripped chains from a rack of M16s and tugged two from the housing, before clipping a magazine into each weapon, stashing two more in their clothing. They each grabbed a nine millimetre from the cabinet, buckling the holster, before locking up and walking off toward the site supervisor's room.

'Do we need to wake him, Commander?'

'Why should we have all the fun?' smiled Messaris. 'Besides, he may have early starters in the mine.' He thumped on the door as he shoved it open, turning on the light, startling the sleeping manager.

'Have you anyone in the mine this morning?' Messaris demanded.

'What?' The manager struggled to understand the intrusion as he grabbed for his glasses. 'What the hell do you want?'

'I said, do you have anyone scheduled in the mine this morning?'

'No, now nick off.' The manager tossed his glasses away and thumped back into the pillow, tugging the sheet over his head.

Messaris retreated, leaving the light on and door open. 'Let's go check the tags; someone may have wanted an early start.'

The two men stalked along the service road to the mine, checking for signs of movement and listening for uncharacteristic noise like restless animals. As they reached the mine clearing they slowed to listen and scan for movement. When they considered it safe, they crept to the entrance. They identified no absent name tags on the board and could hear nothing, but the cage was missing in the portal.

'You think someone might be down there, Commander?'

'Must be.' Messaris cocked his weapon. 'Why else would the cage be down below? Let's wait to see who comes up.'

'How many do you reckon?'

'Your guess is as good as mine. There could be one, or there could be thirty,' Messaris said, walking over to the gate and checking through the wire into the shaft below, seeing nothing. 'What are they doing is my question.'

'Taking produce?' McGuiness suggested.

'If they are, then we had better check the grading shed.' Messaris stepped off with the M16 resting on his hip. 'Give me a whistle if they start coming up.'

'Yes, sir.'

Messaris headed for the grading works, careful not to startle any unexpected visitors. As he neared the building he dropped his weapon into a fire-ready position, creeping forward. He was confident there was no one about — the lights were off and there were no flashing torch beams, but he checked the doors and windows anyway, confirming no forced entry. They were all in the mine, whoever they were.

As he returned to the portal, the cage engaged, pushing the two men back a safe distance into the darkness. They sidled away from each other providing a wider firing perimeter.

¶

Miller now had fifteen minutes to clear the site. The charges were set to fire with ten-second delays for maximum impact on the tunnel structure, collapsing walls and weakening the roof. She reckoned if she hurried she could be back at her truck before the chaos after the first charge exploded and back on the road within the hour.

She tossed her knapsack aside, discarded her light harness and entered the cage, shoving the button to start the two-minute ascent. She cocked her weapon and flicked the safety off her handguns.

As she began clearing the shaft she checked her watch; she had ten minutes.

'Hold it right there.'

The call chilled her as she unfastened the cage gripping her carbine. She couldn't see anything and didn't know who, or how many were waiting for her.

'Are you the only one?' The accent was South African. 'Is there anyone else in the mine?'

Miller raised her carbine pointing it out into the darkness.

'I suggest you lay that thing down and join it on the ground.'

Miller didn't move, her finger tensing against the trigger. She breathed deeply, readying herself for battle. 'What do you want?'

'I want you to drop your weapon and lie on the ground face down.'

'Or?'

'Or, I drop you where you stand.'

'My friends will be up soon; you can talk to them.'

'Bit hard when the cage is still here, arsehole.' A second voice barked to Miller's right, near the dirt mound.

'Drop your weapon before the count of three,' Messaris demanded, watching her. 'One!'

Miller aroused a favourite movie trope — fire before the end of the count.

'Two.'

She had a rough idea where they were and didn't care about the outcome. Either way, there was just minutes before the explosion.

'All right! You win!' She yelled in a conciliatory tone, hopeful of disarming them for just a moment. Her finger tightened, engaging the carbine in rapid fire toward the voice before switching to the aggressive voice by the mound. As she blasted away she scurried toward the mound. The response was immediate and noise severe as the fizz of M16 rounds zipped passed her. She hit the dirt behind the mound, scrambling to the top to peer over, directing her fire at the source of the tracer rounds until the magazine emptied. She hauled a 9 mm from a side holster and plucked a grenade from her belt, tugged the pin and tossed it toward the men, then emptied the pistol's clip. The shooters dashed for protective cover.

The delay in engagement allowed her time to reload her carbine and she appeared above the mound then emptied the magazine across the clearing before heading into the scrub behind her, running up the hill until she reached the shelter of a rocky outcrop she'd identified earlier. She collapsed behind it, listened, then checked her watch. Two minutes. She reloaded her carbine with her last magazine and listened as the M16s cracked below with the fizz of rounds spraying the area about her. They didn't know where she was, so she waited.

The first blast was a rumble beneath the ground, like a distant rolling thunder. The second shook the ground like a deep earthquake and the third sent an angry roiling ball of fire and black smoke spewing high into the sky from the shaft. Miller grinned as she watched the fireball then detected the men running from the portal toward a four-wheel-drive truck. She needed to get the hell out of there.

As she reached the truck she stayed close to the ground and checked for movement. Detecting none she dumped her equipment into the back and jumped into the cab, tossing a handgun on the seat beside her. Her plan was to drive across country and reach the service track a kilometre or two before the bitumen road. She would then drive to Jabiru, refuel and head to Darwin. She engaged the ignition and it turned but didn't fire the engine. Her breathing quickened as she pumped the accelerator and tried again; this time the engine staggered into motion. She hit the accelerator again and the engine almost stalled before kicking into high revs. She cranked the truck into gear and sped off across country, putting distance between herself and Koning mine, between herself and Country.

She bounced and crashed across rough scrub, a cloud of dust following her. She hoped she could outrun her hunters by reaching the bitumen before daylight and then a three-hour run to Darwin. Within an hour she'd hit the mine's service track with the bitumen, not much further ahead, would make the going easier. As she changed the truck into two-wheel drive mode and planted the accelerator she began thinking about a celebration with friends in Darwin. She smiled at the thought now recognising that if her people were to win concessions from government it would take more than talk.

'That'll will show them.' A satisfied smile creased her as face she barrelled along the track.

Rounding a cutting, she could see lights from a vehicle up ahead, and at the next bend a heavy four-wheel-drive truck blocked the track. She braked, sliding to a stop, raising a thick cloud of dust around both vehicles.

As the dust settled, Miller scanned about, considering an escape route, but she was blocked by unforgiving terrain, so escape was not an option. Two figures stood behind the vehicle with weapons pointed in her direction. She considered her choices. Her weapons were in back and the 9 mm beside her was not up to the job.

'Get out of the truck with your hands up,' a darkened figure called.

Miller didn't respond.

'Get out of the truck, now!'

Checking for her handgun, she thought again about grabbing the 9 mm and rushing to confront them, in all likelihood with dire consequences, deciding against it. She didn't know who was calling her out of the cabin — it might even be Territory rangers. She opened the door and dropped out into what remained of the dust cloud and walked to the front of her truck, hands on her head, waiting for further instructions.

'What the hell did you think you were doing?' a gruff South African voice demanded.

Two silhouettes came before the lights of the four-wheel-drive, prowling closer. She still could not identify them, but heard the sound of a cocking handgun.

'I'm not armed.'

'So what?'

Miller heard the loud bam and felt the thud in her chest lift her and slam her back onto the bull bar. She was unconscious before she hit the dirt.

3

'Does the defendant have anything to say before I pass sentence?' The words resonated throughout the packed court. The judge finished his address merely needing to pronounce sentence. Two years after Miller destroyed the East Alligator mine she now faced judgement. The body armour saved her life from the high-calibre handgun but hadn't saved her from the beating, which broke many bones but not her spirit. She recovered in Darwin before being transferred to Sydney for incarceration prior to the trial.

It was a long trial, culminating in a guilty verdict followed by various presentencing submissions made to the court, which was now waiting for His Lordship to state the appropriate sentence for the terrorist responsible for an act of terrorism against the Koning diamond mine and radicalising then recruiting twenty-three citizens to join a terrorist organisation. The case dominated national and international media; failed appeals made to the International Court of Justice in The Hague to prevent the federal government having a local court hear the case. Now after four months of evidence and submissions, the judge was about to declare the sentence, but waited for a statement of remorse or contrition from the defendant.

Miller hesitated, then defiantly rose to her shackled feet; hand-cuffed, she gripped the brass bar before her. She surveyed the court, triggering anxiety in the public gallery. Officers of the court doodled or shuffled papers as they waited — they'd heard it all before and, no doubt, would hear it all again. Just another angry high security criminal in ill-fitting green prison garb, with wild black hair pulled back into a severe knot.

'Your Honour, when First Nation people talk of Country it means very different things to them than white man's dictionary meaning. When we talk of Country, we mean the homeland of our clan, and we mean more than lines on a map. We mean the entire landscape and the spirits that awaken when called upon. Country for us is not just places within this vast continent.

'For me, Country means my family's values and ancestral bonds, the natural resources available to us, the stories and the cultural responsibilities we are obliged to fulfil. There is no wilderness in my Country, as described by some during this trial, it cannot be wild for it is our mother, our spirit, our being. There is no wildness in me, purely Country, and that means my entire being. Country gives my life meaning and is the basis of our ancient laws; it explains the origins of the natural world. All things are explained by Country — my Country.

'Your Honour, Australia lives a lie. I don't mean arrogance or disrespect to the court when I say this, but Australia does live a lie. It believes it governs its citizens without discrimination, and the government pats itself on the back when it says it protects the vulnerable within the community. Yet, I am being judged by white man's law, which will punish me for protecting my Country, and this is discriminatory.

'Government doesn't protect the vulnerable. Consider Aboriginal people and tell me there is no discrimination in the government systems supposed to protect us. Your Honour, why is that?'

The judge didn't glimpse up from his notes.

'My people continue to live in frightful conditions throughout this continent. The land belonging to my ancestors is no longer. We are pushed further and further into darkened recesses away from Country as the needs of the majority take precedence. We are conquered and have few rights, and little means to protect our culture and our Country. Our Country has been stolen for the benefit of the invaders. For too long we have been shunted into the background of Australian society. Now we say we must be allowed to live the way we want.

'Your Honour, over the last hundred and more years, traditional peoples around the world have reclaimed their lands from their conquerors. When this subject is raised or spoken about by traditional owners in Australia, our claims are ignored or ridiculed, never considered serious. Maybe we are ignored because it is difficult to obtain consensus when we have over five hundred Aboriginal nations, but this should not be the reason why my people are treated with such disdain and disrespect. Australia continues to ignore the claims of its First Nations. It disregards the oldest continuous surviving culture amongst all the many cultures in our world.

'This promised land of which Australians speak is now a lie for my people. We are three per cent of the population, but we are twenty-five per cent of the prison population because your laws, your police and your courts jail us. You say our country is young and free, yet my people die on average ten years before other Australians. We are not free to live our culture nor are we free to provide for ourselves like every other Australian. Our education rates are low, our health is poor, and this has been the case every year since whitefellas thrust a flag on Gadigal land of the Eora nation.

'We die — our culture dies — and you don't care.' Miller paused for a moment, surveying the room. Doodlers had stopped and turned in their seats to listen, spectators were silent. The judge scribbled notes, continuing to ignore her.

'My people are vanishing from the Earth. I am the last remaining member of the Umbakarta mob. And I'm the last because of the development of the East Alligator diamond mine. We objected to our country being violated, yet your laws and your parliament told us we did not exist, and our traditional ownership claim rendered worthless. We fought your way through the courts and we were defeated. We then fought our way, but regrettably, we were defeated when my mob were massacred.'

Miller's voice faulted. 'My people were massacred by your people and nothing has been said or done to concede this crime.' She brushed her cheek.

His Lordship slunk back into his chair, removed his glasses, peeking at the clock.

'We have vanished from our land and someday this will happen to all nations of our people, and our culture will be lost for all time. Yet, I know that if my people, the First Nations of Australia, were provided a homeland to call their own, taking responsibility for their own people,' the judge glanced at her for a moment, before his notes gained his attention again with a sigh, 'then we could take responsibility for ourselves and never again fall victim to government paternalism. We could reclaim and nourish our culture.

'If we were granted homelands then I'm positive my people would respond and pull themselves from the vice-like grip of poverty and provide us all with a future. But, we cannot achieve this goal alone, it is up to the government to act, something they will never do unless we as a people mandate it from them.

'Your Honour, is it wrong for me to love my own people? Is it wicked to think my Country is my family's because I was born where my parents, and their parents, and their parents lived? Is it evil for me, as some in your media have said, to wish to die for my people and my Country by protecting it as I did at the mine site? I am an Umbakarta Aborigine, and I'm proud of who I am, and of what I can do to save my culture. I was trying to save my culture and my Country when I took on Koning Mining. If protecting our lands and culture means we must fight and die as my mob has done, then so be it.'

'Miss Millergoorra, can I just interrupt you there,' the judge glared at Miller and she stopped talking. 'You have been charged with serious crimes against persons and property. You claim your family was massacred, but that is not relevant for these charges before the court. You have not shown contrition, nor have you provided information to authorities of other terrorist matters you have been involved. This is a place of justice not a pulpit for claims that remain unsubstantiated. Can I ask you to conclude your statement?'

Miller did not respond as she frowned at the judge who continued scanning his papers. Then through gritted teeth, she said, 'As long as injustice and gross inequality exist for my people, then I will continue to fight. If a government wishes to rob my people, then I will fight, and I pledge myself to fight against those who take advantage of us.

'I can assure you, Your Honour,' Miller almost sarcastic in tone, 'no matter where I reside I will always be fighting.' She stood back from the rail, resuming her seat.

The judge glanced up and smiled, satisfied it was over. 'Yes, yes of course you will, and you have plenty of time to think about it.' He then read a prepared statement, 'Nellie Millergoorra, you have been found guilty of committing a terrorist act and inciting citizens to perform terrorist acts. You are hereby sentenced to forty-five years' imprisonment with a non-parole period of thirty years.' The judge stood, and all court officers and some spectators stood. As he left the courtroom, lawyers bowed.

A silence lingered as the sentence was absorbed. Miller didn't move until corrections security led her down the narrow stairs from the prisoner's dock to the cells below for processing.

g

'Prime Minister? Mr Neesham is here for his three o'clock.'

'Come on in, Jimmy.' The prime minister walked around his desk, his hand extended in welcome. 'Very pleased you could come.'

'It's not every day you get an invitation to the parliament, Prime Minister.' Neesham stepped forward gripping the proffered hand. 'It's been a very long time since I've been in here; I like the new colour scheme.'

'Must have been more than twelve years ago — it was done before I was here.' Prime Minister Grobbelaar scanned the room. 'Might be time for a new design — here, grab a seat.' Neesham sat on the lounge. 'Would you like a tea or a coffee?'

The staffer waited for the order.

'Anything stronger?'

'Sure.' Grobbelaar checked his watch. 'What would you prefer, a brandy?'

'I'll have a beer if you don't mind.' The staffer went to a bar fridge tucked away in a cabinet and lifted out a bottle, flicked the off top and reached for a glass. 'The bottle's fine love, no glass required.'

'Prime Minister?' The staffer lingered after handing the bottle to Neesham.

'No, I'm fine thanks, Julia.' Grobbelaar sat at his rigid chair beside the lounge. 'How's the new building going in Alice?'

'We have designed it to try and keep most of it in open air. Sort of like a traditional meeting space with a roof.' Neesham glugged a long draught, then wiped his mouth with the back of his hand. 'We have a fire pit in the centre with strong updraft ventilation, so it will be very effective for Congress meetings.'

'That's great, I always knew you would get them organised.'

'It's like herding cats,' said Neesham, as he took another mouthful of beer. 'But, you'd know all about that, you suffer from the same problems here in the parliament.'

'It's a little different,' Grobbelaar scoffed. 'We know which side we're on.'

There was a slight uncomfortable pause as each waited for the other to speak. Neesham took another draught to mask his nerves.

'Jimmy, do you know why I wanted to see you today?'

'You're going to increase the funding for the Congress?'

'Not quite,' the prime minister laughed. 'Don't you have enough? I thought we increased your salary last year?'

'It's never enough for the things I want to do.' Neesham's tone hardened. 'You've had a good deal with me running Congress, but I suspect we could be doing more.'

'If we paid you more, Congress would achieve more outcomes?'

Grobbelaar sat back into his chair and rested a foot on the edge of the marble coffee table. 'I didn't realise your salary and Congress outcomes were linked.'

'There's plenty of challenges in retaining the secretariat leadership and sometimes it gets expensive to maintain the votes.'

'Jimmy, you have worked well with us and we want you to continue, but we don't have a money tree we can shake whenever you need cash.'

'Congress is showing signs of reviving the homeland idea, especially since the mining leases were extended to Koning. If you want me to curtail enthusiastic voices then perhaps you need to address the finance model,' said Neesham. 'Otherwise, I can't guarantee I can hold them back.'

'This is one of the reasons why I wanted to talk to you.' Grobbelaar stood and stepped to his desk, returning with a sheet of paper. 'I have been advised by the federal police that Millergoorra will be released this month. Her parole has been approved and she will be released into a transitional housing program for two months, then free to do as she pleases. She'll have a personal probation officer assigned to her for a couple of months to help her transition and keep her out of trouble.'

'Really?' Neesham put the empty bottle on the coffee table and sat back, spreading his arms along the back of the lounge. 'I thought we agreed she was going to do the full time.'

'International pressure. She's almost a celebrity amongst the liberals and the social justice darlings on twitter.' Grobbelaar referred to his briefing paper. 'She passed the discharge requirements with flying colours, which is in stark contrast to her application five years ago.'

'Time flies.'

'Especially when you have a movement campaigning for her release. They think thirty-five years is enough. After all, she's almost sixty — an old woman.'

'I can assure you, she isn't old. What does Koning have to say about it?'

'He's still a bit miffed.'

'Miffed?' Neesham laughed. 'It must have cost him millions.'

'It did. Now he reckons the site's production value is dropping and if he has to close it, he will. He wants to use the closure as a bargaining chip to secure coalmine licences.'

'He can't use his people like he did last time; that's not on.'

'Things change. He's older and wiser now, and willing to work with traditional owners.'

'I can help.'

'I heard.' Grobbelaar smirked at Neesham. 'According to files, you got a nice little earner out of that site.'

'As I said before, controlling the Congress takes money.' Neesham smiled back. 'If I didn't help Koning get the outcome he wanted, we wouldn't've got our campus.'

'That's true, and you wouldn't live where you do.'

'If it wasn't me then it would have been someone else,' Neesham countered playfully.

'I have no idea, I wasn't there. I just know you've become a wealthy and powerful man because of it.'

'Yes, you may well say that,' Neesham crossed his legs, 'I couldn't possibly comment.'

'I also know Millergoorra will be a handful for us. She's already received publicity about the mine.'

'How can someone get publicity when they're in prison?'

'According to this briefing,' Grobbelaar waved the sheet of paper, 'she has regular visits from Amnesty, Greenpeace and an organisation called WIAC, whatever that is.'

'World Indigenous Arts Council.'

'What do they do?'

'I'm surprised you haven't heard of them. They're a bunch of UN-based snowflakes who advocate the retention of Indigenous culture, art and language. They've been very successful in overturning decisions concerning ownership of traditional artworks. They were effective in having the British Museum return carvings and sculptures to the Fijian government.'

'No wonder I haven't heard of them.'

'They take their role honourably. They even have a program in Wales to restore Welsh place names.'

'We would never approve crap like that here, not under my government.'

Neesham sat forward. 'This is why the government needs to remain in control of the Congress. We can stop them from coming in and making the liberal lawyers richer.'

'You think Millergoorra would be promoting this type of activism?'

'I suspect she hasn't lost any of her fervour for Indigenous rights and justice.'

'How do we play it?'

'Release her on condition she go back to Country and not involve herself in other communities.'

'That'll never work,' Grobbelaar replied, frustrated. 'The mine Koning wants is in Arnhem Land.'

'No, trust me on this.' Neesham sat forward. 'She has family land there, she won't be any trouble. One way or another she'll do as I say.'

'If you can moderate her activities then I'll try and get money for your Congress.'

'Do better than that, Prime Minister, otherwise I might use her to drive unrest and then you'll be up shit creek.'

Grobbelaar eyed Neesham smiling grudgingly. 'Which ancestors are you tapping into right now? The Irish?'

'I'm always open for a deal.' Neesham sat back smugly. 'Now, how about that brandy?'

¶

A small crowd of journalists and interested supporters had assembled on the nominated day, uncertain of the exact time Nellie Millergoorra, the notorious terrorist, would step from Silverwater prison after serving thirty-five years. She had become a *cause celebre* after the controversial attack on the East Alligator River diamond mine. Recent demands to the United Nations for her release were attracting international attention and the government wilted under the pressure to release her.

Celebrities and even the UN Secretary advocated publicly that it was time for her release, given her crime was property damage with no loss of life and her ongoing incarceration was not in keeping with penalties for similar crimes in other countries.

Miller was taken from her cell during the morning. After thirty-five years her possessions could fit in a garbage bag: journals, a bible and a small woven doll presented to her ten years earlier by a departing inmate. All the possessions that had made her life easier were given to other inmates. She was taken to a dressing room where she was given an ill-fitting cotton frock from a used-clothing depot, uncomfortable underwear and a pair of cheap black Chinese sneakers. Her prison garb was taken from her and she was put in a holding pod to complete paperwork, the metal doors clanking behind her, a sound she had never become used to.

Once official papers and release forms were completed and signed, she was led through caged corridors until a door was opened and she was asked to step through. As she sauntered forward she lingered examining the correctional officer waving her through. 'Have a good day, Mr Hopkins.'

'You too, Nellie, all the best.'

And that was it.

The heavy door slammed behind her and she was out of the home that had taken more than half her life. She didn't know what to do. A small crowd was waiting outside the fence line, so she marched to them. She squeezed through the rotating metal security gate and was outside the complex. A sudden burst of voices calling her name, asking questions frightened her and she backed away.

A young woman pushed through the throng, stood in front of her and faced the media. 'Ms Millergoorra will have nothing to say until a press conference tomorrow at the Amnesty International offices in North Sydney. Until that time, please respect her privacy.'

Miller had met Simone O'Donohue a few times during visiting hours and was impressed by her assertiveness, particularly in someone so young. It reminded her of a time when she too cared about things. Now she just wanted to be left alone. Simone placed an arm around Miller's shoulders and led her toward a car waiting by the kerb. Once they were on their way, Simone turned from the front seat with a cheesy smile.

'Well, that was a little intense. How are you feeling? Excited?'

'Jumping out of my skin,' Miller reacted glumly. 'Where are you taking me?'

'The government has provided a community house for you. I've been assigned to manage you for the next few months and we are going to have a great time,' Simone said, beamed, almost crawling into the back seat. 'This is Reg, by the way; he's our driver whenever we want him. He doesn't say much, do you Reggie?'

The driver shook his head.

Miller wasn't interested. 'When can I go home?'

'In a month.'

Miller gazed out the window at the buildings flashing past and recognised nothing. She hadn't spent much time in cities before she was incarcerated, and it was all new to her. Not like the rain forests of her country and the sparse land of her people.

'Is there anything you would like to do?'

Miller considered the question and flicked through her mind the many things she hadn't done for decades. 'I want three things.'

'Shoot and I'll try and get them for you.'

'I want a long hot bath to try and get rid of this stench I have. I haven't had one for a long, long time.''

'I can manage that for you.'

'When I'm doing that, I would also like a few freshly squeezed juices. Not the bottle type they serve in prison. I would love a ginger and carrot, and a celery and apple. I haven't tasted mother's produce for years and I've missed her. Some nuts would be great as well.'

'That will be no problem,' said Simone grinning. 'Nothing else, a wine perhaps.'

'No,' Miller gazed at her and shook her head. 'The last thing I need is a phone and Jimmy Neesham's number.'

'Why do you need that?'

'I have a job to do and he can help.

4

The hidden house amongst the beach jungle was still there, nothing much had changed over the years. Friends and distant relatives lived there for short periods over the thirty years, holidayed and repaired it when needed, and Miller felt free once she stepped from the four-wheel drive recognising its roof amongst the foliage. The nearby community, almost fifty kilometres away, protected it, cared after it, and prepared it for her return.

'How do you feel?' Simone asked as they later stood on the beach watching out past the heads.

'I never thought I'd see this place again,' Miller murmured. 'I'm going to take a swim.' She hauled off her clothes, dropping them at her feet, turning to Simone. 'Coming?' then ran into the water, diving through a wave.

Simone was reluctant but surrendered after Miller was in the water, dropping her trousers and shirt, kicking off her underwear and running after her client. She dived in and stroked over to Miller who was treading water with a broad smile on her face. 'This is fantastic.'

'It was my life and helped me whenever I needed to renew my thinking.'

'Does anyone come here?'

'Not really. It's difficult to get to, so the adventure tourists never come. It's just me and whatever is about the place.' Miller floated back to shore and stood letting a few waves break over her.

Simone walked back to shore and sat at the water's edge feeling refreshed; she watched Miller cleanse herself, then collected her clothes and walked back to the lodge in search of a towel. Miller wasn't far behind, veering off to the outdoor shower and calling Simone to join her. The water was warm, and Miller reached for the shampoo left by a holiday maker.

'There should be towels in the cupboard over there,' Miller pointed to a wooden box. 'I prefer to drip dry.'

Back on the front verandah she said, 'Would you like a drink? There may be supplies here. I asked a cousin to stock up a week or so ago.'

'Do you have wine?'

'Maybe, I'll check. Come through when you finish.'

Simone wandered onto the verandah wrapped in a towel, shook the cushions on the lounge, collapsing amongst them. She watched as Miller appeared with a bottle and two glasses.

'My cousin has done a great job; there are supplies for a week or two.' Miller passed her a glass and splashed a generous measure of chardonnay. 'Did you enjoy the shower? It's great, isn't it? I've missed it.'

'It's just the best, and to have one out here is crazy.'

'Showers are the next best thing to a bath, don't you think? I made sure I had a gas resource to provide some of life's little luxuries.'

'Living out here would be terrific.' Simone took a sip of wine.

Miller lay in the other lounge and tasted the wine. 'It's more than living here though, it means much more than that.'

'How do you mean? I would have thought living out here would be the best thing for someone who wants to get away from the constant chatter of people.'

'It's hard to explain to anyone who doesn't get the connection we have with the land. Country is very important to me. I suppose if you are a Christian, then it would be the same as your god. It's like coming to church every day and living with God.'

'Really?' Simone thought about it. 'That's interesting — I've never heard it expressed in those terms before.'

'This is the problem — when native people are conquered, the dominant culture dismisses the culture of the conquered.' Miller took another mouthful.

'Is that always a bad thing?'

'Spoken like a person from the dominant culture.' Miller glimpsed over at Simone. 'I don't mean to be impolite, but what makes you think your culture and the way you live is superior to mine?'

'I have nothing to compare.'

'You do now, by being here.'

Simone didn't respond. She sat up and tugged off her damp towel flicking it over the end of the lounge. 'I suppose history tells us progress comes from building upon what we have.'

'On the assumption progress is good,' Miller smiled, 'on the assumption your laws are best practice and on the assumption your culture is the one to which we should aspire.'

'History says western culture is better.'

'In China? What about Japan? Look what western culture did in the Middle East, you can't tell me they left a positive mark. No, I reckon western culture has a lot to answer for.'

'What are the alternatives?'

'Give it back,' Miller sat forward and picked up the bottle from the table between them. 'More wine?'

'Yes please.' Simone held up her glass. 'The government won't give it back, they can't.'

'They did in Timor, Papua . . . even Mexico got their independence from Spain. So, why not here?'

'Australia would never give it back. America didn't.'

'We could if they partitioned a homeland.'

'Not probable, not with the current prime minister, and remember what happened in Spain all those years ago.' Simone sat up. 'Anyway, where would you establish a homeland? I bet you don't say Tasmania.'

'It doesn't matter, just so long we have absolute control over it.'

'What, just carve a block of dirt out of the country and call it something else?' Simone chuckled. 'Like Lesotho?'

'There's that example, but there are others,' Miller took a sip of wine. 'There is international precedent and that's the point.'

'What part of Australia are you thinking?'

'The whole lot,' Miller chortled but with an underlining serious tone.

'Never happen — anyway what would you do with the rest of the population?'

'They can immigrate somewhere else,' Miller sniffed. 'Norfolk Island sounds good.'

They laughed, and Simone drained her glass, reaching for a refill.

'No honestly Nellie, where would you do it? You'd have to try and get all your people to agree and that would be mission impossible.'

'The Northern Territory. It has desert and tropical regions, wetlands and established cities. Some of it is a virtual snapshot of what the land was like before you blokes got here.'

'I was born here.'

'Not you, your ancestors,' Miller laughed. 'this is what you blokes are missing, you have no roots anywhere. You have no ancestral connection with the land — and you never will. This is why nationalism is so important in Europe.'

'I'm not Australian?' Simone was sarcastic.

'Of course you are sweetie ... but Australia is a British construct — just like a satellite city — it has no connection to the land.'

'It'll never happen.' Simone stood and stretched as Miller watched her. 'What can I get you to eat?'

'There's a few pieces of meat in the esky we brought; that and a bit of salad would be great.'

'Is it kangaroo?' Simone placed a hand on her hip. 'I mean, we may as well get into the traditional foods.'

'Get stuffed, you cheeky sod.' Miller slapped her backside as she scurried past to the kitchen.

After a meal of salad and steak and another bottle of wine, the noise of the night settled around them with demands of travel catching up.

'I have one bed with a mosquito net and you're welcome to share it,' Miller said, yawning noisily. 'Otherwise, sleep out here, but put plenty of repellent on yourself.'

'I think I'd prefer to sleep with you,' Simone said, slapping at an insect.

'Do you snore?' Miller lugged Simone from the lounge staggering to the bed together. 'I do, mostly after a few wines.'

'I don't know, tell me in the morning.'

§

Jimmy Neesham liked the colonial building on the Esplanade because it conveyed a sense of grandeur and colonial privilege, his office overlooked Bicentennial Park and the Darwin waterfront. He didn't care for air-conditioning and the coastal breeze lifted the cotton curtains from the tall open windows cooling his office, and his mind. He'd established his headquarters decades earlier when appointed by the federal government to provide secretariat services to the United Aboriginal Congress, the increasingly ineffective gathering of the Indigenous nations. His position provided him with status and limited power to make decisions and act on behalf of the Congress; and yet, he wanted more — more money and more power. The government appointment meant he was available to meet with delegations — typically world leaders seeking photo opportunities — review policy and provide recommendations to government about new laws that might affect First Nations.

The annual delegation of influential Chinese businessmen made visiting Neesham a priority today. They will wine and dine him, hoping to continue their influence and maintain support for their investments in Aboriginal territory. It was Jimmy who opened doors for the purchase of Darwin Harbour, and it was Jimmy who helped them negotiate with traditional owners in far north Western Australia for the establishment of an open-cut iron-ore mine. The traditional owners were rewarded with the project, lavishly provided with housing and jobs for many families. Jimmy pocketed a handsome commission for his efforts. They considered him their man and he felt little guilt accepting their money. He had bills to pay and a lifestyle to fund. Unlike the government, the Chinese were generous and valuable supporters.

'Mr Jimmy, we are aware the government is seeking bidders for the underground coalmine proposed for Arnhem Land,' said Mr Teo, the leader of the annual delegation now assembled with his group around a table in Neesham's large office.

'I've heard that.'

'We can confirm South Africans will receive preference within the bid.'

Neesham was surprised. 'How do you know that?'

'We know everything. For instance, we know the government will approve the deal with the South Africans.'

'If what you are saying is true, then this will be good for my people in that region.'

'We respectfully request you ensure you block the development,' Teo said, without any change in tone or inflection. 'We believe it would not be in the interests of China or Australia for the South Africans to have access to the rich minerals in the Northern Territory.'

Neesham was stunned, involuntarily swallowing, his mouth felt dry. 'I'm not sure I have the capacity to do that.' Neesham cleared his throat, shifting in his seat. 'When it comes to mining policy the government doesn't listen to Aborigines.'

'Mr Jimmy, it is in our interests to lock the site up for a number of years, fifteen would be our preference, but ten years would be satisfactory.'

'Why?'

'We do not want a new coalmine producing for the international market. This will increase world supply and reduce prices for our own coal — you understand?'

'Yes, I see, but as I say, the government never listens to us on these matters.'

'We want this new development not approved.' Teo had not moved, his fine hands clasped in front, as he considered Neesham.

'I just said, we have little influence.'

'Mr Jimmy, you are not listening,' Teo forced a thin smile. 'We want you to assure us this mine will not be productive for ten years, at the very minimum.'

Neesham glanced around at the others, for the first time wondering if they spoke English. He nervously smiled. 'How do you propose I do that?'

'There are two ways we would prefer you stop the mine.' Teo raised his hand wiping his forehead with a precisely folded white cotton handkerchief. 'We will support your objection application to the United Nations.'

'I have no confidence that action would work, the UN is useless.'

'Again, you are not listening.' Teo lifted a leather satchel and tugged out a sheaf of papers, tossing it across the table. 'This is your application to the UN Environment Security Council seeking an injunction on the development of any new mine.'

Neesham stopped the sliding wad, scanning the contents. 'Impressive.'

'China will support the application and we will ensure the other permanent members on the council support your submission.'

'You have that influence?'

Teo beamed. 'Oh yes, we are the world power now and they listen to us.'

Neesham dropped his head and riffled the pages like a deck of cards. 'What's the second option?'

'You take ownership of the debate, which will explode in your media, and through native title negotiations you delay and defer as much as possible allowing the UN to consider the application and approve a treaty.'

'What makes you think it will explode in the media?'

'Mr Jimmy,' Teo sighed, 'we will drive social media debate, set up false advocacy sites and push the issue to the community. This is what happens when we want something done.'

'I don't have the room or the resources here for that sort of campaign.'

'We will do it from sites in China.' Teo muttered to the others and they laughed. 'We have been doing it for years.'

Neesham examined the men opposite, dressed in cream suits and dark ties, wilting in the heat. They had finished their glasses of water hoping for a quick resolution, so they could return to their air-conditioned rooms.

'What's in it for me?'

'There are two clear options for you to consider — one, if you get the project delayed we will pay you a personal commission of five million dollars.'

Neesham tried hard not to react to the news keeping his face still. 'That sounds promising,' he said.

Teo ignored the response, narrowed his eyes and with intent, said, 'If you don't stop the mine, then we will end our relationship with you and pass your file to the federal police.'

'What file?' Neesham gulped, checking about for water. 'What's in it?'

'Everything,' Teo said. 'You have been very generous to us, and in return we have been more than generous to you. Unfortunately, most of our relationship could be considered unethical and perhaps should be reported.'

Neesham nervously laughed, 'We don't have to do that.'

'Then I would suggest you devise a plan to delay the coalmine for a number of years.'

Neesham gazed at the men, considering options. Five million was not a bad little earner. He forced a broad smile, stood and leaned over to Teo with his hand outstretched. 'Gentlemen, I think we have a deal.'

§

Lewe Koning was a man who always got his way. He would bark instructions to frighten staff; he would shout at politicians to change policy; and, he used force when needed to ensure his interests were protected, sometimes lethal force. He had a reputation for doing deals with governments in Africa and funded a paramilitary unit to protect his interests throughout the world. His goal was to dominate world mining, retaining interests in diamonds, gold, iron ore and other minerals, and now coal. China was the biggest threat to his market share, but so too were governments he could not influence, and so he worked hard seducing politicians to ensure his needs were met.

Proud of his dual South African — Australian nationality, he understood when he dealt with successive Australian governments they were in the grip of collective community guilt. Guilt about the environment; guilt about climate change; and, guilt about the conditions in which many Aboriginal people lived on traditional lands. He argued this guilt impacted government policy, hampering development, and disadvantaging Indigenous Australians needing community and government support.

He was prepared to share the wealth of his mining interests, but he would never tolerate being told by the natives what to do.

In Africa he was harsh on the local people, but in Australia he recognised the need for a more nuanced diplomacy to achieve his long-term development plans.

His heart remained with his homeland of Eastern Transvaal in South Africa, but figured Australia was his cash-cow for the legacy he planned for his family.

Koning called upon the prime minister whenever he was in Sydney, enjoying the opportunity for a glass or two of whisky and a chat about current affairs and politicians creating a fuss. He was big man, assertive and arrogant, with zero respect for politicians, until he discovered Rene Grobbelaar, his protégé. Now he had someone in whom he placed his faith and trust.

Grobbelaar was the great-grandson of South African immigrants who left for Australia leaving behind their resistance to the establishment of the apartheid regime, his Afrikaner great-grandparents settling in Perth establishing a large family and thriving business interests. After successful university studies, Grobbelaar joined Koning Mining as a geologist, working in the north prospecting for minerals, specialising in diamonds.

Koning recognised Grobbelaar's qualities, choosing to mentor him, teaching him the art of the deal, to negotiate ruthlessly, and always think family first. When a political opportunity presented itself, he encouraged Grobbelaar to run for the federal parliament after Koning secured preselection in a safe seat, then funding his election campaigns. He was now as close as anyone can get to the ultimate seat of power — it took twenty years and less than two million dollars, one of his better long-term investments.

Koning drained his glass, sliding it across the coffee table for a refill. The prime minister splashed a good measure and stretched over the table to hand it to his benefactor.

'Tell me, Prime Minster,' Koning settled back into the soft leather lounge chair, 'are you going to approve my licence for the new mine?'

'You're in the mix. I remain concerned about traditional owners.'

'Fuck those kaffirs,' Koning snapped, almost spilling his whisky. 'Why can't they stick to bark paintings or whatever else they do. They tried to stop the East Alligator, but lost, big time.'

Grobbelaar directed his gaze at Koning, swirling his whisky, sniffing the aroma before saying, 'The woman who blew up your mine was released recently.'

Koning eyed him from beneath his bushy eyebrows. 'I thought you said she would die inside.'

'I did say that,' Grobbelaar shrugged acknowledgement. 'The international advocacy groups got involved, and the UN had a say; then, without warning, the parole board let her out. Not my decision, I'm afraid.'

'Is she likely to cause a problem with the coal licence?'

'Yes. Given her history, I would expect nothing less.'

'Stuff her,' Koning retorted. 'I should've taken her out when we had the chance.'

'Lewe, that sort of talk is from a bygone era,' Grobbelaar smiled, 'no one uses a gun to get their way anymore.'

'Not in this country, that's for sure. You're all a pack of wimps,' Koning declared, then said, 'if she starts to get in the way, this time we shall deal with her.'

'I have her under control,' Grobbelaar reassured him. He sipped his whisky and went on, 'an activist group has made an appeal to the UN, supported by the traditional owners, but the Congress will do as we direct them.'

'You had better get it done,' Koning said. 'This will be good for the country and good for us South Africans, so don't let me down.'

'I remind you, I am the prime minister of Australia.'

'It doesn't matter, boy. Once you have Boer blood in you, you're always Boer.'

'I'm Australian first, Lewe,' Grobbelaar said, then softened as he considered Koning. 'Don't worry, we'll make it happen for you.'

'Just don't let those black bastards get in the way of my plans. I need to know I can have access to minerals for another fifty years. You owe me on this.'

Grobbelaar ignored the implied threat. 'You won't live that long.'

'It's never about me — it's only ever about the company and providing a legacy for my family and my country.'

'I'll do my best for you.'

'Do better than that boy.' Koning slid his empty glass back for a refill.

5

Simone rested a hand on a restless Miller's knee to calm nerves. Neesham had agreed for her to speak if she kept to script, which he first approved. The amphitheatre was at capacity, many delegates keen to listen to what the Umbakarta woman would say and her explanation for bringing discredit to her people with her actions so long ago.

'How are you feeling?' Simone asked.

'Nervous,' Miller smiled. 'I'm not sure I have the right to be in this sacred place and to speak about the things I want to raise.'

'You'll be fine,' Simone placed an arm around her, but Miller was not so confident. She was still skittish around people and uneasy in crowds with her rehabilitation taking longer than she would have liked.

The smoke plume drifted up into the large vent in the roof above the enormous fire lit whenever Aboriginal nations gathered to discuss business. They came from all over Australia to Alice Springs, seeking consensus to recommend policy to the government. They travelled from the tropics of far north Queensland's Kuku Yalanji country, the sometimes bitterly cold Tahuni Lingah country of Tasmania, the Noongar nations of the west, and the desert people of the centre. Their politics and demands often conflicting, but they welcomed the opportunity to speak their business, even if they seldom agreed.

The Congress was proclaimed more than fifty years earlier once amendments to the Australian constitution were made recognising the first peoples' dominion over the land before European settlement. The self-governing political structure around the Karrakatta was formed to bring the nations together. It had been built on good intentions back then, but it was now little more than a talkfest and a platform for ambitious leaders to build profile within Australian politics and media. They came twice a year for five days and spread themselves around the amphitheatre surrounding the fire to listen and learn what others were undertaking to improve conditions for their people. There were often passionate speeches from leaders complaining about lack of progress. It was a common theme, and Miller realised not much had been achieved at the Karrakatta in the thirty-five years she had been away.

Called upon to address the Congress, Miller was welcomed as she walked to the speaker's stand and prepared to address the circle of delegates. 'We live in a land of opportunity,' Miller said, and then paused. 'We live in a land that welcomes peoples from all of over the world. They come here to prosper and lead a privileged life.' She paused for effect again. 'Australians are a lucky people living in a lucky country and most work hard to ensure future generations will also prosper.' Miller scanned about the Congress, all eyes focused on her.

'How stupid were we? They came and stole our land — no consideration, no respect, and still no thought for recompense. They came to build a prosperous life for themselves and developed this country into one of the wealthiest in the world. It may come as a surprise to you to know that I believe if this country had been left to us, then we would not have developed this land as they have done, and we would not be the wealthy nation we are today.' An angry shout from the back interrupted her, but she went on. 'The Aboriginal nations of this land would never have agreed on any strategy, any idea, or any action that might have brought us good fortune in the modern world. We owe whitefellas — this is the sad truth I have come to believe.

'We have succumbed to their will to live in a culture of despair constantly raising this sad business of defeat. In return, we stretch out our begging hand seeking payment from the government, telling them we are victims of their invasion. We continue to take their handouts and we lose our identity, our language and our culture

— because, delegates, you fail to agree on anything of substance that could save our culture, and you never say no to the government.' Sounds of unrest swept through the delegates, in particular the delegation from Western Australia.

'You have let your people down. You have allowed the Europeans to do whatever they like, and you have let them execute a subtle genocide on our culture.' Miller paused for a moment, her head bowed. 'To be black and proud in Australia now means an immigrant from Sudan or other African countries. Black immigrants to our land are stronger advocates and achieve more than any of the First Nations. Why? Why have you let it go? Why have you been defeated? Why have you given up?'

'Sit down woman and show respect,' a council elder barked from the front row.

'Uncle yells for me, be quiet, he says,' Miller pointed to the man. 'Yet, for years no one raised their voice about what we need to survive. I can tell you, and indeed I warn you, if you allow this servitude to the superior culture to continue, then we will have nothing left and our legacy will be the cave paintings from long ago. Tourists from all over the world will point and gape at the long-lost traditions of the people who once inhabited this great southern land. And they will wonder why we no longer exist.

'They say climate change will be the biggest moral challenge ever to face humankind, and everyone speaks with passion about what must be done to protect us all. A virus caused disruption to many countries killing economies and the international community worked together to eradicate it. The question I ask is this — we are facing our own destruction and we are letting it happen — why?

'You have debated the concept of a homeland before. You have debated, and debated, and debated, and yet you still have not made a decision about protecting our people, our culture and our dreaming.' Miller paused and listened to the uncomfortable silence, then lowered her voice. 'Many years ago, I fought for my mob. I drove a spear in the ground and said, "no more". No more disrespect from white fellas, no more dishonesty, no more ignoring my culture, and no more telling me what to do in my country. I stood up and said no more, and I stand before you today asking you to now stand and say — no more.

'No more living in the cultural of poverty. No more assimilation, no more foreign culture. No more servitude to laws that do not respect us or our country. No more disrespect of our land, and no more subjugating our rights as traditional owners.

'I want you to stand with me and fight for our rights. To stand with me and fight for a homeland. I want you to stand with me and say no!' She paused, panting for a few moments. 'Will you stand with me and fight for our culture? Will you stand with me to take back our history and live our future? Will you stand with me and let Aborigines determine our future so that our ancestors can take pride for protecting them?'

Miller stopped talking and stepped back from the lectern. No one spoke. She gazed out at the delegates, awkwardly waiting for a response. An elder in the centre of the audience stood and shouted, 'The Kulin nation stands with you.'

Another elder stood and yelled, 'The Yorta Yorta stand with you.'

Delegates whispered, Miller smiled, nodding appreciation.

Congress members began standing and yelling their commitment, then all delegates were on their feet yelling affirmation to the call for a homeland. The acclamation was thunderous, transforming the meeting into a celebration. A number of delegates came to the fire and began stomping out a ceremonial dance.

Miller stepped down from the podium and strutted to the beaming Simone, and po-faced Jimmy Neesham.

'That was terrific,' Simone said as Miller stepped into her open arms and hugged her. 'You've convinced me.'

'What the hell do you think you're doing? That wasn't the speech you gave me.' Neesham held a different view.

The United Aboriginal Congress elected an executive Council of Elders every three years to represent the Congress to government and complete urgent business between the two annual assemblies. They built a lavish meeting room in the same precinct as the ampitheatre to meet and discuss progress of the assemblies and develop communication frameworks for reports to government. Constructed from several converted shipping containers linked together to form a respectable suite of offices, safe from the ravages of weather and vandals.

Government-funded agencies never missed out on the latest technology and the meeting room was adorned with a giant screen capable of linking video conferencing to anywhere in the world. Twenty councillors eased into cinema-style seats for prearranged meetings with the prime minister or other government officials. A sophisticated communication network was setup, with cameras and microphones before each Elder in attendance.

At the adjournment of each Congress, the Council of Elders advised the government of motions passed and important business debated so the government could respond to media requests and urgent business. As the councillors settled in, with Neesham at a desk down front, the screen flickered, and Prime Minister Grobbelaar appeared from a cabinet anti room. Alongside him were the attorney general, Mary Whittington, and Minister for Indigenous Affairs, Patrick O'Toole.

'Hello, are you there?' Grobbelaar fiddled with controls, pointing a remote-control wand at the screen in Canberra.

'The council is here, Prime Minister, and we thank you for joining us. We see you and your colleagues very well,' Jimmy Neesham responded.

'I see and hear you, too. Thank you for coming — and might I say, I remain impressed with the manner in which you continue to bring together the Congress of First Nation peoples and the work you do in leading it.'

'Thank you, sir.' Neesham referred to his notes. 'After five days of discussion we wish to put to you our motions and recommendations for your government to consider.'

'Fire away.' The prime minister smiled, confident nothing would be approved or accomplished unless he agreed. It was a political commitment he had made to the electorate when he became prime minister, but he never revealed his disregard for the tedious nature of its outcomes.

'The Congress discussed the amendments to the constitution from many years ago. In particular, we remain concerned there still is no prohibition on racial discrimination incorporated within the document, and the ongoing impact this has on Aboriginal people.'

'We have discussed this issue many times.' Grobbelaar sighed, anticipating this would be the first point raised. 'We remain convinced current laws allow for adequate protection against racial discrimination. Mary, would you like to add anything?'

The attorney general cleared her throat and lean forward. 'Yes, thank you Prime Minister. The government has considered this proposition many times over the years, and indeed, the government has referred this to the United Nations Human Rights Council for their opinion. Their advice confirms we do not need to amend the constitution as current laws provide adequate protection.'

Grobbelaar added. 'Can I just suggest your Congress give it a rest for a while. The government will not respond on this issue, and if it went to a referendum of the Australian people, I suspect it would not get up. Emotion for this issue has dialled way back since it was first raised years ago. There are adequate protections for you under other legislation.'

'Mr Prime Minister?' Councillor Appleton from Cape York spoke. 'We respect your view that Australia believes it has done enough to protect First Nations, but we do not agree. We do not want to keep coming to you begging for crumbs, we want equality of law, of community, and of culture. We remain subservient, as we have been for almost three hundred years.'

'I'm sad to hear that you still believe you are not equal,' Grobbelaar said, staring straight into the camera. 'This land is yours to share, and our community is yours to join.'

'This land was ours, and you stole it from us,' Appleton asserted. 'You have been here for three hundred years; we have been here for sixty thousand.'

'This is not an attitude that fosters reconciliation,' Grobbelaar snapped. Some of the council members laughed, riling the prime minister further. 'You laugh, but your people remain hostage to this idea of rights.'

'If I may, Prime Minister,' Mary Whittington moved to calm and reshape the discussion. 'We have acted on your Declaration of Recognition and this will sit outside the constitution as a statutory instrument. This will overcome the need to have the constitution amended.'

'We appreciate this,' said Neesham. 'In addition, we have had, for the first time, a unanimous declaration of support for the establishment of a homeland territory.'

'You are kidding?' Grobbelaar laughed.

'No, we are not,' snapped Appleton.

Neesham jumped in, interrupting the tension, 'We have moved motions like this before, but they have never been unanimous.'

'So now you all want to establish a homeland state? Is that what I am hearing?'

'We have spoken about this sovereignty issue many times with you and previous prime ministers, and we have worked for many years on a submission to the United Nations,' Neesham said.

'It's never going to happen.'

The elders were clearly unimpressed.

'Sovereignty is important to us,' barked Councillor Kerr from Western Australia.

'Sovereignty is not homeland — we are not giving up any land for you to do whatever you want, I can assure you.'

'Prime Minister,' Neesham said. 'We would like the government's support in approving the establishment of a homeland state, but also supporting our submission for statehood before the United Nations.'

'What makes you think the UN would ever approve such an outrageous proposition?' Grobbelaar scoffed.

'They have done it before,' interjected Appleton.

'Timor-Leste, which the Australian government supported,' Neesham referred to his notes. 'Israel, which continues to receive your government's unequivocal support, although the Arab Council has revoked its recognition. Namibia, and the list goes on,' Neesham gazed into the camera. 'Conquerors have relinquished land to traditional owners. It can happen. Lesotho is a good example of how a state can transition, or even Eswatini for that matter.'

'Not on my watch,' Grobbelaar said with a disdainful sweep of his hand.

'Where were you thinking of establishing this homeland?' Whittington asked.

'We have always considered the Northern Territory would be ideal. It would provide clear secured borders and allow us to establish a democratic government and economic model that will support our people.'

'What? And you just give up native title everywhere else?' O'Toole asked, waggling a pen between his fingers.

'No, far from it,' Appleton snapped. 'Australia has a continuing responsibility to all its citizens, including First Nations. Governments have a duty to maintain and continue current laws. What we ask is for sovereignty within our own homeland.'

'Just like Lesotho and Eswatini,' Neesham added.

'Why the hell do you keep talking about African countries?' Grobbelaar asked.

'I know your family was born there.'

'*I* wasn't,' Grobbelaar barked. 'My family comes from the Transvaal.'

'Same thing.'

'If you were South African you would know the difference.'

'And if you were Aboriginal you would know why homeland is important to us — or perhaps you already do,' observed Appleton.

Grobbelaar sat back in his chair and rocked for a moment. 'What else?'

'As you know, Prime Minister, the United Nations have been campaigning for many years to limit new coal mining licenses. They have accepted our submission about the Arnhem Land underground coalmine, and as you no doubt know, they asked you to sign a no-mine treaty with traditional owners.'

'Is that it?'

'With respect, Prime Minister, we have discussed this motion for you to sign the treaty in Congress and we would like to present it to you,' Neesham said.

'With respect to you, Jimmy,' Grobbelaar sighed. 'These matters are not up for discussion. Licences for a new mine are approved by my government. We will begin negotiations with the traditional owners in the fullness of time as required under the Act. We will not enter into any discussion with you or the Karrakatta.'

'We have a UN motion seeking your government sign the treaty,' Neesham objected.

'Let me assure you, Jimmy, and all of your colleagues there, the new mine will be shipping coal within the year.'

'This is not in keeping with the formal agreement between the Congress and government,' interjected Appleton.

'The government is required to listen, there is no obligation to act.'

'Then why do we go through this charade twice a year?' Kerr snapped.

Neesham was getting annoyed and waved his head side to side as he perched forward on his chair. 'The government funds the Congress. We negotiated a constitution for us to operate and the government agreed they would allow us to participate in the political process ...'

'Solely on social policy, Jimmy,' Grobbelaar snapped. 'Not on UN treaties or laws pertaining to the management of national resources. You have Native Title laws, you don't need another voice or legislated instrument about these things.'

'You are responsible for the delivery of services to our people,' Appleton responded.

'State governments have that responsibility.'

'We want a say about these things, Prime Minister,' Neesham said, exasperated.

'Not my issue — you have your Karrakatta and you get to address the parliament once a year, I can't give you any more than that, and I won't be signing any UN treaties, I can assure you.' Grobbelaar replied, waiting for a response and getting none. 'If that is all you have, I will say goodbye.' The prime minister leaned across to the control unit, stubbed a button and the screen in Alice Springs went blank.

'This is not a negotiation. He expects us to come cap in hand, saying *please sir*,' Appleton said, shocked by the prime minister's sudden dismissal.

'We have never been in a position of power since they got here,' sighed Neesham. 'Maybe we have to fight to get what we want. Their courts aren't going to do it for us.'

'The international community could be supportive if we focus on homeland sovereignty,' Appleton said as he stood to leave. 'They've done it before; there is not a single reason they can't do it for us now.'

§

'What the hell was all that about?' The prime minister telephoned Neesham within ten minutes of the meeting. 'I was under the impression a deal is a deal, and you would keep a lid on the enthusiasm.'

'Millergoorra got them stirred up.'

The prime minister slapped his desk. 'You told me she was an old woman and not to worry,' Grobbelaar thundered.

'She put a proposition to the Congress about establishing a homeland, and this is the first time they have supported it — everyone did.'

'You black fellas have been banging on about sovereignty forever. What's changed? What started them thinking about this homeland nonsense this time?'

'Well, frankly, you have.'

'Get stuffed, Jimmy,' Grobbelaar barked. 'I have looked after you for years and your sole job is to control them. You have let me down.'

Who's getting the mining licence?'

'Koning Mining.'

'The South Africans?' Neesham felt a twinge in his wallet. 'You're asking for trouble.'

'Who do you reckon is going to give it to me? You?' the prime minister taunted. 'Or do you reckon some other group will stop it? Lewe Koning will wipe any resistance from the table, you know that.'

Neesham considered the issue for a moment. 'I want more money.'

'You want more money?' Grobbelaar mocked. 'How about you get the job done as we agreed and then I might send you more money.'

'I want four million.'

'And I want a head job from my attorney general, but I've got more chance of getting that than you have of getting four million.'

'If you want me to sway the Congress, you'll need to pay.'

'Jimmy, do as I say, or you will never get a cent from me again.'

❡

Miller and Simone returned to Darwin on the Ghan, stopping off for a brief visit in Katherine. It was an opportunity for Simone to see more of the country she had heard so much about living in Sydney, but never had the opportunity to visit.

'I'm beginning to understand why you have such a connection to the land.'

Miller smiled, 'That's nice, sweetie, but a month in the outback doesn't even come close to the way I feel.'

Simone smiled at the rebuke. 'Can I ever understand how you feel?'

'Nope.'

'How come? Surely, I can feel the same things as you?'

'Ever been in love?'

'Sure.'

'How did it feel?

'Like, I couldn't give it up — it was addictive. I just wanted to gaze at him and touch him all the time. I couldn't get enough of it.'

'That's how I feel about my Country. I ache when I'm not there and I embrace everything when I am. It's like I am not whole if I am not there.'

Simone considered what Miller said. 'You must have felt terrible locked up for so long.'

Miller shook her head. 'You could say that.'

Simone grinned, studying Miller for a moment. 'I've enjoyed this gig. I've learnt so much.'

'Time's up, is it?'

'It will be in two weeks; I think you're able to manage yourself now.'

'I could have told you that when we met, but I've enjoyed having you around.'

Simone smiled. 'I hope I have a body like you when I'm sixty.'

'Black?'

'You're not black, more of a comfortable honey.'

'Comfortable?' Miller snorted. 'First time I've been called comfortable. I often make people very uncomfortable.'

'No, I mean, you have a great body and almost no grey hair. Did you work out much in jail?'

'Every fucking day for thirty-five long years.'

'Where did you find the time?'

'Are you kidding me?' Miller almost fell off her seat as she tried to control her laughter.

'Yeah, I am,' laughed Simone as she joined in the mirth. They took some time to settle down before Simone asked between chuckles. 'What do you think will happen with the Congress motions?'

'I don't know, it's different this time.'

'Will the government respond?'

'They'll respond, I just don't know how.' Miller gazed out at the landscape rushing by the window. 'It was unanimous for the first time.'

'What would you call this new country?'

'I don't know, something everyone can agree on — Arnhem Land might get a run.'

'Ooh, I know — what about Dream World?' Simone beamed, wide-eyed.

'You say some crazy shit, sometimes.'

¶

As the train eased into Darwin, Miller switched her phone on and it sparked up with news of thirteen missed calls from Neesham with eight recorded messages. She ignored the messages and rang him.

'Where have you been?'

'I took the train back to town, what's up?' Miller smiled as she studied Simone stretching for her bag. 'Where are you?'

'I just finished a meeting with the prime minister and the AG.'

'And? Did he agree to the motion?'

'Grobbelaar has fucked us over and won't even consider any motion from the last meeting.'

'Why?'

'Does he need a reason?' Neesham snapped. 'He's just like all the others, and we have to play Uncle Tom to their rules.'

'I told you, before you ever got involved with this Congress shit, you would achieve nothing.'

'Yeah, well maybe it's taken me this long to get the message.'

'What do you want to do?'

'Give me a week to think about it and pull a few favours. Come and see me next Wednesday,' Neesham instructed. 'Have you got a place to stay?'

'As I understand it, the government is paying for a room for my parole officer until my bond is finalised in a couple of weeks, so I will bunk in with her.'

'Oh yes?'

'Oi — single beds, you dirty bastard. You can't help yourself, can you?'

6

The wintry breeze chilled Neesham as he pushed through the door and stepped into the Steam Packet Hotel, a small pub as old as Melbourne's first settlement, in Williamstown, a small bayside suburb. Neesham hated Melbourne winters, he never seemed to get warm no matter how many layers of clothing he wore, so avoided the horrible city as much as possible. As he stepped through the entrance he let the door bang shut, rubbed his hands to warm them and meandered to the bar.

'Pint of draught, thanks mate.' He waited for his beer, checking about the room to see if he recognised the person he was meeting, but it was empty. The beer was cold and he took a mouthful, then a second, before propping himself on a stool. He jerked his phone out of his jacket, scrolling through his twitter feed, entertaining himself as he waited.

The door opened, and a cold gust swept past him as two men entered, dried brown leaves following before the door swung shut. They searched about, saw Neesham and sauntered over. 'Are you Neesham?'

'Yeah.' He stood. 'Mr Messaris is it?'

'This is Terry McGuiness.' No one shook hands. 'Let's go to the back room, it'll be quieter there. Two beers, thanks mate.' The barman nodded and the men slipped into a darker room away from the main bar. 'How do we know each other?'

'I dealt with you quite a few years back when you worked for Koning Mining.' Neesham sat at a corner a table. Messaris and

McGuiness took a chair with their backs to the wall. 'It was around forty years back. The incident with the traditional owners out near the East Alligator.'

'I was a lot younger then.' Messaris glanced at McGuiness and chortled. 'We both were.'

'You dispatched them.' Neesham winced at the memory.

'Oh, that's right, you were our mole.' Messaris gawked at McGuiness. 'This is the Judas who got his thirty pieces of silver.'

'We got the lot that day, except that bitch who blew us up,' McGuiness laughed. 'Crocs had a smorgasbord.'

'She's out of jail and causing trouble,' Neesham said.

'I killed the bitch, well I would have if she wasn't wearing armour,' McGuiness said.

'What brings you to us?' asked Messaris.

'I have need of your expertise.'

'Christ, man, take a gander at us — do you think we're in shape to do any fighting?' Messaris laughed. 'We'd be lucky to run fifty metres, and I haven't been to the gym for years.'

'You look in shape, both of you do.' Neesham checked over his shoulder and leaned into the table as a waiter delivered the beers. 'I don't want your brawn; I need your military skills.'

'Why?'

'I need to convince someone to sign a piece of paper.'

'That sounds like muscle to me,' suggested McGuiness.

'What sort of paper?' Messaris sipped his beer.

'A UN treaty to stop coalmining in Arnhem Land.'

'Koning has the licence to mine up there,' Messaris said to McGuiness.

Neesham sipped his beer, then said, 'I want to stop him.'

'The individual who can stop him is his mate, the prime minister.'

'That's who needs to sign the paper.'

Messaris sat back, picking up his beer, glancing over to McGuiness, who shrugged. 'That would be a big ask. What's in it for us?'

'Fucking-over Lewe Koning doesn't excite you?'

'It doesn't pay the bills.'

'I can get you two hundred.'

'Nowhere near enough,' interrupted McGuiness.

'What would be a good figure for you?' Neesham asked.

'Double that,' Messaris said.

Neesham paused. 'I can do that.'

'You want us to convince the prime minister of Australia to sign a treaty banning coalmining in Arnhem Land?'

'Yes.'

'Simple,' mocked McGuiness. 'How do you expect we do that?'

'I would have thought you could use a number of methods, but he needs to sign the treaty as proposed by the United Nations within two months. If he does, then the mine will be deferred for a decade and that's enough time for me.'

'Enough time for what?' McGuiness asked, as Messaris gazed at Neesham, cranking his mind around the idea.

'This is important for the First Nations and allows us time to build influence.'

'This is about Aboriginal rights?' Messaris tugged his nose.

Neesham avoided his gaze, taking another sip. 'Yeah, of course.'

'Bullshit!' Messaris said. 'If you're the same guy who did over his family for cash, then there's a money-making scheme in here somewhere.'

'I would have thought you'd be pleased to get rid of Koning.'

'There is no love lost between us, and yes, that would be a plus.' Messaris shrugged. 'But if you have a deal, why can't we share it?'

'I can assure you, I have no deal — anytime, anywhere.'

'We'll see.' Messaris peeked at his colleague and received a slight nod. 'Let me assure you,' he said with menace, 'if we find a money-making scheme happening behind our backs, then we will take steps to get what's due.'

Neesham swallowed hard, which didn't go unnoticed, then dismissed Messaris's suggestion with a wave of his hand.

'Are there limitations?' McGuiness asked.

'I don't understand, what do you mean?' Neesham asked.

'Is there anything you don't want us to do?'

Neesham shifted in his chair, 'Well, don't kill him.'

The South Africans howled at the suggestion.

'What support do we have from the kaffirs?' Messaris asked.

'Millergoorra wants involvement and she has others willing to join the *revolution* if you need them.'

'Does the bitch know about us?' McGuiness asked.

'She didn't see you when you cleansed her family, and you didn't give evidence against her — she never saw you. I suspect she doesn't know who you are.'

'Why don't you get her to do it then?'

'She's a revolutionary; in all likelihood she'd just kill the prime minister.'

'Let me get this straight — you want us to get a UN treaty signed by the PM; you are going to pay us four hundred, and if we implicate Millergoorra in the conspiracy you'll be very happy?' Messaris sought confirmation.

'Whoever said you weren't a smart man?' Neesham smiled. 'It'll be almost impossible, you know that don't you?'

Messaris sighed and finished his beer. 'That's why you want us.'

'As I said, I don't want your brawn, I really need your strategic military brain.'

'When do you need to know?'

'Let's catch up next week in Darwin and I'll have Millergoorra there.'

'Is she still a tidy unit?' Messaris wondered.

'She's almost sixty, what would you expect? Anyway, you're too old to get it up,' McGuiness said, slapping Messaris on the shoulder as he stood to leave. 'Unless you take a pill.'

Messaris also stood. 'See you next week. Pay for the beers, will you?'

As Neesham waited for a taxi to the airport his phone sounded.

'Mr Jimmy, it's Teo.'

'Mr Teo, how can I help?' Neesham checked about him.

'Just making sure we are on schedule.'

'We are ahead of schedule, and if I can do a deal then the UN treaty will be signed within weeks, three months, maximum.'

'You will be paid when the treaty is signed.'

'It'll be done, but I need one million now to pay contractors.'

There was no response, apart from the sound of rasping breath, so he waited. Teo responded. 'I will transfer one million today into your normal account.'

Neesham responded with a fist pump. 'Thank you.'

'I remind you that if the treaty is not signed, we will take action against you.'

'I understand.'

'Very good, goodbye, Mr Jimmy.'

¶

'Why would the prime minister sign a piece of paper thrust under his nose?' McGuiness was stretched out on the couch.

Messaris poured himself another glass of a smooth Barossa red. 'Because we ask him nicely. We just have to figure out how to get it in front of him.'

'It's impossible, we've been at this all day and we have nothing.'

'Calm down Macca, we'll think of something. Do you want this last piece of pizza?'

'Wait a minute!' Tyrone Perkins yelled from the computer desk in the corner.

'What?' McGuiness growled.

'First of all, that pizza slice is mine.'

'Was.' McGuiness scooped it up and took a bite, regretting it — it was too spicy.

'What have you got?' Messaris asked the computer whiz.

'How do you know I have something?'

'Because you implied it, so what is it?'

Tyrone offered his idea. 'We take the prime minister's power away.'

'Such a young fucking idiot,' McGuiness sneered.

'I'll have you know I am not an idiot, I have three degrees and a doctorate in IT — I bet you left school when you were young, you dumb arse.'

'Tyrone, just calm down and tell me your idea, please,' Messaris said with a soothing wave to McGuiness.

Tyrone calmed himself with a deep breath. 'I think I know how to take his power away, and before he can get it back, he needs to sign the treaty.'

'How?'

Tyrone beamed. 'We shut the grid down.'

'What grid?' McGuiness asked without glancing up.

'The power grid — we take his power away.'

'I'm listening,' Messaris said with a slight note of scepticism in his tone.

Tyrone was excited and bounced around the room. 'What would the prime minister fear most?'

'Losing an election?' Messaris replied.

Tyrone smacked the back of his hand into the palm of the other and pointed at Messaris. 'Correct! And what would make him lose an election?'

'Voters not voting for him?' McGuiness joked.

'And why wouldn't they vote for him?' Tyrone came to the lounge, picked up the red wine and poured himself another glass, checked the pizza box and flopped into a chair, disappointed. 'Governments stand and fall on national security — history tells us if the people feel threatened then the government falls.'

'So?' Messaris asked, unsure what the boy was getting at.

'Grobbelaar is a smart politician, right? He'd know that if the people of Australia felt unsafe he would lose the election next year,' Tyrone said. 'We make them feel unsafe by turning off the power.'

'Okay, smart boy, how do we do that?' McGuiness asked.

'The grid is operated by various sources of power — coal, wind, gas and such like.'

'What? Are you suggesting we blow up a power plant?' McGuiness sneered. 'You have rocks in your head.'

'We don't have to.'

'Okay, what do we do?' Messaris sighed, losing patience.

'The national power grid is fed by all these different sources and is managed by a central operator. They provide the power to the retailers and they use various interconnectors to control the power supply and surges of demand — for instance, if Adelaide needs more power, it asks the national operator and power is drawn from the grid and fed to Adelaide.'

Messaris thought through the information, sipping his wine. 'If we stop the grid then Adelaide goes into darkness?'

'We can't stop the grid, but we can stop the supply to the city by hacking the system, and in essence turning off the interconnector.'

'How the hell do we do that, smart-arse?' McGuiness was still sceptical.

'We hack the market operator's administration system and divert the power away from a city to the grid for as long as we want. I reckon I can code algorithms to shield us.'

'Causing chaos,' Messaris smiled, winking at Tyrone.

'Precisely,' said Tyrone, chuffed by the response.

'How is that going to cause chaos?' McGuiness asked.

'If you were a criminal and you knew the power was going off at a certain time, on a certain day, what would you do?' Messaris asked.

'I would go for as much cash as I could,' McGuiness responded.

'Imagine, for a moment, if everyone had the same thought when security systems go down. If folks came into the street to cause trouble — Chaos?'

'Exactly!' Tyrone smiled. 'But, it's more than that. Essential services will be down, hospitals switch to their own power, but that doesn't last for ever.'

'We create anarchy chaos in the streets and threaten the prime minister it won't stop until he does what we want. The worried prime minister panics and pleads with us to come and see him and asks us to stop cutting the power supply — and when he signs the treaty like a good little boy, everything goes back to normal,' McGuiness mocked.

'Something like that,' Messaris smiled. Tyrone was smiling and nodding in agreement.

'It's bullshit. It'll never work,' McGuiness said. 'For starters, he would never fall for a cheap trick like that, and secondly, they would override the system, cutting us out. Third, they will find us and stop us.'

'If we stage it like a grand opera,' Messaris began, waving his hands about like a conductor, 'starting with one city to let them know we can do it, then building to a climax by shutting down other cities ... Grobbelaar will want to stop the anarchy, I bet you. If we had rabid foot soldiers, like the kaffirs, out on the street causing trouble and threatening the community, the prime minister would be panicking, I promise you.'

'What happens if the fat lady sings too early in this opera — we're stuffed,' McGuiness said.

'Got any better ideas boofhead?' Tyrone quipped.

McGuiness sat up. 'Who the hell do you think you're talking to?'

'Settle down boys.' Messaris sat forward in his chair. 'I like the idea. Let's see what we can come up with scoping it out further. Good work Tyrone.' Messaris slapped the young man on the knee and fell back in the chair with wine in hand. 'Always thought you were smart.'

§

Neesham chose a private dining room upstairs at Darwin's Char restaurant to meet the team he thought could guarantee the coalmine not proceed. The Chinese were patient, but he knew from experience they wanted results for the money they invested with him. He was running out of time and beginning to feel desperate for a result.

Compared to the wintery chill of Melbourne, the weather was glorious and the restaurant was the ideal place to lavish largesse on his guests to convince them to work together. His plan was simple enough — force the prime minister to act under an ultimatum of some sort. He had the United Nations on his side, so he just needed the prime minister to appreciate the benefits of doing a deal.

The private room looked out onto outside tables and across the Esplanade to the water. He enjoyed bringing guests here and felt a pleasing tingle of self-importance when he was treated well by the staff. The louvered windows were open and a breeze eased the heat of the day.

He was first to arrive and asked for water as he waited, gazing through the trees to a large container ship sailing into port.

'Neesham!' Messaris declared as he stepped into the room. 'A little warmer than last week.'

'This is just one of the many benefits of having an office in Darwin, although I try and get out of the place during the wet season.'

'You know Terry, and this is Tyrone Perkins.' Tyrone extended his hand. 'He's the smarts of the operation and believes we may be able to accomplish what you want.'

'Ah, that gives me a good feeling.' Neesham smiled accepting his hand. 'Welcome, please grab a seat and tell me what you'd like to drink.'

'I'll have a large beer.' McGuiness sat at the end of the table with his back away from the door.

'A couple of beers please,' Neesham instructed a waiter. 'I suppose you'd better bring a bottle of white wine and glasses for everyone as well.'

'Anyone else coming?' Messaris asked as he sat gazing out the windows. 'That breeze is nice.'

'Millergoorra is coming with a few ideas, hopefully.'

'Jeezus Christ.' Tyrone stood and watched as two women appeared in the room.

'Ah, Miller,' Neesham smiled, 'glad you could come, and Simone, nice to see you again.'

Miller was slow to acknowledge the welcome; she didn't know the other men and it seemed all eyes were on Simone, dressed in a light cotton frock, almost sheer against the light. As the group settled, Tyrone manage to sit next to Simone, Miller next to Messaris with Neesham at the head of the table, opposite McGuiness.

Miller smiled at Messaris. 'Have we met before?'

'No.' Messaris showed no sign of recognition. 'I would've remembered a beautiful woman like you if we had.' He flicked a glance to McGuiness and winked.

The waiter returned with the beers and poured water and wine.

'I want to thank you for coming and I hope we can resolve a few things today.' Neesham raised his glass. 'Here's cheers.'

'Why am I here?' Miller was the solitary one not to pick up a glass.

'We want to discuss the proposed coalmine in Arnhem Land and what we can do to stop it,' said Neesham.

'That's a typical Aboriginal response,' Miller said. 'More talk and no action. Talk, talk, talk, talk. Here's cheers.' Miller grinned at Simone and sipped her wine. Simone smiled across to Miller, raising her eyebrows with a slight querying nod of her head toward Tyrone next to her. Miller scrunched her face.

'Conan and his team have a few ideas; I'd have thought you'd be interested.'

'The only way to stop Koning is to blow him away,' Miller offered. 'Squash him like a gnat and blow him away.'

'Violence never works,' Messaris said.

'It did for my family years ago. They tried to prevent a mine from going ahead and Jimmy here, and me, are the soul survivors.' Miller turned to face Messaris. 'I survived the attack and ol' Jimmy here, snuck away for a few hours.'

'What are you suggesting?' Neesham asked.

'Nothing, you survived and now look at you — sitting on top of the political tree.'

'Just the administrator for the Congress, I don't run it,' Neesham demurred.

'Don't undersell yourself cuz, you're now the main man.'

Neesham shifted in his chair. 'What's brought this on?'

Miller didn't respond and squinted out over the table to the water as the others watched and waited. 'Ya know, I was thinking about your discussion with the prime minister. And I was thinking we're just banging our heads against a wall.' Miller paused and glanced at Neesham. 'They are never going to give us sovereignty and they will never formalise the Council of Elders or even the Congress. We've lost it, and we'll never get it back.'

'Lost what?' Simone asked, concerned for her friend.

'Our land — our culture. It's gone,' said Miller, gazing out the window, distracted.

'This is rubbish, Miller,' Neesham snapped. 'You just got here and already you're talking crap. You haven't even listened to what Conan and his team have to say.'

'What's he got to say?'

Messaris didn't respond, drumming his fingers on the table, cupping his face with his other hand. McGuiness drained his beer and Tyrone stole another glance at Simone.

'Do you have a plan, Conan?' Neesham asked.

Messaris sat forward and skimmed about the table. 'Well, I think we should lower the stress levels a little bit — so let's eat first. What do you recommend, Jimmy? What about you, Miller?' He winked at her and smiled. 'I'm a vegan in my old age.'

'Vegan is an Aboriginal word,' said Miller matter-of-factly, smiling at Messaris.

'Oh yes? What does it mean?'

'Can't hunt.'

The tension was smashed as the table broke into laughter and menus opened. Miller stretched out her leg and tapped Simone on the foot. When she glanced up, Miller cocked her head toward Tyrone, pursed her lips and faintly nodded. Simone blushed and wriggled in her chair.

'You blokes sound South African. How long have you been out

here?' Miller asked, nonchalantly scanning the list of food.

'We left the army about forty years ago and a bunch of us decided to come live here.'

'Special services?'

'Commandos, why do you ask?'

'Koning uses a crew to protect his interests and he seems to hire former South African paramilitary types.'

'Are you making a point?' McGuiness demanded.

'No,' smiled Miller. 'It's just interesting that you know Jimmy. How did you and Conan meet, Jimmy?'

'We needed security about ten years ago for Congress,' Neesham lied. 'We've used his security company ever since.'

'You seem a bit old stuffing around guarding fat Aborigines. Why aren't you laying on a beach somewhere?' Miller asked.

'Pension doesn't get you very far these days, so we lend our minds to strategic projects and we have young bucks like Tyrone here to do the heavy lifting.' Messaris smiled, dropped his hand under the table tapping McGuiness on the knee.

'Heavy lifting? The only heavy thing I'm picking up these days is my iPad,' Tyrone said.

'You don't work out?' Simone teased. 'You look as if you do.'

'Ah, what do we have here, Terry?' Messaris joked. 'It seems our little mate has found himself a friend.'

'Nice.' McGuiness wasn't interested. 'I'm going to have the barramundi.' He snapped his menu shut.

The banter continued as the group tossed around ideas, political statements and jokes as they worked their way through lunch and two bottles of wine. Coffees followed, and Simone shared a dessert with Tyrone. The discussion became more political and the issue before them was nudged into the light.

'So, how do we get the prime minister to act?' Neesham asked.

'Whatever we do must be authentic and lawfully binding. In other words, he has to do whatever we want him to do of his free will,' Messaris said.

'He's never going to sign a UN treaty. He's promised he never would,' Miller said.

'He will if he is forced politically and has no other option,' Messaris said.

Miller smirked. 'The only thing any man knows is the rule of the gun. Let's just take him out.'

'You're kidding, aren't you?' McGuiness asked.

Miller didn't respond.

'Nell, you are kidding, aren't you?' Simone asked, leaning toward her.

'She's kidding, but she might have something there. What she's saying is that we change the government, or have the prime minister resign,' Messaris said, smiling at Miller. 'She's not saying to literally kill Grobbelaar, she's saying kill his prime ministership.'

'Am I?' Miller smirked.

'I'm not getting involved in anything that has violence associated with it,' Tyrone said, as McGuiness scoffed, grabbing his napkin to cover his mouth.

'We can't do that, so why bother playing this stupid game?' Neesham interrupted.

'We have a plan,' Messaris declared. 'We think it will change the prime minister's mind.'

'Did you want to listen to this Simone? Or shall I meet you for a drink later?' Miller asked.

Simone ran her fingers across her lips, thinking through her options and the implications. 'No, I'm good.' She dropped her hand into her lap and as Messaris began to speak she ran a finger along Tyrone's leg, which had him jolting upright.

'I believe in chaos theory — so what I want to do is create so much chaos that Grobbelaar will have no alternative than deal with us and endorse the UN agreement.' Over the next twenty-four minutes Messaris outlined the plan to hack the energy distributers at the interconnectors, which will cut the power to various regions of the country. They needed to coordinate civil unrest by recruiting agitators to organise demonstrators in the streets during the blackouts, threatening community security with the fear of anarchy and applying political pressure through the media to threaten the prime minister.

Miller examined Tyrone when Messaris stopped speaking. 'You can do all that from your computer?'

'Once I have the codes and the algorithms, I can make anything happen.'

Simone clasped his thigh.

'The item missing from this scheme is an Aboriginal,' said Messaris. 'That's where you come in — you have to lead it in the media and be the spokesperson for the public campaign we initiate.'

Miller, resting her chin on her hand, asked, 'How would something like that work?'

Messaris glanced at Tyrone and nodded. 'Do you want to step us through it?'

Tyrone shifted in his seat and glimpsed over his shoulders to check for anyone who might be in earshot. 'It's quite easy. Social media allows us to use influencers, who can galvanise large numbers, and once they begin spreading our message we then have an active campaign to change opinion.'

Miller frowned. 'That all sounds too pie in the sky for me.'

'It's easy, Nell,' Simone smiled. 'Tyrone just identifies people with large followings who use Facebook, Twitter, and most likely Instagram, and pitches a message they will either like or comment on — once they do that, their network will do the same and all of a sudden we have thousands of followers talking about the campaign to have the treaty signed.'

'Millions, as a matter of fact,' Tyrone smiled.

'How long will it take to organise?' Miller queried.

'We need to make it happen within a few months,' Neesham said, surprising Messaris.

'Tyrone will need help,' Messaris sniffed, nodding.

'What does he need?' Neesham asked.

Tyrone scanned about the table, settling on Messaris who nodded encouraging him to speak. 'I'll need another geek like me.'

Maybe she had too much wine, but Simone said, 'I can do that.'

'What do you know about computers? You're in justice.' Miller raised her eyebrows.

'I majored in computer science and have a master's in engineering with an advanced diploma of applied electrical engineering.'

'The hell you do,' Miller smiled.

'She'll do.' Tyrone said, grabbing her hand resting high on his thigh.

'Where do we base ourselves?' Miller asked.

'It doesn't matter, but I would prefer we're close to the prime minister when we start the campaign, so let's go to Canberra tomorrow,' Messaris suggested.

'Who funds that?' Miller asked.

'I have an account,' Neesham responded.

'Thought you might,' Messaris said.

'Here's a toast then.' Neesham held up his glass and the other's raised theirs. 'To Aboriginal sovereignty, and no more coal.'

'Hear, hear,' Miller said then sipped from her glass. The South Africans didn't respond.

7

The office above the greasy hamburger joint was frigid. Tyrone sat at his bank of computers with a doona wrapped around his back, a woolly jacket, beanie and fingerless mittens. A single bar electric heater radiated its meagre warmth under his desk, but he was cold and his breath steamed. He was working long days, only stopping to sleep, but the results he was accomplishing were very encouraging, confirming the outcomes he'd predicted were achievable.

The prime minister and his government were never going to respond to threats and power blackouts, but they could be convinced by an intense political campaign targeting specific voter groups, influencing polls and votes — they were politicians after all.

The campaign strategy was to create a social media movement around the unfairness of government policy toward aborigines and the impact coalmining has on the environment. Facts can be distorted using emotional language, reflecting and supporting bias, encouraging protest — all within the remit of the whiz-kid, Tyrone Perkins.

Once the group relocated to Canberra, Tyrone initiated a social media campaign mobilising protests about the proposed mine seeking signatures on petitions demanding a stop coalmining. He initiated five petitions, each worded differently to attract a variety of ages and community groups; the response was overwhelming. Within a few days, he secured three hundred thousand responses and the pressure for government action was building.

Community social media activism is popular with political activists and Tyrone's methods were used in other campaigns. Less brawn and more intellectual engagement made a difference in campaigns these days, something Messaris and McGuiness failed to appreciate.

Tyrone focused on government members in marginal seats, those most vulnerable to swings in public support, and his new team of social media activists bombarded them with questions and complaints about the involvement of South Africans in Australia, generating a nationalism buzz, touching on innate racist fears of losing control of their country. Racism was a hot topic politicians with small electoral voting margins tried to avoid.

Already two targeted marginal seats government members had stepped out into the national media spotlight, questioning the government's decision approving a licence to an international company when there were plenty of good Australian miners who could do the job. Why a politician with an electorate more than three thousand kilometres from a proposed mine site should be raising concerns about the licence wasn't questioned, but Tyrone knew each politician was hurting in their electorate.

Politics is never about the issue, it is about agitation for votes. If voters were mobilised about a policy in an electorate remote from the issue, they could affect government policy if their ambitious local politician wanted to remain in the parliament. Their power was at the ballot box and marginal seat members knew it, so responded when their constituents demanded.

Tyrone labelled himself a social movement entrepreneur because he could mobilise action to stymie a government announcement, a company's plans, or cause chaos during elections. He regarded the shallowness of opinion in modern communities manipulable, influenced by what they saw and read on social media. Tyrone grasped the concept that voters, in particular young voters, were motivated by feelings. Many of them addicted to social media and he nourished that addiction by providing simple answers to complex issues, triggering emotional responses motivating his followers to act. He was a wizard, a geek with special skills, and Messaris paid him well for those talents.

Tyrone could hear someone thumping up the wooden stairs and knew it was his new girlfriend. 'Hi gorgeous, what have you got for me?' His eyes didn't move from the screen.

'I've got you one with the lot with a side order of chips and a coke.' Simone placed a paper bag beside him.

'Ah, that's so nice of you. Did you get yourself something?'

'I had dinner hours ago. What are you up to?' Simone stood behind him, her hands on his shoulders, checking the screen.

'I worked on those algorithms you left me, and I've boosted our followers by a further fifty thousand. Twenty-five per cent have already sent an email to the prime minister complaining about the mine decision and requesting him to recognise the UN's recommendation.'

'Are you using the first nation argument or the environment?'

'I'm using this idea that coal is the bogeyman, and the Great Barrier Reef is under critical threat — drives the dumb bastards feral all the time.'

'The Barrier Reef is nowhere near the proposed site of the coal mine.'

'And, your point is? It doesn't matter what we tell them so long as they act.'

'Why don't we use the traditional lands argument?'

'No one cares.' Tyrone tore at the paper bag. 'Well, they do, but they relate to the environment more. They think the rich getting richer is more important than the plight of aborigines.'

'What do you want me to do?'

'I'm into the energy market operator's mainframe, and I have access to the interconnectors. I just need to check the security walls connecting our IP addresses back to us.' He fingered out the bag of chips and shoved a couple into his mouth.

'You are the best,' Simone smiled.

'I'm trying to impress you, and this is the way I think I can.'

'Don't underestimate yourself.' Simone sat next to him, tapping at her keyboard. 'If I backtrack and program a couple of additional firewalls around our codes, will that be enough?'

Tyrone bit into his burger and through a mouthful of food said, 'Once we are done with security we'll be ready to move to the next stage. I'll email Conan and Nellie later and let them know.'

'Will we have a break then?' Simone swung her legs toward him, leaned back in her chair and smiled.

'Are you asking me out on a date?'

'It's been a couple of weeks; I think it's time we *had* a date.' Simone swayed her knees.

Tyrone stopped chewing and watched. 'All right, let's work till midnight then call it quits, is that okay?' He started chewing again, cramming a chip into his mouth.

'Two hours, sure, I can wait that long.' Simone snapped back into the desk. 'Now give me that doona, it's bloody freezing.'

¶

'The kids reckon we can go now.' Messaris was meeting with Miller and McGuiness at a café in Manuka, a small village precinct near Canberra's parliamentary district. The sun was out but a chill drove them inside to the warmth and a smell of fresh ground coffee.

'I reckon the prime minister could be ready for a chat. He's taking a hammering in the polls,' said McGuiness as he scanned the national broadsheet's latest results. 'It says here that almost seventy per cent of voters think he should sign the UN treaty.'

'Doesn't mean squat to him — the poll he worries about is election day.' Messaris sipped his espresso.

'How do you think this will play out?' Miller asked.

'You go and have a chat to him. You set out your needs and then demonstrate your fire power,' Messaris said.

'How do I get to see him?'

'Good question. My boy Tyrone has scheduled you into his diary for the day after next, for a meeting before question time.'

Miller slumped in her chair. 'How did he do that?'

'Around two weeks ago he hacked into Grobbelaar's chief of staff's laptop when she was out having lunch here in Canberra. He was almost on the next table and put the entry in. He's a wizard that kid.'

'I don't understand, he stole the laptop and then handed it back?'

'He has a hacking code — don't ask me what. He can enter any unsuspecting computer if he is close enough to use its wireless connection.'

Miller thought for a moment. 'Two days?'

'Nervous are you, Jeddah?' McGuiness sneered.

'Don't you talk to me like that, you moron,' Miller snapped back. 'Show some respect.' A customer on the next table glanced up but feeling an air of menace emanating from the three of them, returned to her newspaper.

'He doesn't mean anything by it — relax.' Messaris silenced McGuiness with a wave. 'He's Afrikaans, old habits die hard.'

'Next time I won't say anything, I'll just react — clear?' Miller spat.

'Gee, I'm really nervous,' McGuiness mocked. 'I'm virtually shaking.' He lifted his rock-steady hand.

'Settle down, both of you,' Messaris hissed. 'Look at you — two old farts, thinking you're young revolutionaries.' Messaris laughed. 'We're supposed to be wiser with age.'

'It's not working for him.' Miller's aversion to McGuiness remained strong as she glared at him.

Messaris waited a little longer. 'Do you think you should take anyone?'

'If you aren't coming with me, then I better invite a few willing brothers from Sydney for the drive down.'

'This is an Aboriginal project so we white fellas think we should not be associated with it,' Messaris said. 'You demand action and reassert the threat.'

'He's not going to listen to me, I can promise you that.'

'The prime minister is already feeling political heat in the polls, you just have to get him to focus on political outcomes if he doesn't cooperate. We need to give him a good reason to sign the treaty.' Messaris finished his espresso with a quick snap. 'Just get him focused on the main political game and don't raise other matters such as this sovereignty bullshit.'

'It's important for my people.'

'Maybe it is, but we need small steps, not these giant leaps you want to take.' Messaris gawped over to the waiter and pointed to his cup, suggesting another. 'Listen, I'll make sure a headline in the national paper gets him focused on you and the polls — just make sure you give him a good enough reason to act.'

Miller smirked. 'How will you do that?'

Messaris tapped his nose. 'I have influence. Now piss off and let's talk tomorrow. Get your boys here. Make sure they look the part. We want this to be the start of peace talks not the start of war.'

¶

Parliament House is thick with security when in session. To enter the building requires close scrutiny — identification checks, scanned entry, and in rare cases a security pat-down. Miller was summoned to one side as she stepped through the metal detector and asked for further identification. She was then directed into a side room and advised by two female officers they would perform a pat down, which she did not resist. A convicted terrorist raised the red flag whenever she moved through a security checkpoint. She was the only visitor in her delegation singled out.

Once the delegation stepped out into the marbled entrance they ambled to another security post to advise the prime minister's office of their arrival for the scheduled meeting. Security gave them clip-on numbered passes and advised them a staffer would be along to escort them to the PM. The group of five waited for ten minutes before a chirpy officer from the prime minister's office greeted them.

'I'm sorry, the prime minister wasn't expecting you and his senior adviser has requested we make another time. We would also like you to submit your reasons for wishing to meet with the prime minister.'

Miller decided bluff was better than retreat. 'That's fine. We also have a meeting with the opposition leader this afternoon. If the prime minister regards our meeting as unimportant, then I'm sure the media conference we will be holding later today will be an opportunity for me to explain to him what he missed out on. He should tune in.'

'What's the nature of your meeting with the opposition leader?'

'I'm afraid I can't disclose details, but it's about national security.'

The staffer shifted on her feet, gnawing at her lip as she gazed at a smiling Miller. 'Wait here.' She stepped back and telephoned for instructions. It wasn't long before she returned. 'Okay, follow me.'

From the front parliament's entrance to the prime minister's suite is a five-minute hike, through two further security checkpoints where the staffer swiped her card, then across the huge atrium below the national flag fluttering on the well-known enormous flag pole high on parliamentary hill. The delegation was ushered into an anteroom, a security officer joining them. As they waited, a uniformed federal police officer, with a loud crackling two-way radio unit, entered the room and stood by the door.

'Miss Millergoorra, I believe,' Prime Minister Grobbelaar swept open double doors and stepped into the room, seeking to shake Miller's hand. 'Please join me in my suite.'

The delegation timidly entered.

'Please sit down.' Grobbelaar waved to chairs circling a meeting table. 'I have asked Attorney General, Mary Whittington, and our Indigenous Affairs Minister, Patrick O'Toole, to join us in case they can provide a response for you. Please make yourselves comfortable.'

'Thank you, Prime Minister,' Miller said, as the delegation sat opposite the politicians. 'We appreciate the opportunity.'

'Not every day a convicted terrorist comes calling,' chortled Grobbelaar, eyeballing his attorney general. 'Now, what's all this about.' Grobbelaar wasted little time. 'How the hell did you manage to book an appointment with me?'

'Pleasantries over then?'

'As if I would ever have the need to see you.' Grobbelaar leaned toward her. 'You're nothing but trouble, and if it were up to me you would still be in jail.' He pushed back into his seat. 'Now what did you want to talk to me about?'

'We're here to talk to you about the proposed coalmining license in Arnhem Land and discuss our reasons why the UN treaty should be signed.'

'Why didn't you just send a letter? This is now a waste of time.'

'We think we have reasons why you should consider our request.'

'Who the hell are you to come and tell me what to do — you have no authority and represent no one.'

'We represent the mob from Arnhem Land. My people are … were, traditional owners until Koning Mining declared war and massacred us, then plundered our land.'

'Alleged. Never proven,' Grobbelaar snarled.

'They started a war and I sought retribution.'

Grobbelaar clenched his fists. 'What you did was an act of terrorism and you were found guilty and served your time — not enough in my view.'

Miller sat back in her chair and waited a moment. 'Now you're at it again, but this time we'll win.'

The prime minister, agitated, shifted to the edge of his chair. 'Are you threatening me? Are you threatening the Australian government?' Grobbelaar strode to his desk snatching at the phone. 'Get the justice minister in here as soon as you can.'

'No, I'm not threatening you. I want to help you.'

'Help me? I don't believe it — help me?' Grobbelaar barked. 'Have you got a screw loose?' He returned to the table. 'Are you barking mad? Who do you think you are?'

'You must be a little tense today, prime minister — I get that, the polls aren't good, are they?' A colleague tossed newspaper clippings on the table and the stapled bundle slid across to the prime minister. 'According to that headline, you will be out of a job this time next year.'

Grobbelaar shoved them aside and O'Toole collected them. 'These polls mean nothing.'

'The campaign against you has just begun,' Miller said. 'We have two complementary campaigns working against your government to ensure you lose support in vital marginal seats, and the popular vote, which means your senate numbers are threatened.'

'Why are you doing this? O'Toole asked.

'You're the minister, you should know,' Miller smiled, maintaining her gaze with Grobbelaar. 'We want to stop the mine from going ahead and have the government sign the UN treaty.'

'Why should we sign a treaty?' O'Toole persisted.

Miller shifted her gaze from Grobbelaar to the minister. 'First Nation people want a say in how our Country is managed and governments should not have the right to arbitrarily approve mining rights without proper consultation with the owners.'

'You have the Native Title Act.'

'You're kidding ... the Act provides little protection for the land and forces owners to negotiate not deny access.'

'You think a treaty will change what?' O'Toole asked.

'It gives us more power — we make the decisions, not the government using laws they enacted.'

'The argument you're pushing is not sustainable and the electorate will never support a United Nations' intervention,' Whittington said, as Justice Minister, Marilyn Hodge, entered, taking a chair at the end of the table.

'Fact is, voters will do what we tell them to do,' Miller smiled, Whittington averted her eyes.

'What is it you want?' Grobbelaar asked.

'I want to work with you to end this community unrest and increasing hostility toward your government and allow you to win the next election.' Miller smiled again. 'You believe me, don't you, when I say I want to work with you?'

'Even if you were the incredible woman of influence you say you are, and I very much doubt that, then why would I want to do any deal with you?'

'Because, Prime Minister, I will take your power away.' Miller sat forward, clasped her hands in front of her and smiled. 'Literally and figuratively.'

'Sure, sure — and pigs have flown to the moon,' snapped Grobbelaar, losing patience.

'What is it you want?' Whittington asked.

'Two things,' Miller flopped back into her chair, 'we want the UN treaty signed, with the immediate cancellation of any plans and agreements to begin coalmining in Arnhem Land.'

'Not going to happen, I can assure you,' Grobbelaar said.

'And the second request?' Whittington asked.

'A homeland state — full support of the government to make an application to the United Nations to sanction an Aboriginal sovereign state.'

For a moment the politicians didn't move, not even to glance at each other; they were speechless. The prime minister then bursting into laughter.

Miller raised her voice to speak over him. 'We want the government to agree to these two requests, and in return, we will not take away your power.' Miller scratched her bottom lip with her thumb. It was a bold request and she knew it would be treated with disdain, but an ambit claim sometimes gets through.

'A homeland?' Grobbelaar mocked. 'Where do you think you will establish such a thing — Sydney, perhaps?'

'No, we would like to claim the Northern Territory, which is sacred Aboriginal land.' Miller sat back. 'Just like the Jews claimed Palestine.'

'This is a joke — you are joshing me, aren't you.' Grobbelaar laughed out loud. 'You want your own sovereign state?'

'How do you see this working, Miss Millergoorra?' Hodge asked.

'Constitutionally the commonwealth can do whatever it wants

with the Northern Territory. We are suggesting you proclaim it as an Aboriginal homeland and allow us to govern ourselves.'

'You already have the Karrakatta Congress, which is supposed to provide First Nations a link to the parliament,' Hodge said.

'You can't be serious?' Miller shook her head. 'You know Congress is a talkfest and achieves nothing of substance. Governments don't treat it seriously, and even though we achieved recognition in the constitution, it means nothing. We remain disadvantaged and dispossessed.'

The ministers said nothing until O'Toole asked, 'Does Congress agree with you?'

'They support a homeland.'

'How will that resolve the conflict with five hundred different points of view?' Grobbelaar mocked. 'Your mob is hopeless at making decisions.'

'We all agree to sovereignty and if we had a partitioned independent state then those who want to move there can, just like the European Jews did last century.'

'That is a very different scenario, as you well know,' the prime minister said. 'We just declare a first nation homeland and every Aborigine moves there?' He wasn't convinced.

'Don't be stupid, of course not. You will still need to have a First Nation policy providing government services, just not in the Northern Territory.'

'It's a stupid idea,' Grobbelaar checked about his colleagues for support. 'No one will ever support it.'

'People will support it if they are given enough reasons. It's happened in other countries and there is no reason why it can't happen here,' Miller replied with spirit.

'You think they'll support a convicted terrorist?'

'Mandela was called a terrorist.'

'You ain't no Mandela, I can assure you,' Grobbelaar chided.

'Neither are you,' Miller returned the put-down, then smiled. 'But, you could be and bring a legacy that could ensure the history books record your magnificent leadership.'

'Yeah, right,' Grobbelaar ridiculed the comment and dropped back into his chair, glaring at Miller.

'What happens now?' O'Toole asked.

'As I said, we want the treaty ratified by the government within four weeks, otherwise we shall ensure the government loses the next election,' Miller said. 'And, we want the government to commit to launching a legal process for the establishment of an Aboriginal homeland, that's all.'

'Ain't ever going to happen.' Grobbelaar shook his head.

'Or?' Whittington asked.

Miller waited until she had eye contact with the prime minister. 'Or we take the government's power away.'

'How do you propose to do that?' Grobbelaar asked.

'We increase our community campaign and provide compelling reasons for a change of government. After just a few weeks we have taken four points from you in the polls. You can't continue to ignore the issue of the UN treaty. The polling and negative press will become diabolical for you until you sign it.'

'So, what? When they go to vote they will think of jobs and the money I can put into their pocket,' Grobbelaar said. 'They won't be voting to provide Aborigines with more power, or a homeland. I can assure you, that guilt trip has long gone.'

'This is a long-term strategy for us. We're going to continue to undermine your government and place you in a constant state of political unrest. We're more focused with our issues now and we know how to get what we want,' Miller said. 'But, and this is important for you to come to terms with, to ensure this campaign takes weeks and not years, the government will be at war with the community. We are going to take your power away.'

'You're not making any sense,' said a confused Hodge.

Miller reached into her pocket dragging out a phone. She jabbed at it, placing it to her ear. After a short time, she said, 'Close Canberra.'

'What the hell is this about?' Grobbelaar sounded anxious.

'You think you have the power in Canberra?' Miller paused, then smiled slyly. 'I now have the power.'

'I've had enough of this shit. Time for you folks to leave. This is a joke.' Grobbelaar stood. 'I've had a shake-down before, but this is ridiculous.'

The lights flickered then went off, before coming back on.

'Canberra no longer has power,' Miller declared.

'Bullshit, that was just a supply fault.' Grobbelaar strode to the window inspecting outside.

Whittington checked her phone. 'I have a reduced signal.'

'Your telecommunication system in Canberra no longer has power from the grid.' Miller smiled, enjoying the confusion of the politicians. 'Only the New South Wales operators can supply coverage at the moment.'

'How come we still have power?' Hodge asked no one in particular as she gazed at the ceiling lights.

'Parliament has its own back-up generators,' O'Toole said.

Grobbelaar picked up his phone and prodded a button, 'Can you check the Canberra power supply administrator and get an update?'

'As I said, Prime Minister, I have the power.'

As the prime minister sat at his desk his phone buzzed and he engaged the speaker button.

'Prime Minister, the grid has failed and the entire Territory is without power.'

Grobbelaar grimaced. 'Any reason?'

'Supply discontinued. They think something is wrong with the administration network.'

Grobbelaar called off and glared at Miller. 'You're so damn smart — get it back on.'

Miller swiped the phone and prodded a button and after a short delay, she said. 'Put it back up.'

'Anything we can do to her, Marilyn?' Grobbelaar strolled back to the table and resumed his seat.

'Sure, we can hold them for conspiracy, sedition, perhaps an act of terrorism, and we could charge them with extortion.'

'I would counsel a cool head,' Whittington interjected.

'Well, if these morons just caused this then we have to do something,' Grobbelaar said.

'Or we could go into negotiation with them.' O'Toole smiled at Miller.

'Or we could take them out the back and beat the fucking crap out of them,' barked Grobbelaar.

Miller didn't respond, she just gazed at the prime minister, enjoying the moment.

'Miss Millergoorra,' Whittington ignored the prime minister and focused on Miller, 'what happens now?'

'In five days, we begin a campaign of turning off the power in every capital city. We would expect this loss of power to cause significant inconvenience in each city and in some cases the state. We will advise the media of our plans and believe this will trigger demonstrations against the government. We anticipate anarchists' involvement, and they may take things a little too far, stretching local law enforcement . . . we're planning chaos in the community and we think Australians will blame one person.' Miller shifted in her seat sitting a little straighter. 'We know we're in the right here; the UN agrees with us. The people agree with us when they know the facts, and unless you want to go down at the next election I would suggest you sign the treaty.' Miller stood and tossed the phone onto the table. 'We will communicate with you through this phone. I realise you will need to discuss this — and you'll need to give Koning the bad news — but rest assured that unless our demands are met, your cities will turn into anarchy before the end of the month.'

O'Toole stood and walked up to Miller, 'Is there no other way?'

'You of all people should know we are serious. If you want to retain your power, then sign the treaty.'

'Fuck off,' yelled Grobbelaar.

'This will not turn out well for you,' Hodge offered as Miller began to leave.

'This is hard ball politics,' Miller said. 'The game you all play so well when it comes to us. Just let me reassure you, we are playing for keeps and if you want to win — then sign the treaty.'

'There must be a better way?' Whittington said. 'Can we talk about it?'

'For over thirty years I sat on my arse thinking about better ways to protect my culture, my people and my land. I hoped the Congress would make progress while your government kept me locked up, but you still laugh at us, especially him,' she pointed at Grobbelaar, 'my people deserve better than promises and goodwill. We have talked for decades, now we want action. Sign the treaty.'

¶

'That went well, don't you think?' Whittington asked as the others resumed their chairs.

'It was a waste of time, quite frankly. There is no way we will do anything that bitch wants us to do.' Grobbelaar scanned his ministers. 'Marilyn, engage the feds and have them begin surveillance on her. I want to know who she's working with. Get them to track how these bastards got to the power grid. I don't want it to happen again, is that understood? Patrick, get on to Neesham and find out what his story is — the moron needs to stop this bullshit. Whit, what will happen if we don't sign the treaty? There is no possible way I will ever agree to this.'

'Even if we lose support?' Whittington asked.

'We'll never lose an election on this issue, trust me. White folks will never support black fellas, not on this.' Grobbelaar shook his head. 'If these cretins think they can walk in here and demand a homeland ... what the hell were they thinking?'

8

Neesham felt a little lethargic, the three-course meal weighing on him with the wines dulling his senses, but it was the aroma of the whisky that made him feel sleepy, as he lay back in the soft leather chair. A veil of cigar smug hung above the three men as they sought a resolution to the issues before them, puffing on the finest Cubans presented to the prime minister by the embassy. The prime minister insisted Neesham and Lewe Koning join him to discuss the egregious demands of Millergoorra, and the men were relaxing in Grobbelaar's private lounge.

'Victoria is never going to reopen the Latrobe Valley to coalmining, the greenies have made sure of that, so we need this new field in Arnhem Land,' Koning said, as he sipped the generous splash of whisky. 'It's my right to mine for minerals and that's what I'm going to do.'

'No concern about traditional owners and their rights under native title laws?' Neesham asked, blowing a stream of smoke toward the ceiling. 'You think you have more rights than they do?'

'Of course, I do; I've paid them too much already.' Koning sighed, having to explain his rights yet again.

'The trouble we have is with Millergoorra and her group. How do we stop their campaign?' Grobbelaar asked.

'I would recommend you sign the treaty, Prime Minister,' Neesham said, reaching forward to ash his stogie in the bowl on the marble coffee table.

'How much?' Koning asked.

'How much what?' Neesham responded.

'How much is it going to cost me this time to have the local kaffirs agree to the mine?'

'Not sure they would appreciate being called that,' Neesham said. 'Perhaps a different attitude to the traditional owners might get you what you want.'

'Blacks are blacks — South Africa, Australia, no different.' Koning drained his glass and tilted it toward the prime minister for a refill. 'They think they can build a nation, but they sell out for money. Look at South Africa since they took it back.'

'That sort of talk disturbs me.' Neesham crossed his legs and leaned away from Koning.

'Ease up, Jimmy,' Grobbelaar topped up Koning's glass. 'Lewe is a hard-nosed Afrikaans and hates Indigenous people no matter which country they're from. He says the same things about the Vietnamese, don't you Lewe?'

'Christ, they're worse than the Chinese, those rat fuckers.'

'You see, he's a racist to the core and hates everyone,' Grobbelaar snorted. 'But, without his money we can never develop these mining projects, and he wants to mine coal.'

'Mine coal in China.' Neesham stifled a smile. 'It's time to begin to respect traditional owners and our needs.'

'Jimmy, this is not the attitude we pay you for.' Grobbelaar sat up again offering him another splash of whisky, but Neesham waved him away. 'Your Congress is working, and its elders' council gives you the influence you want.' Neesham glanced away. 'This talk of a homeland is a stupid idea, and we're never going to sign a treaty to end mining.'

'So, why am I here?'

'I want Millergoorra stopped.'

'Sign the treaty and she will stop.'

'How much?' Koning smiled.

'You think you can buy me?'

'We have before,' Koning's smile widened. 'We're just negotiating price.'

'I had my reasons regarding the diamond mine, but I didn't agree to you wiping them out.'

'My men were a little over enthusiastic, I admit that, but I got what I wanted, and so did you, if I recall.'

'Ya think?'

'This is all before my time so it's ancient history as far as I'm concerned,' Grobbelaar interrupted. 'But Jimmy, understand this, we will be mining up north and will not be establishing this homeland bullshit.'

'That's bad news.' Neesham stretched a leg onto the coffee table. 'I'm not sure the radicals will accept that — there's trouble ahead for you.'

'The government will not respond to these threats I can assure you. Nothing will get us to the table to negotiate, nothing.' Grobbelaar grabbed the whisky bottle and splashed a large dram into his own glass and took a mighty swig, wincing as he swallowed.

Koning studied Neesham. 'Jimmy, how much do you want to end this?'

'This is bigger than money.'

'Tell me, what do you want?' Koning insisted.

'I want the mine deferred at least ten years, and I want the Congress and the council restructured so that it has a president — I want the inaugural presidency appointment for an initial period of six years.'

'You're batshit crazy, man,' Grobbelaar laughed.

'If you do that, then I will convince Miller to back off,' Neesham said.

'Is that it?' Koning pressed.

'I also want five million dollars put into an offshore account.'

'So, it is about the money.' Koning sat back triumphant.

'You think I can do all of this without media or parliamentary scrutiny?' the prime minister said.

'If you take a long-term world view, it's a good deal.' Neesham sat up straighter. 'Coal will be back in favour in ten years, and demand will be higher than it is now, so don't sign a treaty stopping mining forever, just announce that you have listened to the traditional people and will reconsider the mining policy again in ten years.'

'Ten years is too long for me,' Koning said.

'Not if you get the licence without any resistance from the traditional owners. Miller will be too old by then and the economy will have changed.'

'It's something to consider,' Grobbelaar said. 'If we agree, we will need to legislate it.'

'Let me tell you this, if you don't make this work then there may be blood,' Neesham said. 'The radicals want action and they are prepared to go all the way. Do not underestimate their determination to get a result.'

'Let them just try — I've wiped out resistance before and I will do it again,' Koning said, his voice low and menacing. 'If she needs dealing with, then let me finish the job.'

'Geezus Lewe, we don't need to do that,' Neesham snapped and then continued in a more conciliatory tone, 'we just defer the mine, tighten up the structure of the Congress and pay the money.'

'Why should you be president?' Grobbelaar asked.

'Because for the last thirty-plus years I have taken shit from my brothers and sisters, and now I think it's time they received some stick from me.'

'Just be careful, Prime Minister, that sounds like a dictator speaking.' Koning smiled.

¶

Messaris and McGuiness were ensconced by the fire at the Walt and Burley bar on the foreshore of Lake Burley Griffin in Kingston. Conan tossed more wood on and the blaze was taking the chill off them. Tyrone was ordering food as they waited for Miller to arrive.

'Is this harebrained scheme going to work, Commander?' McGuiness took a large mouthful of beer and eased himself into the high-backed chair.

'Tyrone is getting significant traction on social media and we've more than doubled our active supporters. The targeted politicians are beginning to speak out more about the UN deal, and the opposition parties are waking up to what's going on and supporting the idea of blocking the coalmine, the populist bastards.'

'What does all that mean?'

Messaris gave a half smile and stroked his face. 'It means I don't have a clue, but I trust the process.'

'It was far simpler years ago.'

'Muscle doesn't have the same effect as it used to, Macca. Victims tend to record everything on their smart phones these days, so standover tactics are subtler, just like Tyrone has been telling us.'

'So instead of threatening them with a gun, we threaten them with a message?'

Messaris laughed. 'Basically. You're a bit of a dinosaur, aren't you?' He smiled at his old friend.

'Maybe. How many Facebook friends do you have?'

Messaris didn't respond to the lame joke. He considered social media fraught with danger for anyone wanting to retain their privacy.

McGuinness took another hefty swig of beer and asked, 'Are there any opportunities for us in this scheme?'

'Half a mill not enough for you?' queried Messaris.

'I'm getting too old for this shit, we need to think about a pension plan.'

'I would have preferred Koning provide it, but shafting us comes at a cost, which is why I like our little plan.'

'Revenge doesn't pay the bills, though, does it.' McGuiness took another large mouthful of beer.

Messaris checked out his friend. 'What do you have in mind?

'I have no idea, but, as you said, if we know the power is off at a certain time there may be an opportunity for us.'

'What opportunity?' Tyrone dropped into his seat after placing his order.

Messaris scanned the area. 'We were just talking about making the most of the power being cut off.'

'Like robbing a bank or something,' Tyrone joked as he placed the order number on the table between them

'Not a bank, but a casino maybe,' Messaris responded.

'Why not a bank?' McGuiness suggested.

'Way too much security,' scoffed Messaris.

'I'm glad you're considering places where they hold plenty of cash and there's not too much security,' Tyrone said, smiling. 'I like this game.'

'So, a casino,' Messaris said.

'What about a racetrack, with all the bookies?' Tyrone grinned. McGuiness nodded. 'Or maybe an armoured truck?'

Both men stared at him. 'What the hell are you talking about Tyrone?' Messaris said, shaking his head.

'Robbing a place where there's plenty of money.'

'What — you think robbing an armoured truck is a smart thing to do?' ridiculed McGuiness.

'Of course, not — but we are dreaming, right?'

'Yeah, we're dreaming,' said Messaris.

'I mean, if we weren't dreaming, then it would be easy to knock off a bank,' Tyrone said, matter-of-factly.

Messaris eyed McGuiness in surprise. 'It's not that easy, trust me.'

'Even if you get the money, you have to keep running.' McGuiness took another swig of beer.

'You blokes are so old school, that's what I like about you.'

'Okay smart-arse,' McGuiness snapped. 'How do the new kids do it?'

'For starters, do something that is undetectable.'

'Like what?' Messaris turned away from the fire to Tyrone who was now being served a mustard hotdog and a side of chips. 'I thought you were going for tapas.'

'Changed my mind,' Tyrone said. 'Anyway, you steal a small amount and they won't detect you.'

'You're a fuckin' idiot — why rob a bank to steal a small amount?' McGuiness snorted.

'If you steal the same small amount many times over then you go undetected.' Tyrone picked up his hot dog and bit off a good chunk, wiping mustard away from his mouth with a paper serviette.

Messaris was sceptical. 'How do you do that?'

Tyrone took another generous bite and said, 'How many credit card transactions do you reckon there are a day in Australia?'

'I wouldn't have a clue, how many?'

'Around twenty million,' mumbled Tyrone.

'So, what?' McGuiness grabbed a hot chip from the basket.

Tyrone glared at him as if to say, get your own. 'If you took one cent for each transaction, how much would you get a day for doing nothing?'

McGuiness snapped up another chip. 'I wasn't good at arithmetic, how much?'

'Around two hundred thousand.'

'For one day?' McGuiness took another chip and sat back.

Tyrone moved his chips further away from McGuiness. 'Over a month that would be around five and half million dollars.' He took another large bite of hotdog and washed some of it down with his soda. 'Small amount from lots of accounts.'

Messaris lowered his tone and asked. 'Are you serious, this can be done?'

'Of course, it can, it just needs the right encrypted program,' Tyrone said, wiping his lips. 'The secret is to take the money between audits, which they do ever month. Write a program that self-destructs, and they will never find you.'

'That's impossible. Surely, they'd pick it up,' Messaris said.

'All transactions go through a central clearing house, there's a fee charged that you see on your bank statement. That's where you take the cent from and send it off to an account somewhere.'

'And they can't track you?' Messaris asked.

'Yes, of course they can, but if you cover your tracks by moving it around, it would be too hard for them to find you. Plus, consumers wouldn't notice a small amount like a cent on a transaction, so no one complains — the banks then let it go because it's cost them nothing.'

'A risk-free theft.' Messaris smiled at McGuiness, who frowned.

'Simple.' He pushed the last of his hotdog into his mouth.

'If it's so fucking simple, why doesn't someone do it?' McGuiness mocked.

'Two points,' Tyrone shoved more chips into his overcrowded mouth, 'perhaps they already have, we would never know, that's one; and two, to get into the system you have to turn it off.'

'For how long?' Messaris queried.

'Ten minutes — thirty max.'

'Where?'

'Ah, that's the difficult part.' Tyrone wiped his hands and tossed the napkin onto the food paddle. 'The clearing house servers are in a basement vault about three storeys below the Reserve Bank building in Melbourne. Security is horrendous no doubt.'

'Bullshit,' McGuiness laughed. 'How do you know this — no one would.'

'Google.'

'If we had access to the servers what would we need done?' Messaris asked.

'Once at the server it is a matter of uploading a program that sits there unnoticed between audits. You just need to know when the audit is.'

McGuiness scoffed. 'Sounds too hard to me.'

Tyrone took a swig of his soda. 'It's possible, but you need to get to the server, and that's impossible.'

'If the power was off?' Messaris queried.

Tyrone thought for a moment. 'They have a manual override, but if the power was off, then chances improve.'

'It's bullshit,' McGuiness said.

'What is?' Tyrone asked.

'It would be like taking money from a baby,' Messaris said. 'A month of one cent pieces and we have five million — is that enough for you Macca?'

'You aren't thinking about doing it?' Tyrone said.

'If there is a power blackout in Melbourne, then there may be a chance, right?'

Tyrone nodded. 'I suppose, but when do we know when a blackout's going to happen?'

McGuiness laughed. 'Are you serious?'

'Go easy on the boy, Macca,' Messaris smiled, then glancing at Tyrone. 'We are turning the power off if you recall.'

'Oh, I see what you mean,' said Tyrone, embarrassed.

'Millergoorra's here, so let's talk about it later.' Messaris grinned at his colleagues. 'But, yes; I am thinking about it.' He stood as Miller and Simone approached and ushered them to their seats. 'How are you, girls? Ready for the next step?'

'Hi boys, I'll have a beer thanks and Simone will have a wine.' Miller nodded at Tyrone, suggesting he attend to the order. 'Neesham is with him now.'

'I don't trust that guy.' McGuiness almost spat the words. 'How cool is he?'

'He'll always back self-interest if it's running.' Miller left the seat next to Tyrone for Simone and sat by the fire. 'How's the campaign going?'

Messaris opened his notes and said, 'We've increased participation on social media and the national media are now running our lines — we just need the prime minister to feel the squeeze in polling a little more. My information is that he does not care about you or the campaign.'

'Let's hit him again and tell the media his leadership is in jeopardy,' Miller suggested.

McGuiness chuckled. 'Geez, for an old girl you get fired up.'

'Once a revolutionary, always a revolutionary.' Miller smiled. 'But, never a mercenary like some.'

McGuiness slid to the edge of his chair. 'What's that supposed to mean?'

'Geezus, for an old bloke you get fired up, Terry,' Miller laughed.

'Let's turn off the lights again,' Messaris spoke over them.

'Do we have to?' Tyrone passed a bottle of premium beer to Miller and a glass of chardonnay to Simone. 'I mean, why Canberra? We're about to enjoy ourselves — why turn the lights off?'

'Where do you suggest?'

'Simone and I think we can turn off Tasmania.'

'The whole state?' Messaris asked. Simone gave a cheesy smile and Tyrone nodded. 'From here?'

'Yep, as we sit here we can take the power away from Tasmania.' Simone smirked. 'We are that talented.'

'Well then, fire up your laptop,' Messaris directed.

'Are we at risk here?' Miller asked, scanning about the room.

'As long as we keep moving and doing things differently they'll never find us,' Tyrone said, as he hauled his laptop from his satchel, prodding the power button.

'Let's place the call.' Messaris nodded toward Miller.

'Wait up,' Miller said. 'What's our plan? What do we need — what does Grobbelaar have to tell us?'

'He has to agree to another meeting to discuss our needs. If he doesn't, then tell him about Tasmania and advise him Perth will be next,' Messaris peeked to Tyrone for confirmation, who shrugged his shoulders and nodded.

'Come on sweetheart, get your arse into gear,' McGuiness snapped.

'All right, all right.' Miller twisted her face. 'What's wrong with you tonight?'

'Just sick of divas not wanting to get a quick resolution. Your job is to get him to sign the fucking document and make sure he knows you will hurt him if he doesn't.'

The phone buzzed on the desk in the next room. Grobbelaar heard it and moved to answer before it rang out. 'Yes?'

'Good evening, Prime Minister. Have you made a decision?'

'Yes, I have.' Grobbelaar flopped back into his chair as the others listened in to his call. 'I have given it a great deal of thought.' He dropped the phone from his ear for a brief moment and smiled at his guests in the next room. 'While I may think there is merit in your need to block the coalmine, the use of intimidation to get what you want does not reflect well on your argument. I have decided to respond to the UN by saying no. Therefore, I will not be signing any treaty.'

'You know there are consequences to your decisions, don't you?'

'Nothing you can do will frighten me.' Grobbelaar sat forward. 'Nothing you say will change my mind.'

'We want the mine licence revoked.'

'I couldn't care less what you want old girl.'

There was a pause, but Grobbelaar could hear someone breathing. 'Tasmania.'

'Tasmania what?'

'Tasmania is now without power.'

'Bull-fucking-shit, lady.' Grobbelaar stood and began pacing. 'You are full of crap. No one can just close down a state.'

'I just did — and that means everything — so think about that.'

Grobbelaar considered it, then said. 'You want blood on your hands do you?'

'It'll be your fault and we'll brief the media on your intransigent position.'

'Fuck you!' The prime minister threw the phone at the couch.

'I do hope that was no one important?' Koning asked.

'It was your bitch, Jimmy,' Grobbelaar shouted. 'She reckons she just turned off Tasmania. Fuck me, who does she think she's dealing with?'

'I might be able to get her to stop, but we will need good signs that the government is meeting our needs.'

'Stuff your needs, Jimmy.' Grobbelaar waved his hands in the air as he paced about the room. 'This ends tonight, otherwise you're history.'

Neesham took a breath to calm himself. 'No Rene — if it doesn't end soon, you may be history.'

Grobbelaar stopped and stared at Neesham, breathing deeply.

'I could wear a ten-year delay, I suppose,' offered Koning from his chair.

'Jimmy, this has to end. I will not be blackmailed like this.'

A quiet knock on the door announced a staff member. She poked her head in and said, 'Prime Minister, there has been a massive state-wide power disruption in Tasmania. It seems the whole state has gone down and there is a total blackout.'

9

The late flight to Darwin landed after ten, but Neesham was keen to tackle urgent paperwork at his office before heading home after his four days in Canberra. He could hear noise from a party at a nearby restaurant as he unlocked the front door, climbing the wooden staircase to the first floor. The large windows of the old colonial building providing enough light to manoeuvre to his office. He unlocked the outer office, moving to his assistant's desk, a shaft of light brightening the room. Leaving his bag by the door, he checked his mailbox, dropping a number of envelopes back into the box before carrying the others to his office. After unlocking the door, crossing to his desk, pulling out his leather chair, flicking on his desk lamp, he sat.

'Mr Jimmy, did you have a good flight?'

'What the hell?' Neesham jolted up, pressing against the wall behind him. 'How the hell did you get in?'

'Ancient Chinese method of Poyzen Zuang, which allows us to scale buildings and open windows that are left unlocked,' Teo said with a cheeky grin, watching Neesham relax, resuming his seat. 'No, just kidding.' Teo laughed. 'I used a master key.'

'You couldn't wait until the morning?'

'I'm returning to China tomorrow. I wanted to ensure our plan is being followed.'

'The prime minister is yet to agree, but he will.'

'This is good news — did the Tasmania event change his mind?'

'He was surprised by the street demonstrations and the damage to services, but he's remains determined not to deal with terrorists.'

'Then why does he not arrest her?'

'She's not the issue, and I suspect Grobbelaar knows that,' Neesham said. 'He's smart enough to know someone would take her place — but I must say, they're throwing a heap of resources at it to stop anyone hacking the power grid, so they can avoid another incident.'

'If he is not persuaded by these threats, how are you going to stop the mine?'

'My fall-back position is a ten-year deferment, which is what you want.'

'It's what we all want, Mr Jimmy.' Teo picked up a small black leather satchel and tossed it onto the desk. 'This is your first payment; spend it judiciously.'

Neesham reached for the satchel. 'How much?'

'Five hundred thousand.'

Neesham opened the zipper, exposing bundles of crisp new notes. Satisfied, he tried to close the zipper, which proved difficult.

'We want the mine stopped before the end of the month.'

'That's a bit tight, but I remain confident.'

Teo stood. 'You have twenty-five days, Mr Jimmy, or we come for you.'

'I'll do my best.'

'Your best is good enough if you stop the mine. Do whatever it takes.'

Neesham dropped his head, paused, then peered up to respond, but Teo had already disappeared.

¶

The politicians were stunned after the briefing, not knowing what to say. The news from Tasmania was grim, the entire state ground to a halt during the blackout.

'Prime Minister, we need to detain Millergoorra and question her about how she's engineering this,' Justice Minister, Marilyn Hodge advised.

Grobbelaar turned to Mary Whittington. 'Would we gain anything if we chucked her in jail?'

'Her crime is conspiracy, but our tracking doesn't have any evidence of her consorting with anyone,' she responded. 'We could hold her on terrorist charges, but my preference is to continue to monitor her and observe who she contacts — she'll soon lead us to the brains behind the operation. The other point to reflect upon is that the media love the crisis and their stories are killing us.'

'Why aren't they after money?' Grobbelaar queried. 'They can't be doing this just to get a mine stopped.'

'Maybe, she is,' Hodge said.

'Can we defer the licence approval for ten years, as Neesham suggested?' Whittington asked. 'Koning has indicated he might agree to a deferment.'

'Neesham would need to prove to us he could end this terrorist shit if we are ever to announce the deal.' Grobbelaar scanned his briefing papers. 'I don't trust the bastard.'

'Can I suggest, Prime Minister, we have Neesham's elders agree to the ten-year deferment before we announce it to the public,' Hodge said.

'What about his money?' Grobbelaar asked.

'We get from him a signed agreement, then we release money into a trust account. It then releases money to him every year over the ten-year period, with a balloon at the end to keep him honest,' Hodge suggested.

'I like that idea, if we can find a way to handle the payments. What about his request to upgrade his position?' asked Whittington.

'He's a fucking bookkeeper, not a leader,' snapped Grobbelaar.

'Yes, but he is our bookkeeper, and he keeps a lid on the Karrakatta so it's nothing more than a biannual talkfest,' Whittington said. 'We don't want them to become anything more than that.'

'Okay, let me call him and organise an elders' meeting for the day after tomorrow so we get agreement on the deferment. That should give him enough time.'

'What do we do with Millergoorra?' asked Hodge.

'Keep surveillance, she may lead us to the others,' Grobbelaar replied.

'Have we any idea how they're doing it?' Whittington asked Hodge.

'They're very sophisticated; we can't track them electronically, there are too many security codes to deal with, and when we do identify an encryption location we find nothing there — which means they know how to send encrypted messages into our system and manipulate our security and firewalls.'

'That's a little dangerous wouldn't you think?' said Whittington, scratching the back of her head.

'Seriously — they're really good,' Hodge said. 'It's meant we've been forced to upgrade our security encryption and other codes, and we're now testing to upgrade our systems even further to contend with these new incursions.'

'These morons are a national security risk?' Grobbelaar asked.

'They have the ability to hack into the power grid, and if *they* can do it, then there's no reason why someone else can't,' agreed Hodge.

'How exposed are we?' asked Whittington.

'We know what we have to do, and we are working on building security walls around the interconnectors, but it's the access to our servers — sending us encrypted messages — that concerns us.'

'Concerns?' snapped Grobbelaar. 'I would suggest you need to resolve this before the end of the week, otherwise, we could be a target for international terrorists, which we don't need.'

'We have our best people on it, Prime Minister.'

'What about the homeland demand?' Whittington changed the subject.

'Let me tell you, we will never, ever, entertain such an idea,' Grobbelaar replied.

'I checked with constitutional experts in the department and Justice Kennedy provide an opinion,' Whittington said.

'We aren't going to agree to this ridiculous idea,' Grobbelaar persisted.

'Fair enough, but it could be done with a simple act of parliament and perhaps wouldn't have to go to a referendum for constitutional change, although I would recommend we consider having one, if we move that way.'

'It's never going to happen.'

'I'm just saying, Rene, you could do it — you have the authority to do it — that's all.'

'For starters, it would create chaos in the Territory — how could we have an independent state in the middle of the country? Issues of security and defence spring to mind. How will they fund this homeland?'

'Mining and tourism?' suggested Hodge, receiving a sharp glance from the prime minister.

'We would still need to provide for them in other states. What would it do to native title and the Reparations Act? Would we still be responsible for them? And, what status would they have with regard to education and health?' Grobbelaar asked.

'Aren't they Australians?' Hodge queried. 'We would be obliged to continue providing for them, although the issue of dual citizenship comes to mind.'

'It would solve this unresolved issue of sovereignty that has been a scab on the nation's soul for decades,' Whittington argued. 'Plus, it could be your legacy –you'd be seen as the father of the new nation.'

'That's crap — I'm a father to my daughter and that's all I want to be,' Grobbelaar laughed.

Whittington sat forward in her chair, 'Prime Minister, the Jews did it in the Middle East, it happened in India, and South Africa have allowed new states to exist. You could make it happen here — if you were of a mind, that's all I'm saying.'

'Well, thank you, Whit, I appreciate your advice,' Grobbelaar said with a mocking laugh. 'But, on this occasion, I won't be taking it.'

¶

As Miller waited for Simone in the park, children ran screaming after a ball, three fluffy dogs barked trying to join in the fun. The two women decided to keep all contact to a minimum since Tasmania, assuming phones were monitored, and they were under surveillance. Miller smiled as she watched Simone cross the busy street from Queen Victoria Market.

'You did that well,' Miller laughed as Simone staggered toward her.

'That is so hard, why they don't put lights there for pedestrians beats me.'

'When someone is hit by a tram they'll act.'

Simone stared out into the traffic. 'I miss your place.'

'Yeah, me too, sweetie.' Miller put an arm around her shoulders. 'What have you got to tell me?'

'We have Western Australia ready, but we want to wait on the others in case they change the algorithms in the next few days. The spooks are chasing us in the system, it's like a game of space invaders, but our firewalls are working okay and withstanding the heat. They have a clamp on South Australia, but we reckon we can crack it.'

'Are you enjoying this?'

'Tyrone's cute,' Simone grinned. 'We're having fun.'

'Yes, but if we get caught then you could do time.'

'Would that mean we do it together?'

'I'm not going back,' Miller said. 'I just survived last time — you know that.'

'I'm so lucky I was assigned to you.' Simone dropped her head onto Miller's shoulder.

'Why so lucky?'

'Well, for starters, I got to travel with you and learn that another culture exists,' Simone put her arm around Miller's waist. 'And I wouldn't have met Ty.'

'You like being a criminal?'

'I'm no more a criminal than you are — I see us as revolutionaries.'

'Freedom fighters,' laughed Miller.

Simone straightened and grabbed Miller's hand. 'I'm doing this because I'm convinced you're right — we owe you.'

'It's not a case of a debt, sweetie,' Miller brought Simone's hand to her lips and kissed it. 'It's about reclaiming culture and having a future.'

'Ty says it's about fighting for freedom, and I agree.'

'You are so beautiful; do you know that?'

Simone eyed Miller. 'I feel as if I've emerged from the greyness in which I used to live, and I like it.'

'Are you sure you want to continue? You could go back to the Justice Department and a quiet life.'

'Meeting you has shifted my thinking and I want to be a part of it.'

'Have you told anyone what you're doing?'

'I emailed work the other day and requested extended unpaid leave — I said I was stressed having to deal with you,' Simone laughed. 'They wrote back agreeing with me and approving my leave.'

Miller chuckled. 'That's funny.'

'I haven't told my family anything, and I'm not on Facebook.'

Miller bit her lip, contemplating her friend. 'It's going to get a little scarier from now on, sweetie, and I don't think we should see or talk to each other for a while. I think you should go back to Sydney.'

'I'm in this to the end, I've told you that.'

'The end may get horrifying, and I'm concerned for you. This is not your fight.'

'I'm an Australian, Nellie, of course it's my fight.'

Miller jumped up, standing before her friend, cupping her face. 'If you insist on remaining, then stay with Tyrone and do as he says. But, keep an eye on his mates, I don't trust them.' She put her arms around the young woman, pulling her close, kissing her on the cheek. 'Make sure you keep moving, make sure your firewalls are working and stop using anything that will attract the spooks — that means phoning friends, using credit cards, anything that will tap into the data system. They're searching for us and pressure will be on us by the time we get to Melbourne and Sydney.'

'I'll be okay.'

'Promise me you won't do anything stupid?' Miller pleaded.

'I should be asking you that.'

'I'll be okay — the person who should be worried is the prime minister.'

'You aren't going to do anything stupid, are you?'

Miller smiled and kissed her. 'I'll be okay.'

Simone turned her head and said, 'Promise?'

'I promise, sweetie.' They hugged a little harder, knowing they might not see each other for a while. 'Thanks for caring, gorgeous. You've met a worthy man, I think, make sure he looks after you.'

'I'm going to miss you.'

'We'll communicate — just be careful.'

Simone brought a tissue from her jacket pocket and wiped a tear from her eye. 'I love you.'

'I love you too, sweetie.' Miller turned and left, cutting through the park, past the children and dogs. She didn't glimpse back.

9

'Prime Minister?' Miller was almost through the park. 'Where do we stand?'

'You stand nowhere. I will not be doing a deal.'

'That's disappointing; that being the case we shall turn another city off the grid in two days, and this time blackout will be for seventy-two hours.'

'You fucking bitch.'

'There's no need to talk to me like that.'

'I'd pick you up right now if I could be certain this crap you started would stop.'

'It can stop — you can stop it. Just sign the treaty.'

'That's not going to happen — but, I tell you what is.'

Miller was intrigued. 'What might that be?'

'Your Council of Elders will be meeting tomorrow, and they will cut you out of any decision — I'm assured they are about to compromise.' Miller didn't respond. 'You see, the First Nations will take the control of negotiations away from you.'

'I wouldn't bet on it.'

'Once you are out of the negotiation loop, we will pick you up, I can assure you,' Grobbelaar growled.

'I'm prepared to bet my life . . . are you?' Miller ended the call.

Miller called Neesham. 'What are you up to, cuz?'

'Nothing that should concern you. We're still working to plan as far as I'm concerned.'

'Then why are you meeting with elders tomorrow?'

'We are discussing the UN treaty and how it will affect us if the government agrees to sign it.'

'What time is the meeting?'

'Tomorrow afternoon — why?'

'I'm on my way.' Miller stepped out into traffic hailing a taxi to take her to the airport.

¶

An elder was on her feet addressing the other councillors from a lectern at the front, as Miller entered the room, gently closing the door. Neesham took notes at a table beside the speaker. As Miller sneaked toward the front, smiling and nodding to others, she listened to the speech, which seemed to focus on appeasing the government with an agreement to defer any mining licenses for ten years.

When the elder asked for questions, Miller was on her feet. 'Aunty Olive, I pay my respects to you and your people. Like you, Aunty, I'm concerned for our people and the manner the federal government continues to disparage our culture and discriminate against us. We deserve better. I have wrestled with this problem for many years.'

'Is this a question or a speech?' Neesham interrupted prompting Miller to glare at him.

She then continued. 'My question is this — why?'

The elder checked about the room, uncertain how to respond. Neesham chewed on the end of his pen.

'Let me help you, Aunty.' Miller walked to the front of the room to face the elders. 'Government suppresses our culture and we need to look after ourselves. If we don't, our people will be assimilated, and we will never regain our identity. Unless we gain proper recognition through a treaty, we will become the forgotten people of this land. We need to make a stand. We need the UN treaty signed by the government, not just a deferment of mining licenses — and we need the government to agree to a process to proclaim a homeland'

An elder stood and said, 'Nellie, it's too late, we have already voted on Jimmy's recommendation to allow a ten-year deferment on the mining licence, therefore defeating the need for a treaty.'

Miller gazed at him, then turned to Aunty Olive, who nodded in agreement. Neesham avoided her gaze when she turned to him.

'Ten years? Is that it? You have agreed to defer mining in traditional lands for ten years instead of negotiating a treaty? You want us to stop campaigning for a treaty and stop negotiating a homeland? Is that the decision you have made?'

There was no response from the group, most averting their eyes from Miller's fierce glare.

'A deferment allows us to prepare a proper and more consultative campaign toward a treaty,' Aunty said. 'We don't need this escalating violence that is happening in our cities because of your activities.'

'You think by delaying mining for ten years you'll get what you want?'

Another elder stood. 'Nellie, we believe we're beginning to get recognition. The Karrakatta is beginning to agree on decisions, and the government is beginning to listen and willing to act on our recommendations. Your crusade is not winning us anything.'

'You think you'll get a say in the decisions of this country?' Miller bounced on her toes. 'The English stole everything from us and now offer empty words in return. Other cultures come here, change our laws adding their community values, but the First Nations remain ignored.'

'It's not like that, Nellie. We have the Karrakatta.'

'Words? After almost three hundred years of occupation and assimilation, all you have to show for a culture of sixty thousand years — are words?'

Aunty Olive looked to the council for support but there was none, Miller's words had stuck.

'The government should not be allowed to treat us like this. White fellas in this country will always treat us with disrespect because they conquered us. They may shake their heads over our troubles, but so what? We're no closer to recognition than we were when we had constitutional change.' Miller glanced around the room; every eye was on her. 'White fellas respond to push back. What I'm asking you to do, is push back, and not do what government expects you to do — if they expect you to defer, then say no. Ask the treaty be signed — then ask for a homeland. The UN is supportive, other countries are supportive, and damn it, even the Australian people are supportive. They want to end the guilt, and they want an end to this cloak of victimhood we live under. I'm asking you to reconsider your decision — don't do as the government has asked — let this fight for a signed treaty and a homeland continue — because, if you do agree to defer mining for ten years, it will mean this opportunity we now have will be lost.'

Some elders dropped their heads, others smiled and nodded. Aunty Olive took a seat beside Neesham who continued doodling.

Miller was ready to stop and listen to what they had to say. 'We need to save our culture. We need to save our people. We need to live — we need a homeland.' She paused and glanced about the room. 'It's worth fighting for — *we are worth fighting for.*'

10

'Where are you?' Messaris had been chasing Miller for a few hours to talk with her, but his calls went to message bank. He was keen to initiate the Western Australian campaign but needed Miller to front a media conference in Sydney outside the parliamentary offices in Bligh Street to add weight to the message they wanted to communicate.

'I'm at Sydney airport. I've just arrived. This flying all around the place is driving me crazy, it's killing me — I'm too old for this shit.'

'Are you ready for the next stage?'

'We may have a problem with Neesham.' Miller jumped into a taxi when it cruised to a stop in the allocated bay, tossing her small bag onto the back seat. 'Somehow, I think he's shafting us.'

'Why, what's happened?'

'I was lucky enough to get to a meeting of elders in Darwin yesterday. They had decided to agree on a motion put by Jimmy to a deferral of mining rather than have the government sign the UN treaty.'

'That sounds like Koning,' Messaris suggested.

'I'd lay odds Jimmy is in it up to his neck, and there is a big bag of cash involved. He's always after money.'

'If they defer they still get what they want,' Messaris said.

'But, only for ten years. The elders had agreed to it — even voted on it, if you can believe that — I think I may have convinced them to change their minds. We'll know soon enough.'

'Good girl. We need to make sure we keep at this campaign of civil unrest and get it to Melbourne and Sydney for a climax.'

'Why?' Miller asked, curious about what he'd just said.

Messaris recovered and said, 'It means you have a better chance of getting what you want — the treaty and the homeland.'

'Homeland has always been an ambit claim, it's the UN treaty I want — mining banned altogether.'

'The Territory has more than just coal and diamonds, why would you want to cut off your nose? A homeland gives you greater flexibility to do whatever you want, no matter the government.'

'We should not be mining, period — it's my Country and we should leave it as it is, that's what my ancestors would have wanted.' Miller glanced at the taxi driver who appeared keen to listen to what was going on. 'Let's talk about it later, I'll be in the city in about twenty minutes. What time is media?'

'Thirty minutes — have you got the notes I texted?'

'I know what to say.'

'Great, then make sure you hit the points I sent you, otherwise WA will be a waste of time.'

'I'll be fine — I'll call you when I get there.' Miller ended the call, slipping the phone into her army camouflage jacket, which she'd picked up along with other essentials from her bolthole in Darwin.

'Are you going to war?' The Sikh driver disturbed Miller's thinking about the media conference.

'What?'

'You look and talk as if you are about to go to war — are you?'

'No, just trying to get my culture back.'

'You have lost your culture?' The driver seemed confused and keen to engage in conversation, but Miller resisted. 'How is it, white people dominate conquered countries? Why do they kill the culture?'

Miller glanced into the rear-vision mirror engaging the driver's eyes. 'They didn't in India.'

'Ah yes, but independence brought with it many harsh times for all Indians.

'You all got homelands, though didn't you?'

'I wouldn't call partitioning the country on religious grounds homelands — my family lost everything.'

'Just like mine.' Miller peered out the window as the taxi rushed along the M1. 'Creating a partitioned country worked for you, didn't it?' Miller was curious.

'It's worked, I suppose, but the Muslims and the Hindus still want to kill each other. In the Punjab, where I'm from, it's a little more complex. That's why I got out. We have a great new life here.'

'New life for you and yet others still struggle.'

'Then you have a fight worthy of having. If they can make two new countries out of British India, now three with Bangladesh, then why can't you have a homeland like us?'

'My point precisely.'

'Gandhi made it happen peacefully. Maybe you can do the same — no?'

'Talk is cheap — an iron fist can make more of a difference.' Miller glanced out the window, killing the conversation.

As the taxi drew up outside the building in Bligh Street, the driver said, 'If you can win the people, your battle will be easier — that's what Gandhi did.'

'Wise advice I'm sure.' Miller took back her credit card, grabbed her bag and got out of the car. 'Let me ask you this, if India is such a nice place, why are you here?'

'Opportunity, madam, this is what Australia offers my family.'

It wasn't the driver's fault Miller's family had disappeared almost forty years ago, nor was it his fault the same opportunity didn't exist for her people, but his comment hurt as she closed the door and the taxi drove off. She watched it go, thinking about how others could do well in this country but her own people remain outcasts. She stared across the street and saw a mingling band of media. She called Messaris. 'I'm here. What time is WA being turned off?'

'Give the government ninety minutes to respond to your demands — so that means at three o'clock the power goes off in the west.'

Avoiding traffic and trotting the last few metres to avoid a bus, Miller crossed the street and stepped onto the kerb. 'I'm here now, so turn your television on — I'll leave the phone on, so you can either listen or watch.'

Miller walked to the media group, positioned herself facing the street, ensuring the Australian coat-of-arms on the wall behind her would be in shot.

'Are you ready?' Miller waited for the media people to settle into place. Five poked a microphone at her, others held up recorders. Two cameras began to roll, another provided a live feed to ABC News 24. After a few more moments, she said, 'My name is Nellie Millergoorra, of the Umbakarta people, and I pay my respects to the elders and traditional owners of this land on which I stand.' She paused for a moment as a bus motored by, its diesel engine drowning her out. 'My people have lived on this land we now call Australia for over sixty thousand years. Those who destroyed our culture have lived here for almost three hundred.

'The Grobbelaar government is forcing its will upon Aboriginal nations to our north, continuing to ignore the failure of government policy and the needs of traditional owners. We want nothing more than open communication, and the freedom to decide who comes to our land, but Prime Minister Grobbelaar and his government believe we are of little consequence to Australia and must obey the will and direction of the government.' Miller paused for a moment, then said, 'But, we say no more.'

'Our prime minister has decided to favour his own people, from South Africa, and his government will provide a mining licence to the Koning Mining Company. They plan to begin coalmining in our pristine sacred lands within the next eighteen months, ignoring our culture and our spiritual claims. Prime Minister Grobbelaar ignores Australia and its traditional peoples to support his favoured South African company, which has pillaged my people's land for three decades searching for diamonds. And now this same company wants to mine dirty coal.'

❡

'Prime Minister are you watching this?'

'Watching what?' Grobbelaar responded to Mary Whittington's call.

'Flick your television to News 24 — Millergoorra is downstairs right now giving a media conference.'

Grobbelaar picked up his remote and switched channels to the news. 'Is she surrendering?' He laughed.

'Far from it, I think she's about to declare war.'

'Well, she looks the part.'

❡

Miller spoke without notes; she had been rehearsing this speech for thirty years. 'The Australian people have a clear choice — they can either accept the grubby money thrown at them by foreigners to buy their silence, or they can join us to fight the Grobbelaar government to protect our First Nations, and recognise our existence, embrace our culture, and work toward fulfilling the reconciliation we've all wanted for decades. Now is the time to act and to stop wringing our hands with guilt, to stop worrying about years of government sanctioned virtual genocide. Join with us to say no to this government's total disregard of Aboriginal cultural and environmental values.

'Our five hundred nations do not want your sit-down money bribes anymore. We do not want your pity or your guilt. We don't want you to feel sorry for us, or to continue apologising for the deeds your elders have done. We don't want your sympathy, and we don't want your money. What we want is dignity. We want our lands back.'

Miller smiled, pausing for a moment to allow her declaration to sink in. 'I know you cannot give us our land back. You cannot give us back our lost culture. But … you can give us a future. You can give us hope, and you can release yourselves of the burden of guilt many of you continue to carry.

'We ask for two things from you — not much recompense to provide to five hundred nations for the centuries of neglect. We ask the government sign the UN treaty banning mining in Arnhem Land. This will provide security and happiness for traditional owners who feel their sacred sites are being violated.

'The second request is to provide us with a homeland. Provide us our own sacred land where we can legislate our own laws, our own culture and our own language. Other great countries in history have recognised the importance of preserving Indigenous culture by providing land for the vanquished and the defeated, and we ask for the same consideration here.

'I cite as an example the establishment of the state of Lesotho and Eswatini in South Africa; there are others and even Israel allowed followers of Judaism from all over the world to establish a sacred homeland. I'm also thankful to my taxi driver this morning who reminded me of the partitioning of India — and, I'm sure there are other examples from across the world where culture has been protected and the security of a homeland established.

'I know Australians are a generous and fair people who will do what is right. So, I ask my fellow Australians to become involved in the debate we are having with the Grobbelaar government who seem more willing to support foreign investment than talk to their traditional people.

'We would prefer a peaceful process, but Prime Minister Grobbelaar dismisses our approaches as if we are the coloured help. I apologise for the actions we will be taking over the next weeks as we assert our rights to fight for recognition. We accept full responsibility for the recent power blackout in Tasmania. We took that action because the government refuses to talk with us and negotiate a resolution that is acceptable for you, and us.

'We want government to negotiate with us. We do not want to cause inconvenience, but we are left with no other option. We want to talk. There is nothing to fear from us — we request your government act now and talk. We advise that until they do, we will continue our campaign of disruption.

'If you agree with our cause; if you agree with our fight for recognition and freedom from the shackles of colonisation — then tell your families, tell your workmates, and if the unions mean anything anymore, then come out on the streets and tell your government you want them to talk to us.

'Western Australia will lose its power in ninety minutes for seventy-two hours as part of our campaign. We apologise for the three-day inconvenience, but we have been inconvenienced for centuries. Queensland will follow. If you want your government to end these inconveniences then speak to your local MP, contact your media, and give the message to the prime minister you are not happy and demand he negotiate, otherwise the entire country will be blacked out.'

Miller left without answering questions barked at her by journalists. She ran through the traffic until she reached a taxi rank and jumped in to the first in line.

'We meet again madam. How is the war going?'

'Operation Blitzkrieg just started — the airport please.'

'You have not followed Mahatma's lead?' The driver seemed disappointed.

'We have been talking for over two hundred years — we don't need any more talk.'

The driver glanced at her. 'The great Winston Churchill once said, that jaw to jaw is better than war.'

'He also said, history is written by the victors. I can assure you, our history remains to be written.'

¶

The telephone rang after Millergoorra finished her speech. Grobbelaar assumed it was the attorney general and chose not to answer. He was still shaking from a surge of adrenalin. He tried to control his breathing as his doctor advised, avoiding the stress of moments such as these. He endured a lot of shocks and surprises during his parliamentary career, specifically when his wife died, but he hadn't felt this type of anxiety before.

The prime minister tried to walk but it was painful; his feet were sore. As he moved about, his joints returned to normal and he sauntered to the sideboard, poured himself a brandy, gulping it down. He poured another, and as he placed the crystal decanter back onto the silver tray, Whittington burst through the door.

'I called; you didn't answer.'

'Would you like a drink?'

'Prime Minister, Western Australia will be in the dark very soon, and we don't know for how long.' Whittington glanced at Grobbelaar, who picked up the decanter with a querying expression. 'No thanks.'

'We can assume they'll be able to hack into the system to manipulate the power grid so it collapses, three days she said — their threats seem to have validity.' The prime minster walked back to his desk and flopped into the chair, allowing it to rock. 'We should let the premier know so he can declare a state of emergency.'

'Shall we pick her up?'

'And, do what? The media would crucify us,' Grobbelaar spun the chair plonking his feet on the desk, 'they are waiting for any excuse to get stuck into us and this could be it, if they support her.'

'We can't let her just threaten us like that.' Whittington dragged out a chair at the front of the desk and sat.

'How the hell are they doing it?' Grobbelaar smelled then sipped the brandy. 'Does anyone know, are we close to finding out?'

'The short answer is no. We know they have gained access to the server and have built firewalls around their entry and exit points, but that's about it. Our best people are on it.'

'Our best people? Give me a break ...' scoffed the prime minister. 'If we had the best people then those who are doing this would be working for us.'

'Rene, this is new for us and we are learning as we go,' Whittington responded. 'The best-case scenario is that once we resolve it, it will never happen again.'

'This will cause a shit storm in WA so let's leverage that. Let's get our communications team to draw up a media strategy. If we are to win this battle against these terrorists, then we have to beat them at their own game and win the hearts and minds of the punters affected by the power cuts.'

Whittington considered the prime minister's comment, then suggested. 'We need Neesham on this.'

'That wanker is a nobody; he talks the good talk, but when it comes to delivering he's never there. But ... I agree — let's get a delegation of elders or some other Aboriginal group we can use to counter this lovey-lovey feel good *they owe us* theme they're running,' Grobbelaar sipped at his brandy, the fumes prickling his nose. He rubbed it. 'The liberals and the lefties will be loving this development. They've been calling for a treaty for decades, so we need to halt them in their tracks with an alternate voice. Otherwise, they'll be out on the streets by the end of the week, with their rainbow flags and signs.'

9

There was little relief from the Darwin heat, which seemed to shroud everyone in a damp steam bath, forcing them to slow down. Jimmy Neesham had slowed right down, almost emptying a jug of iced lemon tea. The air was barely moving, although the overhead fan creaked above him. He was hot, sticky and ready for a cool bath, but couldn't move from the couch. He picked up his glass of ice and tea, sipping it, condensation dripping onto his bare chest, but he didn't care — he was still thinking his way through the media conference and Miller's demands, wondering how long it would be before the telephone calls began, summoning him.

He was playing a high-stakes game and could come out a winner, but there was something Miller had said that worried him. Not so much the words but the tone in the way she expressed it — she was unpredictable and dangerous — she just might do something stupid. The idea of declaring a cold war on the government didn't sit well with him but a hot war was worse. Her campaign could leave him short of government money and end his career. It could also threaten the Chinese money, signing a no-mining treaty might cause them to renege on the agreement, obliging him to return their money. He figured whichever way this campaign played out he needed to protect himself and his finances.

Since his clandestine involvement with Koning Mining, his regret over the violent outcome and been replaced by guilt. He wanted to redeem himself — not to anyone in particular, but to everyone. He wanted to lead his people and not be a gofer for the government. He needed the prime minister to sanction his idea of increased legislative responsibility for the Karrakatta and the deferring of mining for ten years. If Grobbelaar acted on this, it would satisfy the Chinese and bolster to his bank account.

The telephone rang, and he struggled to get out of the couch to answer. 'Jimmy, here.'

'Neesham, this is the prime minister,' a familiar voice boomed. 'Did you see your mate, Millergoorra, speaking.'

'She isn't my mate,' Neesham sniffed as he sat at his desk. 'Yes, I did see her — powerful and motivating words wouldn't you say?'

'I want you and a couple of your elders in Sydney tomorrow to refute her words.'

'Why?'

'I want to show the sensible side of traditional owners. I want them telling a story of support for the government and its policies.'

'That will be difficult. Most folks from the Council of Elders support her.'

'Is there anyone you could get from the Congress?'

'Maybe.' Neesham doodled with a pen. 'Where are we with the deal I put to you?'

'I told you, the mine will go ahead, I already have Koning preparing site plans.'

'Prime Minister, the way I am reading this debate is that you have two clear choices — you either do it my way, or you do it Miller's way,' Neesham smiled, lips tightening as he imagined the prime minister's face. 'If you want a resolution to this cyber-attack against the government, which is an attack on Australia, then I suspect you need to choose who you want to deal with.'

'What's gotten into you Jimmy — have you grown hairy balls?' Grobbelaar teased.

'If you want me and the elders to support you, then you will need to travel to Darwin and meet with us here.'

'You slimy little prick, what do you think you're playing at?'

'If you want our support, then you come to us and make an offer — tomorrow would be good,' Neesham said. 'This will give us time to prepare media statements. If you don't want to deal with me then you'll have to deal with Millergoorra.'

'I don't negotiate with terrorists.'

'Then you had better be here tomorrow with your best offer.' Neesham decided to add a little weight to his statement and hung up on the prime minister of Australia. He dropped the phone and danced around his desk, punching the air.

The shrilling telephone stopped him, and he picked it up, apprehensive it might be the prime minister again.

'Neesham? It's Conan.' Neesham let out a sigh. 'We are about to close WA. Is there anything we need to know?'

'I may have the prime minister agreeing to deal.'

'When?'

'As early as tomorrow.'

'That's no good,' Messaris said. 'I mean, it's good for you, but not good for me.'

'How do you mean, it's not good for you?'

'You are on a need to know basis, Jimmy — let's just say you have led us to the right place, again.'

Neesham was troubled by the comment. 'What are you planning?'

'Nothing for you to worry about, but we're working on a retirement fund, and we would prefer the entire plan followed.'

'If I get a firm offer from the PM tomorrow I may have to call an end to it.'

'You stupid kaffir,' Messaris said. 'It ends when I say it ends.' Messaris paused, then added, 'WA is down in an hour and Queensland is the next target. In the meantime, just play the game with the prime minister and we shall get you what you want.'

g

Messaris tossed the phone onto the bed and paced across the motel room, then back again.

'What's up?' Tyrone asked as he noticed Messaris pacing.

'Neesham might sell us short,' Messaris replied. 'He may try to end it before we're ready.'

'I have the codes ready for Queensland, but I'll need Simone with me to complete Melbourne and Sydney.'

'Are we able to change the grid to do both cities at once?' Messaris stood by the window and watched a car enter the complex and park outside a room two doors down. 'If we do both at the same time it might cover our tracks better in Melbourne.'

'It's possible, but it might cause damage to the grid.'

'I don't care about damage, I just want Melbourne switched off for enough time,' said Messaris, as he watched two men in dark suits get out of the car and walk to their room. 'When will you have the program ready?'

'I need another two weeks.'

'We may only have one,' said Messaris, studying the men. 'Pack up, we have to go.'

'Why? I haven't finalised WA yet.'

'Just do it, will you,' Messaris said, watching and waiting. 'We need to move, now.'

Tyrone closed his laptop, snatched connection cords from the wall and shoved the equipment into his backpack.

'Have you got everything?'

'What about the food?'

'Leave it, let's go.' Messaris opened the door and squeezed out shepherding Tyrone past him, who scooted off to the end of the building where their car was parked, with Messaris right behind him, flicking open the electric locks. They jumped in, fired up the car and sped off, kicking stones up as they hit the exit.

'What's all that about?' Tyrone asked when he thought Messaris had relaxed.

'I'm not sure, but since when do you see blokes in suits book a room at a dingy motel in the middle of nowhere?'

'A little overreaction I would have thought.'

'Does your computer have a connection?'

Tyrone hauled his laptop from his bag and opened it, then said, 'I have three bars, so we should be okay.'

'Then do the job on WA.'

'We'll be early, and it might just be Perth.'

'It'll be okay, just get it done. I don't know when we'll be able to get a connection again.

11

Two white commonwealth cars pulled out onto the tarmac drawing up by the front stairs of the small government jet, used by the governor-general, but often seconded by the prime minister for lightening visits to various parts of the country. It carried thirty passengers but today there were three VIPs and two advisers. The still, hot air hit the prime minister as he descended the steps, tugging off his tie and unbuttoning his shirt. Mary Whittington followed close behind, last guest off the bulky Lewe Koning.

Koning was struggling with the heat, even the full blast of the car's air-conditioning failed to cool him or dry the sweat. He had taken a damp cloth from the plane wiping his face and thick neck. The bulges in his shirt exposed lines of dampness as his body struggled to control the heat. 'I hate this place, always have. It reminds me of Tanzania — that's a shit hole as well.'

Grobbelaar chuckled. 'You made a lot of money from diamonds in Africa and yet you complain about it.'

'I provided the government plenty of money in taxes and royalties and employ thousands. Like yours, their economy benefited from my investments.'

'You didn't make money?'

'Of course, I did, but I was a lot younger and fitter back then. This heat is killing me.'

'Don't worry, we'll be back in the air in a couple of hours and you can sip on a few chilled wines on the flight back to Sydney.

'Prime Minister, the premier of Western Australia has called a state of emergency and asked us to mobilise troops to aid police,' Whittington said, from the front seat, as she wrapped up a telephone call.

'We can't deploy the SAS, but we could use air force and navy personnel over there. Call the defence minister to get them started.' Grobbelaar paused, then asked, 'what's happened? Anything I should be aware of?'

'There's a potential problem with an demonstration at the parliament house — an estimated ten thousand people, mostly Aborigines, are in the forecourt.'

'What are they doing?'

'Speakers are urging the crowd to maintain a peaceful vigil — they are chanting slogans and singing.'

'Fucking hippies,' Grobbelaar laughed. 'No wonder government doesn't take their claims seriously.'

'They would have been moved on by now if they were in South Africa, the police would have given them stick.'

'Aren't the South African police black now?' Whittington asked.

'It makes no difference — authority needs to control the mob, and if the stick is needed it should be wielded.'

Grobbelaar winced. 'I'm not so sure that would work here.'

'Your ancestors would have been at the front of the line pushing them back.'

'My ancestors are Australian.'

'Once the veldt is in your DNA, your homeland is always the Transvaal.'

'My great grandfather spoke of it, but most of my family are Australian.'

'Where are your roots?'

'Australia.'

'*Niemand!*' Koning chastised him. 'You're a *besoeker* in Australia, trust me — your heart is Afrikaans.'

'What's that?' Whittington asked.

'It means, you folks are passing through this country, so use the time and make money out of it,' Koning replied.

'This is my home, Africa means nothing to me,' Grobbelaar said.

'You don't feel it — do you?'

'Feel what?'

'The earth, the land, when you walk on it — you don't feel it, do you?'

'What the hell are you talking about?' Grobbelaar asked.

'The land, it speaks to you when it's your home — you feel it in your feet, in your body, even in your mind,' Koning persisted. 'Go home to the veldt and you'll feel it, I promise you.'

'This is my land.'

'Bullshit it is — it's theirs.' Koning pointed toward a group of eight Aborigines sitting in the shade under an enormous tree as the car ferried them along the driveway to the front of parliament house. 'But they are not capable of doing anything with it. They had it for thousands of years and did nothing, now they want it back — yeah, right.'

The prime minister pondered for a moment the brusque discussion and its link to the battle he was fighting in the national press and social media. His approval rating was taking a dive in the polls; the energy security crisis destroying any marginal support. Once the population understood who was causing the energy crisis, and the issues and reasons behind it, there was a significant movement of public support toward the Aboriginal activists. The radio shock jocks supported the government, but their callers were not. Even pundits thought the community response bizarre, and the prime minister could not recall another time in political history that had been similar — any threat to Australia and its people was always responded to by government with solid and overwhelming support from the community, but not now.

'Thanks for doing this, Lewe, I appreciate it.'

'So long as I get the licence in ten years as you have promised, I will do whatever is needed to get it done.'

'Let's get you cooled down and cleaned up for the negotiation.'

¶

The Council of Elders assigned five members to represent them, although remaining apprehensive negotiating with the prime minister. Millergoorra challenged the meaning of the reconciliation process and her enthusiasm was infectious, shifting long entrenched views within the indigenous community. Government after government promised wealth creation yet delivered nothing. Governments preferred assimilation rather than recognition of culture. There was little evidence prosperity was ever delivered — plenty of talk and still no one cared. White Australia still felt guilty and demanded something be done but few stepped up to do it.

The prime minister waited for Koning with Whittington in an office on the first floor overlooking the water. During his entire political career, this was the first real policy challenge Grobbelaar faced. He remained anxious from a feeling of little control — his principle was to always control the controllables, and didn't enjoy the gnawing of his increasing fretfulness. As he waited he took a blister pack of tablets from his jacket, popped out two, and flicked them into his mouth, hopeful the gnawing pressure in his chest was indigestion.

Whittington helped herself to a glass of water and the prime minister waved her away when she offered to pour him another glass. 'What is your plan B on this, Prime Minister?'

'I don't have one.' Grobbelaar was sitting on the edge of a wooden chair. 'If we defer the coalmine for ten years, that will cost the government hundreds of millions in royalties, but it's better than signing a UN treaty banning all mining. The redevelopment and funding issue with the Karrakatta seems like it's a name change; so, whatever these elders want to do with that seems okay with me. It may cost us more money, but if we get the ten years that will be fine. What concerns me is this; if we agree and the terrorists don't stop — then what?'

'Would you sign the treaty?'

'No.'

'It might save the government at the next election if you did.'

'If I sign the UN treaty under duress then anyone can do the same by threatening the government.'

'What happens if the government is forced to sign?'

'The parliament would never accept its validity. Future governments could override it with legislation at any time,' Grobbelaar stood and ambled to the window, gazing out, watching nothing in particular. 'There is no way we can take direction from unrepresentative bodies like the UN — once we start doing that, the wackos will come demanding we submit to every nutty idea; then we, theoretically lose our sovereignty. It'll be better if we get the ten-year moratorium agreed to with this mob today.'

Whittington fell silent for a few moments, then said, 'The homeland idea has been around for a while now. Have you never considered it?'

'Never,' Grobbelaar glimpsed at his watch, 'I'm not breaking up Australia for a few good headlines.'

'What happens if Lewe doesn't get what he wants?'

'Who knows? Maybe he takes his money and invests in another country.'

'What am I supposed to have done?' Koning plodded into the room as the prime minister finished his comment.

'We were just wondering what you would do if the UN forced us to sign the treaty.'

Koning poured a glass of water and said, 'I would take my money elsewhere — to a country without ownership issues.'

'Then why would you wait for ten years?' Whittington asked.

'It's a no-brainer.' Koning sniffed. 'The licence gives me fifty years of mining rights in the region and doesn't limit me to coal. My geologists tell me the region is rich in bauxite and magnesium, so I can develop pits to extract more minerals and only have to make application for an initial coal licence.'

'One payment to the traditional owners?' Whittington queried.

'With any luck, none.'

Whittington glanced at Grobbelaar as Koning chuckled at the prospect.

'What's taking these people so long?' Grobbelaar asked. 'Can you check please, Whit?'

Whittington left the room to rouse up the elders and get the meeting started. They were needed back in Sydney that evening to meet with defence and homeland security leaders, so reaching an agreement before they left would influence how they managed their next meeting. She stalked along a corridor, finding no one, then checked downstairs, stepping out onto the verandah then strolled around the corner to the back of the building.

She stumbled upon Neesham sitting with five Aborigines, shaded under trees. 'Were we not meeting?' she asked as she wandered down the grassed slope toward them.

'We've been waiting for you.' Neesham stood, holding out his hand to shake Whittington's. 'This is where we discuss business of importance.'

'Not inside?' Whittington indicated the building. 'Were you coming to get us?'

'You would ultimately come searching.'

'The Prime Minister of Australia needs to come searching for you?' Whittington winced. 'Shouldn't it be the other way around?'

'You are on our country, so you come to us,' said a grey-haired man with a long, bushy, white beard sitting with legs crossed. 'Please, come and join us.'

It took some gentle persuasion but fifteen minutes later the prime minister and Koning strolled out onto the lawn greeted by Neesham who asked them to sit. Grobbelaar struggled to lower himself to the ground, his joints no longer as supple as they were, but he settled into a pose that required him to sit erect, his back rigid. Koning resisted, but when encouraged by the prime minister, collapsed onto the grass and was fortunate not to roll further down the slope. He didn't even bother to cross his legs and lay back on an elbow as if he were at the beach. Whittington had little trouble sitting and crossing her legs, despite her frock. The prime minister's staff stood to one side at a respectable distance from the seated group, but close enough to listen to discussions.

'Thank you for the opportunity to speak with you.' Grobbelaar smiled and nodded, hoping for a response. 'We appreciate time is important to you, so we would like to move along. If you have anything to contribute we would welcome it.'

The Aboriginal men said nothing, gazing at the ground before them, making no movement other than to brush away annoying flies.

'We would welcome a comment,' Grobbelaar persisted.

The bushy-faced elder said, 'Our people are forgotten by your people. This has been the same for many years — since before my father and his father were born. We are ignored by you and we see the end to many languages. Our people are losing tradition and knowledge — this sad business must end.'

'What would you have us do?'

'Respect.'

Grobbelaar was silent and glanced at Whittington for support.

'Your law says we have rights — but it gives us no respect.'

The prime minister eyed the men and then glanced at Neesham who sat with his head bowed, wrists resting on his knees. 'How should we express this respect?' he asked.

The elder did not respond. The others closed their eyes, one rocked back and forth as if in a trance. 'Give us a voice.'

The prime minister smiled, bemused by the declaration. 'You already have a voice with the senate committee and you have the Karrakatta Congress. This is what we agreed many years ago when we amended the constitution. Your leaders said then, it was enough.'

'They were wrong. It is not enough. We want to have a voice for our own people.'

Grobbelaar sat straighter, stretching his lumber region, his patience beginning to wear thin. 'What would you have me do?'

The elder stared at the prime minister, waiting in silence. Neesham wanted to intervene so the two parties could continue dialogue, but he did not have the authority to speak.

'Can I just cut in for a moment,' Koning heaved himself up, 'if we deferred all mining in the region for ten years would this help?'

Whittington lost patience. 'They're not talking about mining rights; this is bigger than that.'

'Christ, not the homeland crap again.' Grobbelaar could not help himself.

'Prime Minister, please,' Whittington said, then addressing the elders, 'If I understand you — the government cannot agree to your request.'

'This is not right,' one of the elders said.

'We are legally bound by the Australian constitution . . .'

'We want what was originally ours.'

'I didn't come all this way to sit in the dirt to discuss a partitioning of Australia — is there anything else?' Grobbelaar prepared to stand.

The elders made no attempt to object to their guests leaving. Neesham, realising his prospects were dwindling, interjected. 'Prime Minister . . .' Grobbelaar stopped and waited for Neesham to have his say. 'I have no authority to speak on such an occasion, but you might recall this is the very issue I have been talking with you about. The Council of Elders are very clear on what they want.'

'Well, it's not clear at the moment.'

'We need the Karrakatta reframed. We need more funding and we want the Congress to have a greater say on all policy and legislation concerning us, including a veto clause.'

Grobbelaar considered the elders. 'Is this what you want?'

'We want a louder voice. We want what we agree for our people done. You may listen, but you never take action.'

'What you are asking is effectively another chamber of the federal parliament.'

'We do not want to deal with your parliament, but we want a say on the laws affecting our people.

'But, that's everything,' Whittington interjected. 'You can't have a veto clause on all legislation.'

Neesham interrupted before an elder responded. 'Prime Minister, we are not saying all legislation, just the laws regulating us.'

'If I agree to this new role for the Karrakatta, will you call off this aggressive anti-government campaign?'

'How will you give us a louder voice?'

'We will provide more funding and consider a restructure . . .' Grobbelaar considered the options, '. . . we will allow you to move formal legislation at the Karrakatta that can be ratified as law within the national parliament, on the proviso the government approves and retains its own power of veto.' The elders stared up at the prime minister and nodded. 'We will also ask the Congress to assemble once a year at parliament house in Canberra when my entire ministry will be in attendance to discuss government policy and funding impacting the First Nation population, answering your questions.'

The spokesman nodded and glanced to his colleagues who also nodded. 'We also want the mine licence to stop.'

Grobbelaar glimpsed to Koning who pursed his lips and nodded before the prime minister suggested. 'If we defer an application for ten years so we can negotiate with the traditional owners first, and provide them with new services and increased funding, would that please you?'

'You are saying defer mining for ten years?' an elder asked.

Grobbelaar nodded. 'The government can provide the traditional owners the services they want.'

'You must deliver these things — we must know you will keep your word. There have been many times when governments have promised but not delivered on business agreed.'

'Will the Karrakatta agree to this motion on deferral?' Grobbelaar asked.

'If you keep your word, then we will agree.'

'We will prepare an agreement, and have it delivered to Jimmy by the end of this week.' Grobbelaar now stood, brushing debris from his trousers. 'But, you must assure me, these terrorist acts must stop.'

'We have no control over Millergoorra and her campaign. We will try and do what you want and cease her activities. You must know she is acting independent of the Karrakatta.'

Grobbelaar held out his hand to Koning to help the enormous man to his feet. It was a struggle, but they achieved it with a laugh — it provided them the opportunity to hug and celebrate the deal. Neesham assisted Whittington and the elders prepared to say goodbye by standing.

As the prime minister reached out to shake hands he said, 'Let me assure you, if the disruption to the power grid continues, then there is no deal. Do your very best to end it.' The elders nodded and smiled as their guests moved off around the building to cars waiting in the shade.

Neesham opened the back door of the lead vehicle for the prime minister and Grobbelaar grabbed his arm, drawing him close. 'We'll make formal announcements in a week or so, but if you stuff this up, Jimmy, this will be the end of you. Make sure WA gets back on the grid and we have no more of Millergoorra's terrorist antics.'

'She is her own person, as you well know, but I know how to control her.'

'The federal police are close to a breakthrough on where and how their attack on the energy grid is done, so we can stop it — and when we have that security reinstated we will pick her up — she can then spend a few more years in jail thinking about her madness.'

'When will I get my money?'

'You'll get it when the deal is done, and Millergoorra and her collection of thugs are locked up. Make sure it happens.' Grobbelaar got into the car, slammed the door and the car took off at speed kicking up dust and a few loose pebbles. 'I don't trust that slimy bastard.'

'Then why not get rid of him?' Whittington said from the front seat.

'I may not trust him, but he is all I've got within the murky world of Aboriginal politics.'

'Can you assure me I'll get the licence in ten years?' Koning was struggling to brush himself down again.

'We'll legislate for a moratorium providing native title owners certain rights, including requiring them to deal with your company in ten years, don't worry. Just stay alive long enough to enjoy it.'

¶

'Conan, it's time to back off.' Neesham's call hadn't gone terribly well. The South African resisted the idea of calling an end to the social media campaign and power blackouts, and Neesham felt exposed.

'We won't be doing anything like that until we get what we want, I can assure you.'

'The government is close, and they have threatened terrorist charges against all those involved if we don't back off, now.'

'WA can't come back on for another few hours, it's the metrics associated with the algorithms, and our plan is to have them back up in ten hours.'

'Just make sure this is the last of it,' Neesham said.

'Got what you want from the government have you?'

'The prime minister is talking and the deal we want is almost done.'

'Just because you get what you want . . . the original deal was, we all get what we want.'

'That wasn't the deal when I brought you in.'

'It is now, so I'd be ensuring your back is protected, because it's exposed.'

'Don't threaten me.'

'Jimmy, you're in no position to be making demands — I know you, and I know your past, so don't think you can call an end to this perfect political storm just because you're sitting by a warm fire.'

'We have the mine deferred and a revitalisation of the Congress, so don't jeopardise this outcome.'

'I told you when we started you were not offering enough.'

'What are you talking about? I offered you what I was prepared to pay and now you're saying you want more.'

'For us, this has only been about money and once we get it, we'll stop.'

'I haven't got any more money.'

'When we get what we want, we'll stop,' Messaris repeated.

'What do you want?'

'We want you to sit peacefully for a few weeks and enjoy a holiday.'

'What are you talking about?'

'Your girl, Millergoorra, will be back in the news tomorrow, so listen to her. She'll be talking about the latest government polling — we have community support and we are close to getting the government into a position to agree to what she wants. Everything is going as we planned — so take a break, Jimmy.'

'I insist you end the campaign, at the very least stop the blackouts, otherwise we lose everything.'

'We will not lose everything — if we follow the plan we will get much more.'

'Please, I insist.'

'And, I insist I get the money I want,' Messaris barked. 'Let me assure you, if I don't get what is my due, then you won't be around to celebrate any success you achieve.

12

The prime minister stared out over Sydney Harbour from the verandah, watching the water traffic, enjoying a rare sunny day. A Havana cigar helped relax him and a glass of shiraz swung from his hand as he pondered the political dilemma before him. Australia was under attack and he was impotent to prevent the distress being meted out by a few disenfranchised Aborigines keen to make a point. He'd called his trusted ministers to a meeting to resolve the issue.

The attorney general said, 'I can't sit here all day, I have washing to do and children to care for.' Whittington laughed. 'Do we sign this document or wait for confirmation of a truce?'

'We wait, I think,' the justice minister offered.

'They promised me they would end it.' Grobbelaar ashed his cigar in the enormous rainbow-coloured glass bowl, ignoring the distaste on the faces of his colleagues. 'Why don't we just pick her up? Do we know where she is?'

'We know she's in Queensland, but we're not sure where,' Hodge replied, taking another sip of iced tea. 'She may be the proxy — we're not even sure if she is involved. We have no direct evidence implicating her, other than public statements.'

'It would be hard to make charges stick given her defence would focus on the virtuous notion of sovereignty,' Whittington responded.

Grobbelaar clouded himself in smoke then remarked, 'if we make the announcement deferring the mining and increasing the status of the Congress, would that make a difference? This is what I'm struggling with.' He drew on his cigar again and blew the smoke high into the corrugated roof. 'Have we figured out how they are doing the hacking? Can they do it again?'

'They have an encrypted program subverting the security of the grid interconnectors forcing electricity supply to bypass the interconnector that feeds various power systems in states such as Tasmania and WA. The local power plants can't cope with demand because they don't have enough supply, then the system automatically shuts down, needing retriggering,' Hodge said. 'But, they've hacked that system as well, requiring us to recalibrate the operational algorithms.'

'Why does it take so long to reset?' Grobbelaar asked.

'They introduced a bug into the system that has a number of sophisticated firewalls protecting it. They program it to self-destruct, so they never have to re-enter the system and thus be detected by us — we have no idea who or where they are. They could be in Russia for all we know.'

'Neesham will deliver; he knows his future depends on it,' Whittington said, glancing at her watch.

'I'm not so sure now,' Grobbelaar took a swig of wine. 'When is Millergoorra's deadline?'

'Three hours,' Hodge replied.

'We still don't know which city or state?'

'No, Prime Minister. We have our best system engineers on it, but we are yet to detect activity on the grid or within the interconnectors.'

'I'm sorry to have to say this, Whit, but your husband will need to do the washing and cook the kids' meal tonight.'

Whittington nodded, picking up her telephone to text her husband the latest news. 'I'm sure he'll be happy to do that, and will most likely order in pizza.'

'Where would the world be without pizza?' Grobbelaar smiled.

9

Kombumerri land looks nothing like it did when traditional owners hiked the beaches and hinterland twenty-five thousand years ago. The glaring neon and drunk holidaymakers on footpaths, walkways and beaches are a far cry from the people who cared for and respected the land. Ugly housing estates and architecturally challenged high-rise blocks now announced the wealth of the coastal region and little is left of the culture and rituals of the first peoples. Even now traditional custodians are losing their unique dialect to the neighbouring Yugambeh nation.

Millergoora sat on the beach at Snapper Rocks, the late afternoon sun warming her from the chill of the surf and breeze whipping up across the waves. Six proficient surfers were at work on the well-known break and she gazed beyond them, across the bay, to the tasteless skyscrapers at Surfers Paradise. The irony of her campaign was not lost on her. Europeans had brought development, wealth and tourism to the region, which allowed residents, including Aborigines, to prosper, yet at what cost?

She earlier walked around the point from the mouth of the Tweed River, having spent an hour or two at the Captain Cook memorial meditating and reflecting upon the changes since the explorer sailed the region. There were no reminders of the traditional people, the Tulgi-gin, Cudgenburra, and Mooburra clans, no names or monuments, and Miller accepted there never would be. New settlers with zero connection to the land or respect for the communities living there, named localities after themselves, destroyed vegetation, and built grotesque structures without any thought for the land or its first people.

It was time to make a call. She wandered up to the nearby commercial precinct on the highway. Public phones were rare, but Miller identified one on Marine Parade. She swiped her credit card, dialling the new number Messaris provided during previous communication.

'Where are you?' Messaris asked.

'Gold Coast.'

'You'd better head into New South Wales because the lights go off in Brisbane and the south-east region at five. They'll be off for forty hours unless they can figure out an override and bring power in from across the border.'

'Do I call Grobbelaar?'

'I think you should, but do it from across the border,' Messaris said. 'You may as well use your own phone; they'll track it, clearing you from any involvement from what may happen in Queensland.'

'Neesham called today,' Miller said.

'Oh yeah? What did he want?'

'He told me he had spoken to you earlier in the week and asked you to back off.'

'Interesting.'

'He said the government's agreed to our demands.'

'No, they haven't.'

'It maybe all we'll get from them.'

'You either want to do this, or you don't.' Messaris's voice strengthened. 'Either way, I don't give a damn, because we are going to do Melbourne at the very least.'

'Why?'

'Let's just say there are special interests involved.'

'This prime minister will never agree to sovereignty. He hasn't moved on this at all. It's a good idea but I think it's passed its use-by date with this bloke.'

'He will if he's involved,' Messaris said.

'How will that work?'

'We have a plan in play, I'm just waiting for Macca's confirmation.'

'Are you sure Grobbelaar will respond the way we want him to?'

'Tomorrow night he'll have the troops out on the street trying to win back support.'

'Why?'

'Because of the anarchy we'll cause tonight.'

'What's the plan?'

'Best you remain outside the loop,' Messaris replied. 'The only thing I can tell you is that I have Macca doing good stuff — he has Brisbane organised and he's now on assignment in Bali.'

'Bali? You blokes get around,' Miller sniffed. 'How's Simone?'

'The love birds are never too far from each other.'

'Okay, I'll go call the prime minister.'

'Stick to the script and demand what you want — it's coming together; stop worrying.'

Miller ran her fingers through her hair checking the street. 'The people are with us — well, at least they want it on the agenda.'

'You'll get what you want, trust me,' Messaris said.

'I do trust you, but it seems we are no closer than we were when we started.'

'The polls are killing the government. Your media has been providing great leverage and the blackouts reinforce with punters that the prime minister is not in control — which, he isn't.'

'I just want to get what we planned.'

'We'll get the treaty signed, and I suspect after the next few days the prime minister will want to talk to you about sovereignty,' Messaris shifted his tone, 'don't go soft on me.'

'I'm not,' Miller sighed. 'I just wish we had more support from the elders.'

'Don't worry about them — if you get what you want they will be hailing you the hero.'

'Okay, I'd better go. I'll call you on number five tomorrow.'

❡

The chill once the sun disappeared behind buildings and trees forced the prime minister inside and the politicians made themselves comfortable in the lounge.

'You know something?' Grobbelaar asked, as a household staff member prepared cocktails, 'this place needs a makeover. Have you noticed how the chandeliers don't match?' The others studied the lights. 'They're different; don't we ever think about these things?'

'I suspect taxpayers wouldn't care about lights not matching, they'd rather see us spend money on other things,' Hodge sighed.

'And, there you have it — voters hate politicians, especially when we show leadership and spend money. They call us liars and flakes when we spend money on heritage houses but scream blue murder if we don't spend money on them.'

'Leadership is more about doing what is right,' Whittington joined the conversation, smiling as she took a gin and tonic from the attendant. 'Thank you. Sometimes, governments don't do that.'

'Sticking the verbal knife in again, Whit?' Grobbelaar accepted his whisky. 'You think we are handling this business shabbily?'

'I think you have done a wonderful job in getting an agreement from the elders,' Whittington smiled, raising an eyebrow toward Marilyn Hodge. 'Ironically, the polls would suggest otherwise.'

'They have a social media campaign going crazy against us — but I reckon my polling figures can come back.'

'I'm not so sure they can, Prime Minister,' Hodge said. 'We need an intervention.'

'We need a war,' Grobbelaar said. 'A war on jobless, or a war against drugs — an immigration debate always distracts the punters from the big issues.'

'You're already in a war and the population thinks you're on the wrong side,' Hodge responded.

'What would you have me do?'

'Just consider this partitioning idea,' Whittington said. 'It may never go anywhere, but at least you can lead the debate. The punters will have a change of heart about you.'

'I would never agree to transform Australia in such a monumental way.'

'It could be the right thing to do,' Hodge suggested, with a slight, encouraging smile.

Grobbelaar ignored her. 'There have been a million ideas about reconciliation, but nothing ever hits the political sweet spot. It seems this guilt trip the country has been on for decades will never end.'

'They want sovereignty, so let's give it to them,' Whittington said. 'Once they have it they will never be able to drive a wedge into the goodwill of the population ever again.'

'Fuck 'em,' Grobbelaar snapped. 'They never meet us in the middle, so fuck 'em.'

'Perhaps it is we who should move toward them,' Hodge suggested.

'Fuck you two as well.' Grobbelaar finished his drink, moving to the sideboard to pour another generous dram. 'Anyway, if we sign this deal we won't need to.'

The phone on the coffee table vibrated. The politicians gazed at it, then at the prime minister who picked it up. He punched the speaker button placing the phone on the table.

'This is the prime minister.'

'Have you approved our requests?'

'As you no doubt have been advised, I met with a delegation of elders a few days back in Darwin. We had robust discussion and a number of proposals were agreed — the government has made certain commitments to the Karrakatta. We will be signing formal documents if they meet their part of the agreement.'

'What agreement?'

'We defer mining for ten years. We pay traditional owners a lot more funds, providing increased services to the people involved. We increase funding to the Karrakatta Congress, providing it greater access to the government and the parliament. We believe the proposal will facilitate the Karrakatta to forward proposals for legislation to the commonwealth parliament for ratification — we also agreed the Karrakatta assemble at least once a year in Canberra when the government will provide them full access to discuss policy and funding. This is a momentous advancement for the cause of sovereignty, and I suspect you will be pleased with the outcome.' Grobbelaar paused for a response, there was none. 'In return for these agreed outcomes we have asked all criminal threats to energy security cease.'

'So, nothing?'

'This is a significant deal, Nellie,' Whittington said, moving closer to the telephone. 'Your elders have agreed.'

'I haven't.'

'If you don't yield to this agreement then all bets are off, and we will take action to arrest you on terrorism charges,' Hodge said.

'You know something, ladies?' They could hear the smile in Miller's voice. 'Your government is in trouble. You have your own members out in the national media calling for the government to sign the UN treaty. Every day the media is more supportive of the sovereignty proposition and you are still offering beads and mirrors.'

'Nellie, that is not the case,' Whittington chipped in. 'We have taken no action against you and our policy is that we do not press charges against you and your group; but, if you force us to act by refusing to consent with this agreement, then we will come down hard on you.'

Miller ignored the threat. 'The deal the elders negotiated is not acceptable. At the very least you will need to sign the treaty — there will be no more mining in Arnhem Land.'

'Don't try telling me what will or will not happen,' Grobbelaar barked.

'Hey, Prime Minister, I lost my family protecting our land. I'm prepared to go all the way this time. If I were you, I'd be preparing a declaration to sign the UN treaty, otherwise your government is gone.'

'You know something, Millergoorra? You keep playing these stupid games and there will be no future for you or your people.'

'Can I quote you?' Miller chuckled. 'Oh, wait, I just did.'

'What the hell are you talking about?'

'I'm sorry, I should have advised you this call is being recorded for the purposes of training,' she laughed.

Grobbelaar hesitated and then pushed on, seething. 'Let me tell you this: unless I get agreement from you securing the energy grid, mining will start this year — trust me on that.'

'Brisbane goes off in thirty minutes. Enjoy.'

13

The vibrant colours of Brisbane were extinguished, streets almost deserted, and in those businesses remaining open, torch light and candles illuminating the premises, but no customers. Cars providing the only lights in and around the city.

Messaris directed Miller to put the word out to her allies to form a mob of activists by midnight for a little *'rough and tumble'*. They were encouraged to dress in black, hooded and masked — the international garb of anarchists keen to create as much disturbance and chaos as possible. The assembly point in the botanic gardens hummed with a growing number of excited hushed voices. Thirty minutes after the designated time, Messaris moved to the few steps at the Walter Hill fountain and more than two hundred activists shuffled close to hear what he had to say.

A masked Messaris addressed them in a hoarse whisper: 'We are about to embark on the first step to achieving Aboriginal sovereignty.' A ripple of sentiment washed through the crowd. 'Before us is the parliament of Queensland, a symbol of white settler supremacy. The plunderers stole our lands taking away our rights, oppressing all Aboriginal people and ignoring the sovereign rights of the Turrbal and Jagera peoples. This should never be forgotten. We survived, and we want it all back.'

'You got that right,' someone said, sparking murmurs of agreement.

'The struggle we begin tonight will not deliver much for us, but it will be an important first step in bringing justice for our people.

Tonight, the revolution begins — we may be nearly three hundred years late, but it is a fight we stand ready for. Let us do as our brothers and sisters did in Western Australia, but with one important difference — let us not have a silent vigil, let us attack the parliament and occupy the symbol of white privilege and let us send a message to Canberra that we are not a forgotten people.' Voices raised in agreement. 'Let us, as one, storm the parliament and demonstrate we cannot be ignored. Let us be *loud and proud*.' Messaris strode off the fountain steps, jostling through the crowd that turned as one, following him through the gardens to parliament house.

When the mob reached the forecourt, they rushed the locked iron gates shouting slogans, rattling the gates, creating wild activity. Flares were ignited and tossed over the fence. Security guards assigned to protect the building when the blackout kicked in realised they be unable to hold back the mob if the gates failed. A young, nervous police officer radioed an appeal to his central base, soon after reassuring wails of distant sirens were heard.

Messaris was satisfied with the diversion at the front of the building. The mob was loud and angry. They wanted access, pushing hard against the gates, forcing security guards and attending police to push back and hold until reinforcements arrived. He pinged a message to his colleagues at the rear of the parliamentary complex, to activate their mission to break and enter. Three dark figures climbed the security barrier from the Queensland University of Technology, rushing to the building, securing access by smashing a window. The security alarm rendered useless by the blackout. The operatives wore night vision googles, allowing them to progress through the building unimpeded. They were directed to target the former parliamentary council chamber, daubing it with slogans, then enter the main chamber and set it alight.

After tagging the room, the operatives entered the main chamber, splashing accelerant across the benches and the speaker's chair. As they left, one operative dropped a lit wick onto the parliamentary table, which ignited the pool of liquid, racing flames throughout the chamber. The sprinkler system was well above the chamber, high in the ceiling, and would engage but not before enough damage had been done.

Messaris pressed on his earpiece to listen to the report, grinning when he learned the fire was blazing and operatives were clear. The police riot squad arrived and a battle for control ensued as each party resisted the other. Flags were burned, fire crackers tossed toward police horses, who arrived to support the cordon. Chaos spread as assembled police wielded batons against the mob corralling them from the building and fence line. Many agitators running off through the city, pushing over rubbish bins, igniting fires, smashing windows with steel rods, and a police car was upended. It was a perfect night, so he slipped away.

¶

Mary Whittington made it home and snuck into bed beside her husband after checking the children. It was a stressful job and although she relished the opportunity being the first lawmaker, she missed her family. Her phone buzzed as sleep was about to take her. The federal police commissioner advised of the street activists and civil unrest in Brisbane. She phoned the prime minister and was now pulling up at Kirribilli, ablaze with light.

'What the hell is going on, Whit?' Grobbelaar was addressing eight members of the Homeland Security Committee and the justice minister, when she entered the room.

'I have a report from the Queensland premier who advises me the situation is contained.' Whittington took the remaining seat at the table and glimpsed about her colleagues, none showing any sign of enthusiasm. 'The fire at the parliament is extinguished and they are cleaning up with the help of military generators. First reports indicate this was an opportunistic vigilante attack.'

'Intelligence suggests the main group were organised Aboriginal activists. We are yet to identify who organised them.' A military man, a chest full of coloured service ribbons spoke. 'They daubed slogans throughout the building — *Give Australia back to first Australians*, that kind of thing.'

'Was Millergoorra involved?' the prime minister barked at the general.

'We are unable to confirm her involvement,' the federal police commissioner said.

'Where is she now?'

'The latest report has her in northern New South Wales, south of Ballina.'

'How do you know that for sure?'

'We're tracking her mobile telephone,' the commissioner responded.

'Can we pick her up?' an exasperated prime minister asked.

'I would recommend it.'

Whittington nodded.

'We risk turning her into a martyr — is that what you want?' Marilyn Hodge asked, the prime minster didn't respond.

'If we isolate her from the activism and the blackouts then her message would be muted. The media could change their line of attack against the government,' Whittington said.

'What's the damage bill likely to be?' Grobbelaar asked, eyes narrowing.

'Politically or figuratively?' asked Matthew Roberts, the prime minister's shrewdest political adviser, heading Prime Minister and Cabinet. Grobbelaar swung in his chair, scratching his unshaven face while waiting for an answer. 'The cost of repair is nothing; however, the cost to the government's reputation will be severe unless we handle the response effectively and efficiently.'

Grobbelaar crossed his arms, rocking back in his chair. 'What are you suggesting?'

'We have to end the activism — let's pick up Millergoorra and get boots on the streets before morning.'

'That's an overreaction, is it not?' Whittington sat forward. 'The local police are equipped to keep the peace.'

Roberts sat forward, leaning on the table. 'Once this gets out that it was Aborigines, Queenslanders will want to extract their unique form of payback. The extreme right will mobilise, no doubt. This will inspire the local branch of Antifa thugs to get out onto the streets. They will cause even more trouble on the streets over the next forty-eight hours. And remember this, the All Blacks are due to play Australia tonight. The city is full of disappointed supporters asking for trouble.'

'Are you suggesting we invoke martial law?' Hodge's voice rose.

'If we have to then we should — but, only if we have trouble,' the general resumed the conversation.

'This is madness,' Hodge glimpsed at the prime minister, shaking her head.

'Can we get the power back on?' Grobbelaar asked.

'We have isolated the interconnector and we are working to bypass the hacked bug so energy supplies can be restored,' the homeland security minister responded.

'How long?'

'Unknown at this time.'

'It's obvious either Melbourne or Sydney will be next — how do we protect those cities?' Grobbelaar demanded, almost resigned to bad news.

'We have masked the interconnectors, this will delay but not stop them if they are determined to disrupt the grid,' the minister said.

Grobbelaar rested his elbows on the table, dropping his head into his hands, raking his fingers through his grey hair. 'You are the minister for homeland security and you are advising me our energy supply is not secure?'

'Prime Minister, we have never faced this type of attack before.'

'You people are the security committee and you are telling me Australians are at risk from a terrorist threat?'

The general shifted in his seat and said, 'It's not that simple.'

'You had better explain it to me, because I would have thought keeping the lights on should be simple,' Grobbelaar bellowed, slapping the table.

'Technology and a central national energy operator mean the energy grid is no longer autonomously managed in each state. If someone has the ability to hack the system, then this is what can happen. Once they are in they stay in the system until we find them. This mob are sophisticated and know what they're doing.'

'You're telling me anyone can enter the grid?'

'Not precisely — they may have in the past, but these attacks have caused us to close the portholes this mob used to come in.'

'Well, thank Christ for that,' Grobbelaar growled. 'I suppose we should be thanking them — I mean, if it wasn't for these terrorists, who knows what might have happened — thank God the Russians didn't bother to drop by,' Grobbelaar gazed about the table, 'you folks worry me — Australia is under attack and you have no solutions.'

Those around the table averted eyes or seemed busy taking notes. Whittington offered, 'Prime Minister, it might be time to revisit the demands.'

'There will be no deals with anyone — the deal with the elders is off the table, and there will be no further discussion on the treaty — or this joke of an idea about sovereignty.'

'What about the troops?' Roberts prompted.

'General, mobilise a brigade and get them on every corner of the city. Mary, have the police begin questioning the usual suspects to try and establish ringleaders; they were too organised for weekend warriors. If Millergoorra was involved, we need to know. And fuck it, pick her up and bring her to Sydney — hold her on terrorism charges, which means we can interrogate her for fourteen days — get what you can from her.' Grobbelaar stood, ending the meeting. 'Folks, get the power back on and make sure it doesn't happen again, otherwise retirement could be your next career move. Let's end this shit now.' He stormed from the room, stomping upstairs.

The others sat, watching each other, unsure what to say. Mary Whittington was the first to move, and as she left for her office she thought another day looming without seeing her children.

§

The highway between Ballina and Port Macquarie is an easy four-hour run, especially in the morning when drivers are on high alert. Miller left soon after having a hamburger at the local takeaway café before heading for the Pacific Highway. Messaris wanted her on the move to avoid detection from those who would prefer her in custody, so after a few hours' sleep at Leisure Lee holiday apartments just north of town, she hit the road. She paid cash for her room and kept her telephone switched off removing the SIM card.

When she arrived in Port Macquarie she figured she would find a pay phone near the shopping arcade. After parking the car, she sauntered off searching for a payphone conscious of keeping in the background. She found an operational unit near the information booth. She pulled a slip of paper from her jeans back pocket, stabbing in the fifth number on her list, rolling four dollar coins into the machine.

'It's Miller.'

'Good news and bad news for you.'

'What's the bad news?'

'One of your boys from last night has been picked up and is being questioned.'

'They know nothing, other than receiving a text message telling them to report to the gardens at midnight from a phone number that no longer exists. The coppers will get nothing from them. What's the damage? The papers must be screaming.'

'There was fire and graffiti in the parliament, Shop windows were smashed. No one injured, and no one arrested. Where are you?'

'Port Macquarie, I just got here.'

'The prime minister has been on television this morning calming things down, suggesting the federal police are using all resources at their disposal to bring the terrorists to justice. He expects arrests shortly.'

'Did he say anything about the deal with the elders?'

'No. His comment was that any negotiation with the Council of Elders would take place once the terrorists are in custody.'

'Where's Simone?'

'They're safe in Sydney and ready for the next phase. The government still has little idea of how we go about it.'

'Is this campaign going to work? It just seems pointless at the moment, and I'm confused by the government's response,' Miller said.

'The government's polling has crashed and if an election was held now, the government would lose most of their majority. The media and the population are on our side — they want the government to sign a treaty and negotiate the homeland idea. The prime minister is playing a game of brinksmanship but he's not in control, we are.'

'What does Neesham have to say.'

'Stuff Neesham,' Messaris snapped. 'He's out of the picture as far as I'm concerned. He wanted to defer the mine and not sign a treaty, that's all, which is not what we agreed.'

'You won't get paid.'

'I'll get paid, just let me worry about that.' Messaris paused. 'This is about two things for me . . . stopping the mine, and shafting Koning. If I get that result, then I win,' he lied, 'if you get the result you want, then you win, so let's ignore Neesham.'

'What happens now?' Miller peeped over her shoulder for signs of any potential threat, identifying nothing.

'We have cranked up the social media campaign and we have another online petition attracting significant numbers — we're already at a million. The government will wilt soon, trust me.'

'This is not going to change Grobbelaar's mind.'

'Then we put more pressure on the prime minister, make it personal.'

'How do we do that?'

'Get to Sydney before dark and I'll fill you in on the next steps.'

'I'll be there around six; it should take around five hours depending on traffic.'

'Get rid of your phone, leave it in a bin where you are — make sure you turn it on before you drop it.'

'Why?'

'I reckon they're hunting for you and they'll track your phone — so take plenty of money out of the account from an ATM to make sure they know you are in Port Macquarie, then hightail it out of there. Also, buy dark fatigues before you get here.'

¶

Grobbelaar was enjoying a traditional sandwich and a cup of tea on the patio when Matthew Roberts approached to update him on the politics of the morning. 'Do you want a cup?' he asked as Roberts joined him at the small table.

'No, I'm fine Rene, thanks.'

'You look as if you have grim news.' Grobbelaar took a bite of his granny's favourite Western Cape Gatsby, wiping his lips to clear the sauce, waving Roberts to continue.

'The troops are out in Brisbane. We have no further developments on the energy grid. Neesham wants to see you in a few days to sort out what to do, and, the media hate you — no surprises there. Other than that, it's been a good morning.'

'What do the polls say?'

'They say you have to sort it out.'

'I'm not going to give them what they want — the mine will go ahead.'

'Koning can get another mine — you won't get another chance.'

'What are you saying?' Grobbelaar asked.

'Unless you resolve this, you are done — no, more than just you — the government is done.'

Grobbelaar dropped his sandwich and looked out onto the garden and the harbour beyond. 'Why is this happening?'

'Years of broken promises, perhaps . . . I don't know.' Roberts followed his gaze out over the harbour. 'If you show leadership on this you'll become an international star.'

'Big fucking deal.'

'If you don't you'll be discarded in the waste bin of history.'

'I can't back down.'

'Then see Neesham and sort it out. My advice is to sign the treaty.'

'What? Just because the UN tells me?'

'No . . . because the polls are telling you. Sign it and you'll win, at the very least, the next two elections; keep fighting, as you are, and you'll be retired next year.'

14

The metal of the dinghy was numb on Millergoora's hand as she sat forward, gripping the gunwale, the dark water of the harbour rolling aside as the boat puttered along the shoreline under the bridge toward Kirribilli House. The night sky was obscured by rain clouds yet to drop their load, the only visible lights from early-morning risers in the shoreline apartments and houses. She was chilled and nervous about what she agreed to do.

Her meeting with Messaris that afternoon continued to drive shivers through her, but she agreed with him the campaign had to become personal, and now she was about to make it so. The single engine of dinghy was quiet as it motored past the Jeffrey Street ferry wharf toward the small point and grounds of the official Sydney residences of the governor-general and prime minister.

The tide was at the right height for the flat-hulled dinghy to move close to the sandstone rock face discouraging anyone from approaching the private gardens from the harbour. Miller checked her watch, waved to the nameless man piloting the boat, and swung onto a rocky shelf. The dinghy moving on; if anyone was watching they would not have realised it had dropped off a visitor. As instructed, she waited on the ledge until three-thirty to begin scaling the rocks.

¶

The sedan cruised along Kirribilli Avenue until it reached the dead-end, reversed, then struggled to turn. There were no driveways, and when the driver had driven back and forth without gaining any significant revolution, a man almost fell out of the passenger seat, staggering to the front of the vehicle, semaphoring directions to the driver.

'Nah, stop. Turn it the other way; that's it, now go back.' The sedan over-revved, stalling as it shuddered against the brake. 'Come on. Faster, turn it faster.' The engine then stopped, the driver lowering the window.

'You're so smart, why don't you have a go?' a woman shrieked.

'Sssh, you'll wake the neighbours,' the man responded, swaying in the bath of headlights.

Across the road, at the gate securing the prime minister's property, a guard observed from a darkened corner. He was watching for anything unusual and scanned the street in the direction away from the chaotic drunks trying to get home.

'I thought you said you knew where to go,' the woman yelled.

'Sssh! I thought I did, but I think we took a wrong turn back up the hill.'

'You take over and get this thing out of here.'

As the guard watched, a colleague tapped into his communication set. 'What's all the noise?'

'A couple of drunks having trouble with a car.'

'Suspicious?'

'Hard to say, no one else about — just a woman and a bloke.'

'I'm on my way.'

The man stumbled to the driver's door, opened it, assisting the woman from the seat. She collapsed into his arms and began laughing. 'I think we should get a cab.' Her partner helped her to the bonnet, leaned her against it then moved to get back in the car; but, she dragged him close, kissing him. The man responded. What had been a comedy act of drunk drivers turned into an amorous public display.

The security guard's partner arrived and assessed the situation. 'Oi. You two on the car, get a room will you. Move on.'

The couple jumped apart, surprised by the voice, adjusting themselves. 'Can you give us a hand, mate?' the man asked.

The security guards stepped through a side gate, scanning the vicinity before the senior officer walked to the car, jumped into the front seat, restarted it, and within two deft moves had the car facing in the right direction.

'Thanks mate,' said the man as he helped his partner into the passenger seat. She seemed as if she was ready to pass out. He then jumped into the driver's seat, buckled up and took off, honking his horn twice as he waved goodbye, shuddering up the street.

'I took a note of the number. Should we let the locals know about two drunks on the road?'

'Call it in; they're dangerous like that,' the senior officer said, as they watched it disappear around a curve in the road.

Inside the car the woman sat up and smiled, and the man said, 'I didn't think we'd planned for sex in the street.'

'Oh well, they weren't responding, so I thought I'd push them to see how far they would let us go.'

'What would you have done if they hadn't come out?'

'I was ready,' Simone smiled at Tyrone. 'I could feel you were.'

'Saucy beast.' He parked the car outside a pink apartment block. They strolled around the corner, popping the boot of a BMW 3 series, swapping jackets. Simone tossed her blonde wig in and they were away within five minutes, passing a police patrol car as they turned from Warudu back into Kirribilli Avenue.

¶

Miller heard the honking as she ran up the stepped lawn to the back of the house. Messaris had told her what to do — check the veranda doors: *'who needs to lock doors when there is so much security?'* They were locked. She checked the windows — same result. She knew it was time for a ground patrol and needed to make a decision — she had to get up onto the roof and enter the house through the skylight above the stairs. Should she scale a tree or retreat to the governor's garden shed next door, then cross the tin roofs and Kirribilli kitchens with the hope the domestic staff were sound asleep.

Given her age, she decided to retreat to Admiralty House and the gardener's compound.

The gate was locked but she had no trouble climbing it, jumping over. Her thighs were beginning to feel a little sore, but she ignored the burning, dragged a crate to a corner and was soon on the roof. The gardener's residence was close, and a window overlooked the roof, so she scampered across the tin, then across a high brick wall like a tight-rope walker, and onto the pitched roof of the kitchen. She checked her watch, ducking down, laying flat against the roof as the security patrol worked its way around the gardens. She gazed out onto the harbour, taking in the view and the signs of the approaching dawn.

The tin was cold; Miller welcomed it until the chill from the wintry conditions and her damp clothes started to seep into her. She waited the agreed fifteen minutes, then progressed to the house. The pitch of the roof was steep and the slate tiles would be difficult to climb. The skylight was located between ridges, which meant climbing the main ridge, using the first-floor gable windows, with their own pitched tiling as helpful stages in her climb. She decided to use the windows as leverage and scooted along the verandah roof searching for a foothold near a window. She pushed at the window to check if it was locked, and to her astonishment and gratitude, it moved. She made a muffled noise of delight and relief before checking herself. She slid the window up until it hit a security snib, deflating her enthusiasm. The opening might be big enough for her to squeeze through, but she would need to flatten herself right down.

She dropped her back pack and emptied her pockets, taking off her equipment belt; she figured if she could squeeze her head and shoulders through first she might have a chance of getting in. She decided to lay

on her back and wriggle rather than slide face down. Her ear felt the
ridge of the wooden sill as she pushed through, dragging an arm then
pulling the other through. She was facing the ceiling and hoped to see
the snib, loosen it and push the window up, but it was out of reach. She
fingered for a sturdy grip and thought the heavy curtains were as good
as anything, trusting they would be secured tightly. She inched her way
further into the room, holding fast to the drapes, grateful for her small
breasts, but unsure if her hips would fit. It was too late to retreat — she
was now committed. She would either squeeze through or be stuck
until discovered by the next security patrol.

She grappled with the drapes, wriggling hard, but she was stuck.
She just needed a touch more flesh from her backside through and
she'd be in. She worked her abdominals, sucking, squeezing and
pulling at her hips until she could feel a little movement. She reached
high into the drapes and tugged, and her hips came through followed
by her legs. She collapsed on the floor and lay for a moment on the
plush carpet, breathing, controlling her anxiety. She readjusted her
clothing, then clipped open the security snib, lifting up the window,
retrieving her bag and equipment.

Grobbelaar was alone in the house. His wife had died after a
prolonged illness with motor neurone disease and he'd shown little
enthusiasm for another relationship. His daughter shared the house,
but was holidaying overseas during her university winter break. After
the late nights worrying over the increasing loss of public confidence
in his government he was stretched out on his bed, still dressed, with
a doona covering him.

Miller knew which room, although she hadn't anticipated the
floorboard squeaking under the plush carpet. The bedroom door was
ajar and she listened for noise, hearing the soft rhythmic breathing of
a sleeper. She drew her weapon and crept in. She was nervous as she
lowered herself onto the bed, placing a hand on the prime minister's
knee and shaking.

'Prime Minister?' Miller whispered.

'Wah?'

'Prime Minister, we need to talk.'

Grobbelaar rolled aside, struggling to open his eyes. 'Who is it? What do you want?'

'I'm just going to turn the lamp on.' Miller found the cord and flicked the switch. 'Hi,' she smiled, 'just stay where you are.'

Grobbelaar recoiled, trying to sit up. 'What the hell do you want?'

'We need to talk,' Miller said once more, poking Grobbelaar in the chest with her pistol, forcing him back into his pillows. 'Just relax so we can chat.'

The prime minister struggled then fell back against the wooden headboard. 'How the hell did you get in?' He felt about for his phone to check the time and how far he was from the panic button.

'Before you think about calling for help, I would like to show you something and then perhaps you will settle down and we can talk about a few important things.' Miller tugged out a phone, found a photograph messaged to her hours earlier from Bali and displayed it for the prime minister. 'As I understand it, this beautiful girl is your daughter,' Grobbelaar paid attention, 'the man she is standing with works with me, and if you ring your daughter now she will be pleased to hear from you.'

Miller passed Grobbelaar his phone and he pushed the button for his daughter.

'Hello?' A man answered.

'Who the hell are you?'

'I'm the man in the photograph.'

'Where's my daughter?'

'She's enjoying a good sleep. She was tired and needed a rest after the day we've had together.'

'Can I speak to her?' Grobbelaar glanced to Miller for support.

'Not right now — maybe, after you do what you are told.'

'If you fucking hurt her, I will kill you.'

'You have no idea, moron.' Terry McGuiness ended the call.

Grobbelaar dropped the phone, glaring at Miller who was waiting, still sitting on the edge of the bed.

'Everything will be fine, I can assure you, you just need to understand the importance of the treaty and our need for sovereignty.' Miller smiled. 'As my colleagues recommended, you need skin in the game, so let's talk.'

Grobbelaar appeared mutinous. 'So, talk to me.'

'No harm will come to your daughter, she is incommunicado for a few days with her friends.'

'Why did a man answer her phone?'

'Part of the deal with the trip of a lifetime is no communication, so the phones were collected when they went on board.'

'On board? Where is she?'

'She is off on a great diving adventure with friends.'

'Who is he?'

'He will be your daughter's worst nightmare if anything happens to me,' Miller squeezed a smile, 'he is my security against your poor judgement.'

'This is ridiculous, you can't hold her hostage and make me do anything.' Grobbelaar shoved Miller aside standing up from the bed.

'Prime Minister, you will be working from home over the next few days as far as your security detail needs to know. I am a guest who you know and trust. As I said, anything happens to me and your daughter will not see you again.'

'Are you threatening me?'

Miller smiled. 'No, of course not, I just want to talk to you about the future and what we can do together.'

'I'm not going to do anything with you.'

'Well then, that's a shame because I'm not stuffing around.' Miller fired off a muffled round into the bed then stood in front of a startled Grobbelaar a warm pistol pressed against his chest. 'I told you before what I'm prepared to do, I just want you to reconsider what *you* may be prepared to do.' Grobbelaar stepped back, a little lost, his eyes wide searching for his panic button. 'What say I rustle up some eggs and toast, maybe even a cup of tea, and why don't you refresh yourself, perhaps call the attorney general and ask her to join us.' Miller made her way to the door. 'Just think about your daughter and don't do anything stupid. I'll be downstairs.'

As Miller left, Grobbelaar grabbed his phone, calling Whittington.

¶

The light was improving when Whittington knocked on the front door. Grobbelaar let her in, leading her to the kitchen where Miller was perched at the stone bench on a wooden stool, pistol in front of her, holding a cup with two hands, smiling as the attorney general entered.

'Would you like a cup of tea, Mary?' Miller asked. 'How are your kids?'

'What is this — some sort of tea party?'

'You could say that. Didn't the American revolution start with a tea party?'

'Now's not the time for your jokes,' Grobbelaar snapped.

'I'm just asking if Mary would like a cup of tea. It's fresh.' Miller picked up the china pot, pouring a cup. 'Prime Minister, would you like another?'

'I can't stand this.' Grobbelaar stood, hands on hips. 'Now that she's here, tell me what you want?'

'What's the rush? It's too early in the morning for business.' Miller passed the cup to Whittington and motioned her to sit. 'Would you like something to eat? I cooked the PM a few eggs, but he hasn't eaten them, I could do some for you.'

'Tell me what's going on, Nellie. The prime minister seems to think you have his daughter and you're threatening to do something if he doesn't do as you wish.'

'That's a little dramatic.' Miller smiled, glanced at Grobbelaar then said, 'I told him I wanted to talk about this dilemma we find ourselves in. We are enjoying breakfast, so I'm unsure what he needs to be worried about.'

Grobbelaar wanted to shout at her, but said, 'she has my daughter and threatened to harm her if we don't do as she says.'

'Not correct — I said there would be problems if anything happens to me.'

'What do you want?' Whittington asked again.

Miller dropped off the stool and walked over to the window overlooking the harbour. The Manly ferry was ploughing toward Circular Quay, the lights across the harbour losing their brilliance as the sky brightened. She stared out the window then said, 'Almost three hundred years ago the English entered that harbour claiming the land as their own.'

'Oh Christ, not again,' Grobbelaar groaned, but Whittington hushed him, placing a finger to her lips.

'Three hundred years and not only did you claim the harbour, but all the lands you were yet to see, no matter who had claimed them before you. You fought us, killed us, oppressed us, and then made laws saying we didn't exist.'

'This is history, Nellie. What would you have us do now?' Whittington asked.

'The British were in India for four hundred years, then gave it back. They were in Hong Kong for one hundred and fifty years and then transferred sovereignty back to China. They signed a treaty in New Zealand, but they never considered it proper in Australia. In other colonies, Indigenous people fought to regain their sovereignty, and yet, these same countries remain important to the commonwealth.'

Whittington shared a glance with Grobbelaar, who shrugged his shoulders.

'We want what is right — we want our culture back. We want respect.'

'You already have it.' Grobbelaar was not prepared to concede a single point.

Miller turned to face him. 'Really? You believe that?'

'Nellie, of course, we do,' Whittington interjected. 'Our budgets are focused on improving outcomes. We continue to provide services for remote communities that cost the taxpayer a fortune. We have an equality policy guaranteeing Indigenous participation in all government departments, boards and other government appointments.'

Miller dropped her head and said, 'It's not always about the money.'

'Then tell us, what is it about?' Whittington encouraged her.

Miller took a moment, then said, 'Language, culture, law is not about money.'

'How can we incorporate your culture into Australian culture without incorporating other cultures? We now have demands to incorporate Sharia law and certain aspects of African cultures into our laws. We are multicultural, but we are one. We can't change the rules for you and then not the others.'

'That's the point, you can't. Even though we were here first, we lose again, and my people and our culture drop closer to extinction.'

'That's ridiculous, you are not nearing extinction.' Grobbelaar grabbed a glass stepping to the sink to fill it with water.

'When you came here we had six hundred nations, now many of those are under threat.'

Grobbelaar gulped a mouthful and sneered, 'You have to help yourselves.'

'And there, my friends, is the issue — you see no problem, and therefore refuse to act to resolve them.'

Grobbelaar slammed his glass down. 'We are all Australians, no one is any more or less Australian.'

Miller smiled shaking her head, acknowledging the comment. 'Where on the spectrum of Australian citizenship would you place the First Nation people?'

Neither politician responded.

'Let me help you by asking this — who has the highest death rates? Who has the lowest education rates? Who has the highest health risks? Who is more likely to be incarcerated? Who has the highest deaths in custody rates? Who has the lowest home ownership rates? Who has the highest cancer rates? The highest unemployment rate?' Miller glared at them. 'Any suggestions?'

After a protracted silence, Whittington glanced to Grobbelaar but knew he was not engaged, so asked, 'What is it that you want? The government has agreed to the Karrakatta Congress having at least one parliamentary assembly a year in Canberra — what more do you want?'

'A homeland.'

'That's rubbish.' Grobbelaar sat at the bench and thrust his head into his hands, his fingers rubbing his scalp.

'Partition off the Northern Territory and allow us to run it. Allow us a separate state, let us do our own thing.'

'It would never work.' The prime minister didn't want to listen.

'It did in India, in Israel, in Africa, South America and even closer to us with New Guinea — it can work here.'

'How do you reckon you would fund it.'

'You transition it over, say, ten years.'

'What about the families and other First Nation claims in Australia? Would they still need funding?'

'They are Australians, why not?'

'But, you want a homeland?'

'The Jews still pay their taxes in Australia.'

Whittington interjected. 'This is not something that can be done overnight, here at this bench.'

'Of course, not — but we can draw up an Act of Parliament, have it tabled, debated and voted upon. We don't need a constitutional change to do this because the commonwealth has the power to grant sovereignty and you have exclusive power over the territories.'

Whittington smiled at the brash idea acknowledging Millergoorra's enthusiasm.

Grobbelaar sighed. 'What else?'

'What else, what?'

'How much money do you want?'

'This is not about money.'

Grobbelaar licked his lips and smirked. 'You must be the only Aborigine who doesn't want money.'

'You evidently haven't met too many Aborigines.'

'What else do you want to end this?'

'I want the UN treaty banning mining in Arnhem Land signed.'

15

Grobbelaar led Whittington into his office for a quiet word, flopping into the chair at his large jarrah desk. 'This is crazy. She must be afflicted with something. What are we to do?'

'How certain are you they have your daughter?'

'I have the federal police investigating and they are liaising with Indonesian authorities. We should know if what she's saying has any foundation in around two hours. I've told them to not do anything until we know for certain.'

'Can we assume the deal is off with Neesham?'

'Why don't we get him here. Maybe he has influence over her.'

'What do we do with the media?'

'Keep them out of this — if they get involved there is no saying what might happen. They could turn the public further against us and we don't want fascists out on the street causing problems.'

'Should I advise cabinet?'

Grobbelaar rubbed his face. 'On a need to know basis, I suspect. Let's wait a few hours and assess the need to widen the communication net — the fewer who know the better.'

Whittington sat at the desk watching Grobbelaar work through papers and toss them into a tray for clearing later. 'How did she get in?'

'I've had a word with the feds about that and the officers on the property don't even know she's here. I asked for an examination of CCTV footage, but I'm not sure that will change a damn thing. She's here and we have to deal with her.'

'We just sit and wait for confirmation from Bali before we act?'

'It's the only thing we can do. I can't afford to act against her until I know Marli is safe. We just have to humour her until we do.'

'And if she's not safe, what then?'

Grobbelaar didn't respond.

'What's your view of the demands? The treaty seems okay — it will stuff Koning's plans, but we can live with his disappointment — and the polls would improve.'

Grobbelaar slapped the desk. 'The hell you say — I'm not giving her anything.'

'Rene, if Marli is being threatened then you might need to think of a plan B.'

'We do nothing. I'm not going to surrender on this, no way.' Grobbelaar picked up a pen and tossed it into a tray.

Whittington waited for the prime minister to collect himself. 'What do we do about staff?'

'There's no reason why I can't just stay here and people can come and go. Millergoorra is right on one thing — she's safe while Marli remains under threat. But, when I know she's clear then I will tear her limb from limb.'

'That's interesting.' Miller had approached unnoticed now leaning on the door frame. 'I would prefer you take me out back and give me a good whipping, like you did to my forefathers.'

Grobbelaar fell back in his chair and studied her. 'I need to move forward on this, so how do you see this playing out? Come in and take a seat.'

Miller bumped herself off the door frame entering the office, now filling with sunlight. She sat on a wooden chair at the desk, next to Whittington. 'I know nothing about the federal parliament — total waste of time and money as far as I'm concerned.'

'Most Australians wouldn't think so,' Grobbelaar retorted.

'Yeah, well most of them don't think much about us.' Miller kicked a foot onto the desk. 'Me, on the other hand, I respect my people and my culture.'

Grobbelaar seethed at her blatant disrespect but maintained his calm as he studied her. 'What do you want the parliament to do?'

'People tell me it's possible for you to bring legislation to the parliament and make a law to partition the Northern Territory.'

'Not going to happen.'

'It could if the people tell you it's okay.'

Grobbelaar scoffed, 'How do they tell me?'

'I'm told you could run a referendum to change the constitution to allow partitioning to happen.'

'You are kidding yourself — this idea is crazy.'

'It's crazy because you think so — you have to have an open mind.'

'What happens if we don't give you what you want?'

'Melbourne and Sydney close for three days.'

'When?' Whittington asked her.

'In two days.'

The politicians didn't respond.

'Then we start all over again,' Miller smiled, waiting for a reaction, 'this time with even more anarchy on the streets.'

Whittington swung around to face her. 'These blackouts are causing chaos to business and you are bringing a criminal element onto the streets. The punters are frightened by it all and sooner or later they will turn against you — you can't continue this campaign.'

'Well, you know what to do.'

'Get your fucking foot off my desk.' Grobbelaar had had enough. Miller dropped her foot from the desk. He stabbed a finger at her. 'You trumped-up stupid bitch. What do you think you are playing at?'

'You know something, Prime Minister? I had over thirty years to think about how this country needs to heal its hollow soul — I think this plan will solve your political problems. It'll end the guilt industry, that's for sure. It'll stop this ridiculous victimhood governments wave at us and allow my people independence. White Australia will have a resolution they can agree upon and feel good about their history. Don't underestimate how your people will respond to this — I think whitefellas are crying out for this type of reconciliation and the polls

177

indicate that what I'm saying is spot-on. This is the end game and if you lead it, then the Australian people will embrace it, and follow you.'

Grobbelaar sat back and smiled. 'You think?'

'Territorians won't have to give up their land as white folks did in Zimbabwe. They'll just have a different tax system and an amended set of rules to operate under, business as usual. You're from South Africa, you know independence makes little difference to the economy.'

'I was born here.' Grobbelaar spun away from the desk, staring out the window.

'Your roots are over there, though, aren't they?'

Grobbelaar spun back and gazed at Whittington.

Miller continued. 'This will etch your name in world history for ever more — but if you don't want to do this, the campaign continues, and you will be out of government within twelve months. I'll bet you, a new government will do it — because that's what the people want.'

Grobbelaar glanced back at Miller. 'What makes you so damn sure?'

'The current polls aren't good. The media is beginning to listen to the people and even members of your own cabinet have been making conciliatory noises for new policy thinking.' Grobbelaar cast a peek at Whittington who shrugged agreement. 'The media are reporting your Indigenous Affairs minister has recommended signing the UN treaty and is prepared to consider the sovereignty question. Now that's the leadership we need.'

'It means nothing — he means nothing.'

'Yes, but you know, if these power blackouts become a regular occurrence then your government is gone within the year.'

Grobbelaar didn't respond, conceding she was politically spot-on.

¶

Jimmy Neesham flicked through a book in the newsagency at Darwin airport, waiting for his flight to Sydney. He wasn't interested in reading but figured time would fall away if he focused his mind on distractions rather than the turbulence rolling over the government. He liked reading the first few paragraphs of books to determine the style and statue of the writer, often amazed how publishers picked their winners. He thought many unworthy, yet here they were taking up his time.

'Mr Jimmy?' a voice interrupted. 'May we speak?'

'Christ — do you always sneak around scaring people?'

'You are very busy, and we have not spoken in some time. I came your office yesterday, but you not there, so I need reassurance from you, before you leave to meet with government.'

'How do you know I'm meeting with the government?'

Teo smiled at him. 'Mr Jimmy, we know everything.'

Neesham placed the book back on the shelf, turning to face his visitor, reflecting on his point. 'There is not much to know about me — but why would you need to know what I'm doing?'

'We want the mine licence revoked. We do not want the South Africans mining coal.'

'I negotiated a deferral, but the government retracted once we lost the power in Brisbane.'

'Yes, it is not very pleasant to have your terrorist friends out of your control.'

'First, they ain't my friends; second, they want the same things you do.'

'Yet, you lose the agreement you had with government by closing Brisbane, which means this influence you assure us you have, is not as great as you think.'

Neesham glanced about him to check if anyone was listening. 'I will get what you want.'

Teo stepped forward and held his gaze. 'It's in your best interests to ensure you do.'

'What would happen if the South Africans are out of the picture?'

'Then we would welcome the opportunity of bidding for a licence.'

'You can do that with government now.'

'This is a complex issue for us — we prefer to operate away from the light. We are best suited to the shadows, with agents like you working for us.'

Neesham was annoyed by what Teo said, again checking if anyone was close. 'I'm not your agent.'

Teo smiled. 'You have supported us for many years.' He cocked his head. 'You have taken our money, so we think you are our friend.'

'Yes, but that's very different from being your agent.'

'Mr Jimmy,' Teo sighed, placing a hand on Neesham's arm. 'We are interested in stopping the coalmine. Do what you can when you are in Sydney.'

'I can promise you, I will do my best to do what's right.'

'And, I promise you, Mr Jimmy,' Teo squeezed Neesham's arm, 'if we do not get what we want, then your opportunities will be very limited.'

¶

Neesham shivered in the crisp air of a wintry Sydney twilight as he stepped from the government car sent to transport him from the airport to Kirribilli. He strode to the front door, which was opened just as he was about to knock by a staff member who directed him to the dining room. As he entered, the conversation stopped, the prime minister waving to him to a seat.

'Glad you could get here at such short notice, Jimmy. I suspect you know everyone.' Grobbelaar indicated about the table with a wave. He smiled, and nodded, as he removed a pad and papers from his satchel. Grobbelaar waited for him to settle before continuing. 'I'm sure you know about the troubles we are having with one of yours. We need a resolution.'

'I can assure you — and I have told you this many times before — she is not one of mine. Where is she?'

'Watching television in the lounge, I think. She seems too damn relaxed for my liking.'

'Why are we negotiating with her?' Neesham asked.

'I'd rather not say, until I have confirmation from the federal police. Suffice to say we remain in a period of negotiation.'

'More like a siege,' Matthew Roberts remarked.

'Without the violence,' Grobbelaar added, glancing at his adviser.

Marilyn Hodge, the justice minister, read from her phone: 'Prime Minister, I've just been sent a text which states the federal police will have a report for you within the hour.'

¶

'Why are you doing this?' Simone sat watching Tyrone pattering away at a keyboard.

'It's something Conan wants me to do.'

'You do everything he wants?'

'He pays me — and you, for that matter — so if I can do what he asks, I usually do.' Tyrone stopped typing and stared at her. 'It'll be all over in two days, I promise you.' He reached for her hand. 'Once we are done in Melbourne there'll be no more revolutions, and our clients will have what they need.'

'Clients?'

'Sure — who do you think is paying the bills?'

'I thought Conan was doing this with Nellie.'

Tyrone sat back and smiled. 'My darling Simone, this campaign has a number of architects, but there is one group paying us — and that's the one we answer to.'

Simone let go of his hand. 'We're not doing this to help the traditional owners stop the mining?' This was the first flicker of doubt she'd felt in weeks about what she was doing.

'Of course, we are — amongst other things.'

'What other things are we talking about?'

Tyrone glimpsed at her, considering what to say, tempted to explain. 'You're on a need to know basis and at this time you know everything you need.'

'You are kidding me, right?'

Tyrone stood, stepped away from the computer, padding to a window, gazing out on the city of Melbourne and the Reserve Bank across the street. He leaned into the window frame, cocking a foot onto a knee as he thought about what to say. 'I can't tell you any more than that — please don't force me.'

Simone shimmied over to him, sliding her arms around him, cupping his shoulders, placing her head on his back, offering reassurance, understanding and love. 'We'll be okay. Let's just finish this next one and get out of here.'

Tyrone turned and hugged her, then dropped a brief kiss on her head — he never missed a chance to enjoy her soft warmth.

'Get a room, will you?' Messaris came through the door carrying food and other supplies and they broke apart, a little embarrassed. 'Are we ready to move yet?'

Tyrone returned to his computer, flicking open a window showing the administration menu for the national energy manager of the power grid. 'We're ready to trip the grid in three separate stages, which will send the system into chaos. It will believe it's under attack and shut down. We then direct the interconnectors to isolate power supply to Melbourne, and hopefully, Sydney will be affected.'

'How long will it be off?'

'It's much more complex than the others. They have added a number of encryptions working to stop us — I can't guarantee a time.'

'Best estimate?'

'At least twelve hours.'

'I was expecting at least a day.'

'They have overhauled some of the coding we installed, and access is now much more difficult, but I can get you twelve — maybe more.'

Messaris hesitated and glanced at Simone before turning back to Tyrone. 'And the other party — how long can you guarantee me.'

'They'll have reserve power back on within the hour. I can't give you any more than that. I'll try for longer, but their security system is much more sophisticated than we thought.'

'You're not leaving me much time,' Messaris groaned.

'You need five minutes on site, if that.'

'You're sure this will work?' Messaris sought reassurance.

'You get to the computer while it's in standby mode and download the code before they reactivate, and you'll get what you want.'

'Get what?' Simone asked.

Messaris glanced at her, tapping his nose with a finger and smiled. After a moment he said, 'I have food for you — help yourself.'

¶

Miller was stretched out on a comfortable couch, her boots on the arm, watching the television news, gun on a pedestal table beside her. She had almost dropped off to sleep when Neesham came to join her.

'What is going on Nellie?' he asked as he entered the room.

'When did you get here?' She yawned as she sat up. 'I was expecting you earlier.'

'I was just in with Grobbelaar and his advisers — why have you taken his daughter?'

'He told you that?'

'The federal police can't find her or her mates. Where is she?'

'She is safe and unharmed — she's my insurance policy.'

'You know this is being classified as a terrorist siege, and once it's cleaned up, you'll be back in jail — you know that, don't you?'

Miller fell back onto the lounge and sniffed with disdain. 'You may be a cousin, but I don't trust you, Jimmy.'

Neesham gazed at her, gnawing on his lower lip. 'The treaty may be done but you can forget this ridiculous idea of sovereignty — the PM will never wear it.'

'Then I suspect he'll need to rethink his position — his daughter's holiday may depend on it, if you know what I mean?'

'You're prepared to go to those lengths to get what you want?'

'*I* don't want anything. *I* have not asked for a thing,' Miller snapped as she jumped to her feet. 'My people deserve respect and the one person who can deliver it to them is the prime minister. If he doesn't agree then whatever happens to him will be a result of his failure of leadership.'

'They will never wear sovereignty.'

'I'm not asking for them to sign off anything now. What I want is an honest discussion. I want the Australian people to have a voice about it. I want them to consider the idea, not to throw it in the corner and forget about it, and I reckon that can be done within the parliament.'

'This is crazy.'

'Just think about it for a moment.' Miller stepped past Neesham and began pacing by the window. 'The public will have a view and the politicians will respond. The government can introduce legislation calling for the partitioning of the Northern Territory by proclamation. If it passes the parliament then we win — if it doesn't, then so be it.'

Neesham drifted to the side of the room with his hands in his pockets, considering her idea. 'It'll never get enacted.'

'But, what if it did?' Miller watched him as he circled the room. 'You could be the first president, just like Gusmao.'

Neesham scoffed at the suggestion, but he was listening. 'We agree to the treaty and legislation, which the prime minister presents to the parliament at the next sitting, then we let the parliament decide.'

'I reckon we need the people to get involved otherwise we lose the goodwill.'

'Hey, good idea, let's have a referendum,' Neesham blurted.

Miller stopped pacing and turned to Jimmy. 'We get the government to pass legislation for a referendum seeking the people's view about partitioning a sovereign state.'

Neesham smiled and said, 'If the people decide on a sovereign state then the government would have to act and pass legislation.'

'This is good,' Miller wanted the scheme as Neesham's idea and smirked as she gazed out the window. 'The one thing we have to convince Grobbelaar to agree to, is a referendum.'

'He might be persuaded.'

'Tell him that he can campaign for a no vote if that's what he and the racists want to do. At least he will have a number of democratic steps before proclamation of the new state.'

Neesham paused and considered her. 'What would you call it?'

'I don't know. Call it Arnhem, call it Kangaroo — I don't care, let our new parliament decide, just make sure *we* decide not the white fellas,' she waved her arm, 'we all want the mine not to go ahead, we know that — I even think Grobbelaar will support that idea, but let's go for the grand prize and if we win then world history will be consistent — if we lose, then so be it, but we lose everything. — and I'm not prepared to do that.'

'I'll go and see what they have to say about the referendum idea,' Neesham told her as he stood and left the room.

❡

'It's very simple Prime Minister.' Neesham settled back into his chair. 'Chaos ends with the stroke of your pen. The UN treaty is signed, and you prepare an act of parliament for a referendum.'

Grobbelaar said nothing as he studied Neesham. Whittington took off her glasses and squinted across to Hodge raising a querying eyebrow. 'What is the referendum about?' she asked Neesham.

'Let the people decide,' Neesham said. 'It's easy. Rather than get bogged down trying to decide if a separate state is possible or even legal, just toss it out to the public. You can then say at the very least you tried.'

Grobbelaar didn't respond and gazed at Whittington who smiled, then shrugged.

'Prime Minister,' Neesham sharpened his tone, 'this can be resolved with a promise to move legislation to go to a referendum. What happens after that is determined by the Australian people. There is a long way to go and these are just small initial steps that can solve this thing today.'

'An act of parliament approving a referendum?' Hodge asked.

'A simple parliamentary process that will start the ball rolling. If it fails to get support in the parliament, then so be it.'

'This is a goodwill gesture that I suspect the public will approve, Prime Minister,' Whittington said. 'It opens up debate and if it is approved then there are other legislative processes it will need to go through. It will be years before we see a result.'

The prime minister didn't respond. His eyes darted between his advisers and landed on Matthew Roberts. He nodded at him to speak.

'We are trailing in the polls, badly, and may not recover. This issue of Aboriginal sovereignty has overshadowed Australia for a long time. This may quieten the voices of discontent, which have been nagging the nation for years. Agreeing to at least consider the idea could end these acts of terrorism, your daughter will then be safe, and we will be seen as brilliant statesmen — oh, and women, sorry.' He smiled at the formidable women across the table.

'Prime Minister, we can do the economic modelling — it may be a win-win for the government financially if we partitioned off the Northern Territory — and the legislative process can all stop at any time if the Australian public don't approve,' Whittington suggested. 'It would be huge kudos for the government, and it would provide a legacy that will never be tarnished.'

'No details — just a goodwill statement?' Grobbelaar said.

'You'll have the support of cabinet and most of the party room,' she added.

Grobbelaar waited, watching the others, then said, 'I must admit I'm going soft on not signing the treaty — Koning will just have to wear it, but, I don't like the idea of sovereignty.'

'We don't have to go to a referendum immediately. We can use joint parliamentary committees such as Foreign Affairs, Defence and Trade to conduct a parliamentary inquiry into how proposed partitioning would work and its implications before the referendum legislation comes before the parliament,' Roberts suggested. 'It is then deferred beyond the next election.'

The prime minister pondered the advice, gazing at the table, then nodded, recognising the political delays he could muster to the progress of a referendum.

'I would recommend we also use the Treaties committee for an inquiry and perhaps the National Capital and External Territories to consider the idea,' Whittington said. 'The concept of partitioning off a sovereign state will have plenty of parliamentary debate and discussion before it goes anywhere near the public, which means it may never get up. The optics will be in our favour and resolve our immediate concerns.'

Grobbelaar said nothing and gazed at his colleagues as they sat waiting for direction.

'Let's bring her in and have a chat.'

16

The morning light hit Miller's face, stirring her from slumber and bringing her to her senses. She had dozed off on the comfy couch with the stress of the past days catching up with her. She staggered to her feet and completed a speedy reconnoitre of the ground floor, but there was no one about. She crept upstairs and checked the bedrooms. Grobbelaar was fast asleep, Neesham laying on a bed snoring, and Whittington curled in a foetal position with a light blanket thrown over her. Miller worked her way back downstairs and circled the house once more; nothing seemed out of place. She removed a communications unit from her back pack, pushed a button through various sequences and waited for a connection as she walked to the kitchen.

'Messaris.'

'Conan, there is good news and bad news,' Miller said. 'I would have contacted you a few hours ago, but I thought an old man like you would need your sleep.'

'How's my front line, special forces commando fairing?' Messaris joked.

'You make it sound military — nothing like that here.'

'What's the news?' he asked.

'The prime minister is close to relenting — it worked, you're brilliant.'

'How close?'

'Hours rather than days, and I would expect an agreement this morning, then an announcement once documents are finalised, possibly tomorrow or the day after.'

'No good.'

Miller frowned, shaking her head. 'Why? We have what we want — well, almost.'

'You see? I knew there was a problem.'

'No problems here. The other good news is that we don't need to close Melbourne, or Sydney for that matter.'

Messaris didn't respond.

'This is good news — we did it.'

'Let me think about it and I'll get back to you,' Messaris said.

'What's there to think about?'

'I have my needs and I want to see them met. If I can do that then we are all winners.'

'What needs? I thought Jimmy was paying you to do a job?'

'He is — I just need to think through a few things. I'll get back to you'

The high-pitched static of the communication link disengaging was loud enough to annoy Miller and she pulled the earpiece away. She sat at a stool, pondering the conversation, concerned there could be unknown forces influencing the government negotiations. Maybe Messaris was right — perhaps she did need to get a firmer commitment from the prime minister, otherwise, the advantage she had in this negotiation could be a complete waste of time.

A yawning Neesham walked into the kitchen scratching the back of his head. 'What's for breakfast?'

Miller didn't respond but watched him as he sat on a stool around the corner of bench from her. 'How well do you know Messaris?'

'Reasonably — why?'

'Has he always done what you've paid him to do?'

'He comes to me recommended when I used his services at Congress, but I don't know what he's done in the past. He worked for Koning at one time, I think.'

'Doing what?' she asked, curious.

Neesham was about to respond but thought better of it. 'Marketing,

I reckon.' He got up to fill the kettle. 'Do you want a tea?'

'There's something strange going on.' Miller watched as he worked his way through cupboards searching for cups or mugs before finding a stash in a drawer. 'Not sure what it is, but I think we may have trouble brewing.'

'Speaking of brewing — do you want a tea?'

'Yes, please,' Miller said. 'Where are you getting the money from to pay him?'

He ignored her and went about the business of making tea.

After a short time, she asked, 'indeed, where are you getting your money?'

'Why? Do you want some?'

Miller cocked an eye at him. 'How much have you got?'

'Enough.'

'You've told me everything about this deal, haven't you?'

Neesham was not facing her. 'Of course.'

Miller for the first time felt a stirring of anxiety about not being in control. 'You support what I'm doing, don't you?'

Neesham glanced at her and said with a wry smile said, 'of course.' He passed the mug of black tea to Miller. 'Little cousin, I can assure you, everything is under control.'

⁋

Messaris stepped out of bed, his feet a little sore until he began moving them, easing stiffness from his body before moving into the bathroom. The air-conditioning system was cranked up to twenty-five degrees, just the right temperature for him to keep flexible and ready for action. He flicked on the lights, turning the shower to a tepid warmth, then stepped in, washing off the night. Before he stepped out he switched the water to cold, allowing it to hit his head and wash the warmth away. When he felt the chill hit his ankles he stepped out, switching off the shower.

He towelled himself then brushed his teeth, considering the image before him. His skin was aging, the scars were not as masculine as they had once seemed. His neck gave away his age and he knew there was not much time left for him as a mercenary. Time to retire perhaps, that's what he encouraged McGuiness to consider when they thought through the raid on the banking system. Harebrained it may have been at the time, but he was just a few hours from at least trying to get the jackpot he hoped.

Messaris walked through to his room, banging on the connecting door to waken his neighbours, no doubt in the romantic embrace favoured by the young. He dressed in fresh clothes — a black t-shirt and heavy-duty cargo pants. Once he laced his boots, he walked through to the room next door without knocking.

'Come on you two, we have work to do.'

'We're set for tomorrow — no issues to be resolved today,' Tyrone groaned as he dragged a sheet over them.

'Change of plan, sunshine — we go tonight.'

§

Grobbelaar summoned cabinet to Kirribilli House for a late-morning meeting. They assembled in the dining room, some having flown in from Canberra, and nervous chatter flowed through the room as they tried to get an idea of what the sudden unscheduled meeting was all about.

Grobbelaar entered the room at eleven followed by Whittington and Hodge who took up their assigned places. There were two chairs left empty at one end of the table, closest to the door. The prime minister checked his notes and opened the meeting. 'Colleagues, thank you for attending at such short notice, I appreciate your consideration.' Grobbelaar paused for a moment to compose himself. 'It is my melancholy duty to inform you that the nation is under attack.' The room was hushed; he felt increased tension as all eyes focused on him. 'As you no doubt know, the attack on the energy grid has been well organised and continues to be a major threat to our ability to guarantee power supply.'

Grobbelaar paused and scanned his colleagues. 'Indeed, we are yet to determine the method the terrorists use to disrupt the system. We know they are hacking the operational software, but we have no evidence of the source of the corruption.'

'Who is doing this, Prime Minister?' someone asked.

'We have identified one person.'

'Only one? This is unbelievable. What are the police doing to protect us?'

Marilyn Hodge sat forward. 'We have initiated the terrorism response plan, but these activities we face have not been considered before, so we are flying blind. We are yet to detect how they are entering the energy grid; we have identified one person who is involved, and she is not interfering with the grid.'

'Unbelievable,' someone mumbled.

'Yes, it is,' said Grobbelaar, 'but there's more.' Grobbelaar swallowed hard. 'We have been advised, and this has been confirmed by our staff in Indonesia, that my daughter has been taken and is being used as a bargaining chip.'

'Outrageous.'

'Special Services are en route to Bali,' Hodge advised.

'What do they want?'

Grobbelaar peered around the table. 'This is why I've called you in. The terrorists are Aborigines, apparently, and have a list of demands. They want sovereignty, and they want all mining in Arnhem Land, particularly coalmining, to cease.'

The ministers seemed nonplussed — some scratched heads, others wiped mouths — no one spoke. The prime minister nodded to Whittington who took control of the meeting.

'We have come to an agreement with Jimmy Neesham, the administrator of the Karrakatta Congress and the manager of its Council of Elders.' Few ministers knew who he was, so Whittington pressed on. 'The agreement states that the government will consider the partitioning of Australia and the enactment of an independent state as a homeland for Aboriginal people.'

'Is this a joke?' a minister asked.

'We're not laughing, Roger,' Whittington replied. 'This is a very serious matter.'

Another extended silence shrouded the table.

'Let me spell it out for you,' Grobbelaar grumbled. 'These fuckers will continue to control the energy grid unless we agree to their demands. This means increased violence, such as we saw in Brisbane, and when they are done with Melbourne and Sydney they start another round of the country. Not only that, they now have five million followers on Facebook and a further million on Twitter, all supporting the endorsement of the United Nations treaty to end mining — in other words, if we don't act, when we go to the election next year, on those figures, we are rooted.'

'What the prime minister is saying, is that the threat is real, and we have no other realistic option for a satisfactory outcome other than this proposal,' Whittington said.

'Who is this hero who has us on our knees?' a minister demanded.

'Nellie Millergoorra,' Hodge replied.

'The terrorist jailed for blowing up a diamond mine? The one released not so long ago?'

'Yes, she's leading the assault and the negotiation.'

'Well, pick her up, throw her in jail and toss away the key.'

'It's a little more complicated than that,' Grobbelaar sighed. 'She's using my daughter's safety as her security. Until Marli is safe, then her safety is guaranteed, our hands are tied.'

'Surely, we can bring her in and strip her of her ability to communicate with her mates. This is crazy.'

Hodge grimaced. 'She's in the next room– with Neesham.'

'What the hell?'

'Exactly, Roger,' Grobbelaar smiled. 'Now you understand the dilemma we all have.'

Miller and Neesham waited together in the lounge, Miller fidgeting and pacing, impatient for news from the cabinet meeting, Neesham absorbed in a book he'd pulled from the shelf entitled *Australian Prime Ministers*. Miller sometimes glancing at her cousin, perplexed he did not share her anxiety.

'What's so damn interesting about those morons?'

'History.' Neesham never glanced up.

'What's taking them so long? It's been hours.'

'Who knows?'

'Do you think they'll agree?'

'To what exactly?'

'To sovereignty.'

'They won't agree to that outright, but they'll agree to a process to start discussions.'

'What about the treaty?'

'It's in the bag.' Neesham smiled, knowing he had achieved a significant financial windfall from the Chinese. 'There won't be any mining for at least ten years.'

'It's forever, that's what we want.'

Neesham glanced up and smiled at Miller. 'Nothing's forever, you know that.'

Miller gazed out over the harbour. She watched a large cruise ship sail toward the heads and wondered what life must be like holidaying on such a big ship in a vast ocean.

'How sure are you Messaris will call it off?' Neesham closed the book, checking his watch.

'I said I'd call when the deal is done,' Miller responded. 'He's all set to go tomorrow — that's what we told the media.'

'Did he tell you why he wants to close Melbourne?'

Miller paced the floor. 'Only that he has his own needs.'

'What's that supposed to mean?'

'I don't know, and frankly, I don't care, so long as we're done tonight, I can slip away and let you take all the glory.'

'Not sure they'll let you do that. They'll want to bring someone to justice.'

'Then I expect you to ensure that is not what happens. I'm not going back to jail, I can assure you.'

9

Grobbelaar fell back into his chair with a smile, pleased an agreement had been reached. 'Okay, well done everybody, this is great work — let's bring them in.'

Hodge came to the lounge and announced cabinet would like to finalise the discussions before moving to a formal agreement and asked if Neesham and Millergoorra would care to join them. Neesham stood striding to the dining room, but Miller hesitated then picked up her weapon, shoving it into her belt, before following Hodge to the other room.

'Come in, you two,' Grobbelaar waved them in, indicating seats at the end of the table strewn with documents and papers. 'This is Jimmy Neesham, the administrator of the Karrakatta, which is the United Aboriginal Congress of nations, and Nellie Millergoorra . . . now what do we call you, Nellie?'

Miller sat and stared at the prime minister. 'Your worst nightmare?'

Grobbelaar barked a laugh and fought to control himself. 'That's funny.' Back in control, he said, 'we have an offer for you to consider.'

Whittington took the lead from the prime minister and said, 'the government has agreed to sign the UN treaty declaring coalmining will not proceed in Arnhem Land.' Neesham discreetly pumped a fist, withholding a smile. 'This is on the proviso we have no further interruptions to the energy grid. This time we will not reconsider if you fail to comply.'

'We had two conditions,' Miller snapped.

'If the government has your assurance there will be no further interruptions to the grid and we receive detailed instructions on how you were able to hack the system, then we agree to moving forward on a process for establishing an Aboriginal homeland.'

Miller didn't respond. She watched the prime minister with a steely gaze, feeling her stomach tightening wanting to shout in triumph. Finally, she said, 'if we do this before television cameras when the deal is written, I will make the call to allow your daughter to contact you and you can make arrangements for her to return.'

Grobbelaar didn't respond. He couldn't let her see any emotion, he had to stay cool. More than anything, he wanted to see her jailed, but knew this could not happen, at least not right now. The thought of a terrorist ransoming the government and getting away with it rankled, but he needed law and order in the cities and wanted to reassure the electorate. Support was moving away from his government, and if he waited any longer it would be too late. He hoped this deal would save him.

Neesham smiled and stood, wanting to thank the cabinet before he made a few calls, but before he spoke Grobbelaar thundered at him, 'Jimmy, if these blackouts don't stop, I will have your balls.'

'The next one is planned for tomorrow night, Prime Minister; I'll make sure it doesn't happen.'

⁋

'Conan, the deal is done — call it off and have your colleagues allow the daughter to call her father tomorrow around midday her time.'

'The deal is not done until I say it is.'

'We have what we want, so call it off — no more shutdowns from tomorrow night.'

Messaris thought about his plans then said, 'I can reassure you, Jimmy,' there was a generous smile in his tone, 'there will be no further action from us after midday tomorrow. Macca will have the daughter call soon after, and then we will disappear. Ensure our money is in the accounts before midnight tonight, otherwise the deal is off.'

17

Messaris was keen for Simone to leave the group, given the secrecy of his grand plan, and arranged for her to return to Darwin and wait for them, arguing that she was too much of a distraction for Tyrone. They were now at the pointy end of their mission to pressure the government and this was his one chance to be rewarded so he could take few risks, and distractions were a huge risk.

She didn't mind leaving — even glad to get away — she felt anxiety building between the men. She was petrified of Messaris's erratic behaviour and the tension clouding him. She sneaked a brief quiet time with Tyrone to say goodbye and made him promise to meet her in Darwin. She was worried, and whispered to him to watch his back, little knowing he comprehended the dangers of working with his friend, Conan.

'According to the Reserve Bank's audit schedule, investigative programs end today, and we can gain credible access into the system tomorrow. Are you sure you want to do this now?'

'If we can do it tomorrow, what is the earliest we can get in?'

'Technically, any time after midnight.'

'How long will the window remain open for us?'

'You'll have thirty minutes before they generate their own power and block access. On the safe side, I would say you have ten minutes, max.'

'You're kidding me.' Messaris deliberated on his reducing options, wondering if the risk was worth it. 'How do you expect me to enter the building, get to the computer room and upload the program within ten minutes?'

'Not my issue.' Tyrone fell back from the screen, glancing over to Messaris. 'You always knew this would be a long shot. But, if you can get to the server and download the program then we could be wealthy men.'

'Are you sure this swipe card will get me into the building?'

'Simone took it off their system this afternoon, it'll get you in.'

'Okay, run me through the process again.'

The two men studied the floor plans once more, reviewing the server configuration and access points, considering contingency plans for the next two hours. They knew the security routine, the lift well entry point on the first floor, which would be easier than the ground floor doors; they understood the drop zone was between twelve and fifteen metres, and that was the best information they could find. They worked through procedures and exit plans — it was a long shot and Messaris knew it was risky, but, thought it worth it.

¶

Messaris left the hotel, crossing Collins Street, swiftly covering the fifty metres to the Exhibition Street corner. He jogged to Little Collins Street, ducking around the corner reaching the service lane which lead to the back of the building, pausing behind an industrial dumpster. He checked his watch: ten minutes before *go time*. Tyrone watched from the thirty-seventh floor and confirmed him rounding the corner, then sat at his computer preparing to switch off Melbourne.

As Messaris waited he could hear a rasping sound — someone snoring. He scouted the area around his entry point but saw nothing and settled back beside the dumpster.

There was a scratching noise.

'Gotta smoke, mate?'

Messaris glimpsed up to the dumpster and saw the top half of a head regarding him. 'No mate, I don't smoke.'

'What are you doing?'

Messaris glanced about and saw nothing, 'It doesn't concern you. Go back to sleep.'

'Not every day ya have company in a dark lane.' The vagrant was persistent. 'You up to somethin'?'

'Mate, listen to me — go back to sleep.'

'Gotta a dollar?'

'No, I don't.'

'I betcha ya do if I call the cops.'

'Mate, just leave me alone will you, please.'

'Give me somethin' first — what's in ya bag?'

Messaris stood up and was now eye level with the vagrant. 'Mate, you don't want to disturb me, so go back to sleep.'

'You keep checkin' ya watch — I reckon you're up to no good, mate, so once you go I'll call out for the cops . . . unless ya give me somethin'.' Messaris sighed and checked his watch; it was two minutes past midnight. 'See, I told ya — you're in a hurry. I knew it. Give me somethin' or I start yellin'.'

Messaris glanced about him, sighed, then, losing patience, unzipped his leather jacket, drew out his pistol and held the silencer against the man's forehead. He squeezed the trigger, lowered the dumpster's lid and crouched down, waiting for the power to drop out.

Tyrone was tapping his computer when the call came. He knew it was Messaris, so he ignored any pleasantries. 'They've installed a firewall and I'm having trouble. Should be good to go in about ten minutes.'

'Just hurry up for fuck's sake,' Messaris growled and shoved his telephone back into a side pocket. It was now twelve forty-five.

¶

'Nellie, it's Simone.' She arrived in Darwin, deciding to break curfew to call Miller. 'I'm worried about Ty and I don't know what to do.'

Miller was wide awake; sleep was not an option for her so close to the final resolution and announcement. 'Messaris assured me nothing was happening so what are you worried about?'

'He sent me to Darwin — told me I would be too much of a distraction if I stayed in Melbourne.'

'What are they up to?'

'I don't know, but I had to organise an activated swipe card for a building in Collins Street.'

'Which building?'

'Sixty Collins — I don't know who's in there.'

'You may be right, something could be happening, but I'm unsure you should be concerned about it,' Miller reassured her. 'We're close to resolving this treaty issue, the government has almost agreed to terms, we're just waiting for a formal document. I don't trust the government when they say no further action will be taken on me or the others, and they may begin rounding up everyone involved in this business. I'd rather you kept a low profile. Can you pack up a car and go bush?'

'To the house?'

'Tell no one, not even Tyrone, and take supplies for at least a week, maybe two. Get a bottle of champagne and I'll see you there in a few days.'

'You think everything will be okay?'

'Yes, but I'm convinced they'll try and take action against various people involved, which means you, so make sure you tell no one — and let me say again, that means Tyrone.'

'Okay. I'll see you in a few days — love you.'

'Take care sweetie — love you, too.'

g

'Christ, Tyrone, what's happening?' Messaris was now pacing the laneway, worried about the plan and whether Tyrone was capable of completing his part.

'I'm almost there. They've increased security and it's difficult getting linked to our code — the problem I'll have is not knowing how long the power will be off for.'

'You are kidding me!' Messaris barked. 'How long do you think we can get?'

'Best case two days, worst case two hours.'

'When?'

'Ten minutes I'd reckon.'

¶

'What's so important in Melbourne that your mate Messaris would be interested in?'

'Not sure, why?' Neesham replied.

'He's up to something. What building would be of interest in Collins Street?'

Neesham flicked open his iPad and tapped the address into google maps. 'Got a number?'

'Sixty something, maybe two or four?'

Neesham tapped in the address and a Thornbury address popped up. 'This is no good, how do I get a Melbourne CBD address?

'Try tapping in Melbourne 3000.'

He re-entered the address, this time with the post code. 'It's on the corner of Exhibition Street — as it happens the Reserve Bank building is across the road at sixty.'

'They don't have money at the bank, do they?' Miller asked. 'He's not after gold deposits, is he? Where are our gold deposits?'

'Not sure, maybe I should google it.' Neesham tapped in more information. 'Humph — the Bank of England have them.'

'Fuck me — do they have to have everything we own, those bastards?' Miller snapped.

Neesham ignored her. 'Why would he want to get into a building in Collins Street?'

¶

Messaris checked his watch — it was now two thirty and he could hear rubbish trucks doing their rounds. He felt his phone buzz and checked the screen — a message from Tyrone telling him blackout would start in five minutes. At six minutes the promised blackout began and Messaris was off.

The magnetised swipe card worked and Messaris eased the heavy fire door shut behind him. He scooted up the six flights of stairs in the fire escape to the first level and squeezed open the fire door. The corridor was pitch black. He clipped his night-vision goggles into place and moved to the lift well. There were three doors to choose from, hopefully none had a car at the ground floor. The cars were sent to a higher floor when the building was closed, but in the first lift well the car was at ground level. Messaris poked his head further in and surveyed the other lift wells, seeing door three was clear. He hastily jimmied the doors open and thrust in a wedge to keep them in place. He assembled his abseil anchor and, once the pullies and ropes were in place, positioned himself.

He was four minutes into his mission.

Avoiding the central cables he leapt off into the void, passing the ground-level doors, lowering himself past the two car-park doorways and into the basement. There was still twenty feet of shaft below him. Bracing himself using a foothold and his ropes, he extracted the jemmy from his pack and wedged it in between the doors, forcing them apart. He then fixed it against the doors prying them just far enough apart for him to squeeze through. Once in, he uncoupled his equipment and checked for the central server access point. Tyrone explained what to search for — an ordinary chair and desk away from the major server equipment.

He was at eight minutes.

Messaris spotted a non-descript workstation away from the other stations and headed for it. A blinking emerald light indicated there was power from a battery back-up and one touch of the keyboard lit up the screen. The computer wanted a passcode and he tapped in Tyrone's suggestion — he had four attempts to get it right before the system locked. The first didn't work, nor the second — the third didn't reject but the screen froze. Messaris couldn't believe what had just happened and thought through what to do. The fourth unsuccessful attempt froze access, not the third, and now he checked about for other options — perhaps another machine could do what he wanted. He scouted the other machines, but none had the blinking emerald light.

He walked back to the desk to check if the machine had got it wrong and was surprised to see the screen was black. He touched the keyboard again and the screen lit up, displaying he was into the system. He calmed himself with a few deep breaths. He'd been inside the building for thirteen minutes.

Deftly he drew the USB from his jacket, struggling to get it into position his arm hit the desk and he dropped it. He swept his hand across the carpet trying to locate it but couldn't find it. He fell to his knees and swept again, this time finding it wedged against the desk leg. He jammed it into the machine and pushed the keys Tyrone had instructed him to push, in exact sequence, and waited for something to happen. Again, nothing engaged — then an upload progress graph appeared racing to 96 per cent complete before stalling. Messaris waited.

It was now seventeen minutes since he'd entered the building.

At twenty minutes the upload was complete. Messaris tugged the USB from the machine, tapped the escape button and returned to the lift doors, climbed into his equipment and swung out into the lift shaft. Fifteen minutes later he was out on the lane, packing his equipment back into his bag, rounding the corners into Collins Street then crossing the road to the hotel. Staff advised him the way to his room was via the fire escape, but given he was on the thirty-seventh floor, they advised him to rest in the lounge until the power came back on. Messaris ignored their pleas heading for the stairs, regretting the decision at the twentieth level and needing to rest for five minutes at the thirtieth. The last seven floors took him fifteen minutes and he collapsed onto the bed when Tyrone let him into the room.

'I'm way too old for this sort of shit.'

'Neesham has been calling.'

'Thought he might. Let's pack up and get going. We need to get lost as soon as we can.'

'Any problems?'

Messaris thought about the homeless man. 'Nah — I got in on your third guess, then it was easy enough.'

'Did you close with the alt F6 sequence?'

Messaris hesitated. 'Sure.'

'Are you sure? It won't work otherwise.'

'Sure.' He wasn't.

'Then we are in.'

'When do you think we'll see results?'

'Once the emergency power is on, the system will cleanse itself and our program will be configured into the system. I suspect by tomorrow maybe, after tonights' clearing of funds, we may begin to see a steady flow into the account. We could even see results later today.'

'When can we get it?'

'It needs washing a few times, but I suspect within a week you'll have access to it.'

'In a week we could be in Europe with Macca and we can worry about what we do with it then. In the meantime, we are in the clear.'

'As far as the bank is concerned they won't be onto it until the next audit in a month, and even then, they won't raise the alarm, it's a clearing house. A cent a transaction fee is nothing to them because they don't have to pay for it, the transacting banks will be required to pay, and they'll just pass it onto their customers.'

'We get one cent per transaction on ATM cards and credit cards?'

'I would suggest a minimum of a cool five million should be in the account by the end of the month.'

'Do you think we should have made it ten cents?'

'They'd notice ten cents. How much do you need?' Tyrone was miffed with Messaris's greed. 'It could be more than five.'

'I just love this idea. You're brilliant, Tyrone.' Messaris held up his palm for a high five and his colleague obliged. 'Now let's get out of here.

18

The prime minister sat in a small, dimly lit alcove of Kirribilli's spacious lounge, where he had welcomed the many guests with whom he discussed affairs of state. Now he pondered whether he was doing the right thing by his country and, more importantly, if it was the right political strategy for his own career. He sniffed at a large brandy balloon in which a good cognac was mellowing.

Mary Whittington approached, sidling up with a gin and tonic in hand, the ice clinking as she took the large winged chair beside him. 'The PMC are putting together a formal agreement and should have it to us within three hours.'

'We wait,' Grobbelaar sighed staring into nothing, the burden of leadership draining him. 'I was just thinking, Whit, perhaps it's time for me to give it away.'

Whittington considered the prime minister, sipped her drink then said, 'Not sure why you would want to do that — you're still at the top of your game.'

'I need to spend more time with my daughter — I'm scared for her.'

Whittington patted his arm. 'We're doing our best to get her back.'

'Yes, I know that, but it doesn't make it any easier.'

'The country needs you right now, Rene; the party needs you.'

'It's moments like these that you begin to question whether it's been worth it.' The prime minister twirled his brandy. 'Losing Sonja was hard, but I cannot lose Marli — she's the reason I do what I do.'

'She'll be okay — trust the specialists.'

'This bullshit has affected me. I'm not in full control and it makes me nervous.'

'We are responding to the issue, and I think we are doing well considering the challenges we have.'

'I'm worried about Marli.' The prime minister took a large dram and swallowed hard, the alcohol biting his throat as it went down, as punishment for placing his daughter in danger. 'I should never have allowed her to go without security.'

'We'll have her back soon — a Special Services squad will be there tonight. They'll get her back, I can assure you.'

'Fact is, you can't assure me of that and I'm not certain if I'm doing the right thing by agreeing to this deal.' The prime minister cocked an eyebrow and glanced over to his attorney general. 'Why are we doing this for them?'

'The treaty will be fine; the government can revisit the decision in ten years. The sovereignty thing is nothing more than an agreement to seek an agreement, nothing more.'

'The polls have gone against us over this energy crisis and I'm not sure we can recover — I think I may have to resign as leader to turn them around for us.'

'That's nonsense, Rene. If the government responds positively to the treaty and the energy crisis goes away, the public will support us.'

Grobbelaar sipped his cognac. 'I'm not convinced. If a government can be manipulated as easy as these bastards have done, then we are always vulnerable to campaigns on any social issue.'

'Most campaigns aren't able to shut down the power grid,' Whittington said. 'Maybe we should have a greater awareness of what's important within the community rather than always focusing on the budget and economic performance — government is not just about balancing the books.'

'Perhaps,' Grobbelaar sighed.

'This will turn out as a historic decision we are making. It's time we put this whole guilt industry to bed, and at the same time provide a future for our First Nation people. You will be remembered for this.'

'Like Mandela?'

Whittington smirked, 'I would think de Klerk would be more appropriate.'

'No one remembers him — he ended apartheid, but the terrorist is regarded as the peacemaker. Go figure.'

'If we manage this properly you will be the father of Aboriginal sovereignty.'

Grobbelaar forced a smile. 'Not Millergoorra, or Jimmy the weasel?'

'I would not have thought so — maybe in their history, but not in Australia's, or even the world's.'

Grobbelaar smiled more broadly. 'I don't do this for the recognition, Whit.'

'Rene, we all have giant egos and if you can feed it with some recognition along the way, then why not?'

Grobbelaar sniffed. 'Would you like another drink?'

'I won't say no, thank you.' Whittington held up her glass as Grobbelaar clambered out of his chair. He glanced at his daughter's framed photograph as he passed, turning away, trying not to think about what she might be doing and if she were in danger.

The prime minister passed a clinking glass to Whittington, stretched his long weary legs across a leather footstool and slumped back into the corner of the winged chair. 'If we do this deal today, and we get Marli back, can we detain Millergoorra and charge her with terrorism?'

'Why would you want to do that? That may confuse our supporters.'

'She's created all this trouble, breached many laws and scared a lot of people, and I want to punish her. No one threatens me.'

'If you want a martyr for the social warriors to get excited about, then go for it. Otherwise, I would advise you just to let her disappear. Neesham won't involve her.'

'They're family.'

'And like any family, there are disputes — can't you see they have disagreement — they always seem on edge when I see them together.

It seems obvious to me, but I may be wrong.'

'No, I can't — they're as shifty as each other.'

'Neesham wants the treaty signed, it's Millergoorra who wants the homeland.'

Grobbelaar raised a leg then dropped it frustrated. 'Stuff this homeland idea. Do we need to go through this charade?'

'If we seek agreement within the parliament to take the idea to a referendum then the whole thing may yet fall over. If parliament approves the idea, Australians won't, I'm confident of that.'

'It rankles to even be talking about it, let alone agreeing to seek parliamentary support to hold a referendum on the issue.'

'Yes, but this may still be good for us,' Whittington sipped her gin, 'we will come out winners on this and the next election will be ours — what happens after that doesn't matter.'

'If one hair on my daughter's head is damaged by these people then everything is off,' Grobbelaar snarled. 'They'll get nothing. They can rot in jail.'

'Let's assume she's fine, for the moment at least — and if she is fine, then this deal will be good for us.'

Grobbelaar sniffed at his glass. 'Bullshit.'

Whittington persisted. 'Just think about this deal. We have no issue with the treaty, and we have sunset clause to do a review on it in ten years.'

'Make sure that it is in every form of communication. I want Koning to know there may be an opportunity for him in ten years — if he lives that long.'

'His company will still be here, so let's not worry about him.'

'He donates a lot of money to us.'

'Yes, yes, I know all of that, but the people are saying let's do the deal. So, let's do it.' Whittington paused, taking another sip. 'The real bonus is this idea of sovereignty.'

'It'll never work. They can't protect what they've got, so how do they expect to manage a separate state?'

'Who cares?'

'Perhaps those poor unfortunates living there?'

'Rene, just think about the pluses for a moment if the referendum ever does get up.' Whittington held up her hand and began listing off the political benefits. 'The guilt industry stops, or at the very least is diminished. The Northern Territory is partitioned and taken off our books. We avoid the demand for representation within the Australian parliament. We save heaps of money and we get big ticks from the international community.'

'It'll never pass the parliament.'

Whittington shook her head. 'Oh, I think you're wrong. I think the gutless opposition and the Greens will agree to the referendum, hoping the people knock it back. If they do, then the issue dies and never comes back, but if they don't and vote yes, then we can develop a great homeland for our people.'

'Not our people.'

'Yes, they are — we owe them.'

'You see — this is what I dislike about all of this,' Grobbelaar waved an arm. 'They had the place for thousands of years and did nothing with it. We come along and three hundred years later we are one of the world's best economies and a destination for folks who want to have a go. Yet, we are still required to feel guilty for coming here. Now we're being forced to give them their own country — I just don't like it.'

A door opened shafting light into the room and Matthew Roberts moved to advise the prime minister. 'Melbourne has closed.'

Grobbelaar didn't react, he just stared at Whittington with disbelief. She shook her head, saddened by the news. 'I have the defence minister on his way and a conference call with the premier and her emergency team is planned in fifteen minutes.'

'What is the response from our friends?'

'They remain asleep upstairs and I suspect they are unaware. Do you want to see them?'

Grobbelaar considered the request, gnawing his lower lip, gazing at his attorney general. 'It sounds like they might not have known this was going to happen, which is interesting. Let's meet first and then bring them into it.'

¶

The heavyweights of Australian politics charged with the security of the nation sat around the dining table for a conference call briefing from the Victorian premier advising them of the current state of emergency called for Melbourne. It was morning — the sun had not yet risen — but everyone was alert.

'It goes without saying that if you want me to assign troops then we could have five hundred army personnel in the city within four hours.' Grobbelaar glimpsed to his defence chief for confirmation and the general shrugged, nodding agreement. 'We don't want the same aggravation we had in Brisbane, say the word and we will place them on standby.'

The Victorian police commissioner responded. 'It's a little premature at this time, sir. We have our force on the ground and we are coordinating riot squads to manage any street demonstrations and violence that may erupt when the community realises there is no power. It's not the activists we are concerned about, it's the criminals.'

'We stand ready, if you need them, our special services are awaiting the green light.

'Prime Minister,' the premier interrupted, 'do you know how they are hacking into the system and can we reverse what they've done?'

'It's a good question, Sarah. Let me ask Marilyn to respond.'

The justice minister sat forward. 'We have identified their entry points into the energy manager's system and the national grid. We have closed further opportunities for them to re-enter, so this could be the last of their cyber-attacks,' Hodge paused for a moment, checking her notes, 'we are yet to identify the algorithm they have used on this occasion and we can't be sure when we can reopen the system.'

The prime minister interrupted. 'What's the best estimate?'

'We don't know,' Hodge replied. 'We are still working on it.'

The group discussed the crisis for a further hour before the conversation switched to what to do with the Aboriginal demands. The politicians wanted the agreement finalised the previous evening to stand but the prime minister and his security chiefs were more aggressive and wanted the agreement cancelled with the two sleeping beauties upstairs taken into immediate custody.

Matthew Roberts seemed to pitch the mood of the majority when he said, 'Prime Minister, the punters in Melbourne will be annoyed when they can't get their cup of tea this morning, but they won't blame the Aborigines — they'll blame you. They have indicated they want you to end the conflict with the First Nations and they expect you to make good the promise of reconciliation.'

'They haven't kept their end of the agreement,' Grobbelaar protested.

'It doesn't matter, the punters don't know that. The polls are telling us to do the deal.'

'Prime Minister,' Whittington interrupted. 'The UN treaty deal is a good thing and allows you to position our government as a guardian of the environment — so that's two wins for the price of one agreement. Plus, the referendum may not be approved by the parliament, let alone a majority of voters in a majority of states if it ever gets to the electorate, so let's press ahead with the plan.'

'We just keep Melbourne in the dark? That doesn't seem like a fair deal. Do you reckon it's a fair deal, Sarah?'

The premier surprised everyone when she responded. 'Of course, we want our power back on and we don't want civil unrest, but I have to say, I would agree that signing the treaty and agreeing to a referendum process to establish a homeland would be a tremendous thing for our nation. It would be wonderful.'

Grobbelaar sat with pursed lips, head tilted back as if in disdain. The others waited for his response. 'Okay, get the morons up and let's have a chat about energy security and getting the government back in control.'

Miller didn't respond to the shove in her shoulder. She was in a deep sleep, exhausted by recent events, and didn't take kindly to a second much harder shove. 'What the hell do you want?' She swung her arm out and dropped it over her eyes to protect them from the blazing lights in the room.

'You are wanted downstairs, get a move on.' The trooper showed no sensitivity; as far as she was concerned she was dealing with a terrorist who deserved zero respect. 'They are waiting for you; you have ten minutes.' The booted woman in combat fatigues marched from the room.

Miller dragged herself up, stumbling into the ensuite for a hasty wash before lurching downstairs. Neesham was waiting outside the closed door of dining room secured by the trooper.

'What's up?' Miller asked. 'I thought we were convening for media at ten?'

'It seems they want to discuss something to do with the deal — I don't know.' Neesham's shoulders were hunched as if he were cold, his hands thrust deep into his pockets.

The door swung open and the trooper snapped to attention, stepping to one side. Whittington smiled and invited them in. They entered the room as if preparing to see the headmaster. Their uneasiness increased when they saw uniformed personnel at the table alongside various other people they didn't recognise and sat as directed.

Grobbelaar stared at Neesham and then switched his gaze to Millergoorra before shaking his head. Neesham surmised there must be something wrong; Miller, on the other hand, responded with the force you would expect from a combatant.

'What's with the stupid face, Prime Minister?'

Miller brought Grobbelaar to the edge of his seat.

'You think this is a joke?' Grobbelaar replied.

'No, I don't, but you've been in pain for a few days — my people have been in pain for generations.'

'You made promises to the government.'

'And you have made promises for hundreds of years.'

'You haven't kept yours,' Grobbelaar snapped.

'Neither have you,' barked Miller.

'We've kept our promises,' Neesham joined the conversation.

Whittington said, 'Melbourne went off grid four hours ago.'

No one responded.

Miller held the prime minister's fierce gaze.

Neesham coughed and said, 'That's not possible. We stopped any further action.'

'The entire city and suburbs of Melbourne have been switched off by an incursion within the national grid and we have assigned troops to the street. We do not expect any of your people to give us any grief,' the general said.

'Wait up,' Miller was distracted by what she had just heard. 'The power is off? This isn't us.'

'Are you sure about that, Nellie?' Whittington asked.

'Pretty sure. We said we would stop the blackouts and that was our direction to our people.'

'Then you have rogue elements within your organisation who just put an end to the agreement we negotiated,' Grobbelaar stated. He paused, watching the two Aborigines. 'You have twenty-four hours — make the power grid operative and restore the security you have dismantled, advising us of your methods. And this must never be allowed to happen again. Are we clear?' He was seething.

Miller glanced to Neesham who shrugged, his eyes flicking about.

'Are we clear?' Grobbelaar demanded, raising his voice, slapping the table.

Miller returned Grobbelaar's gaze, increasing the tension around the table.

'Crystal.'

19

Driving is rarely fun for those on a mission, especially on long journeys with few rest stops with a need to reach a destination as soon as possible. Messaris's plan was simple enough — get to a safe place, cover tracks and begin to plan a life of retirement. Tyrone was happy to follow; Conan was the father he'd never experienced, the patriarchal leader he'd craved, and since a teenager he would do most things Conan wanted him to do.

They hit the road soon after Messaris' return, making good progress toward Adelaide, where the plan was to take a flight direct to Darwin. As they came through the Adelaide foothills Messaris switched on his phone and wasn't surprised to read the missed call messages roll out onto his screen. They were all from the same number, so he selected one flicking it onto speaker phone, so Tyrone could share the news.

'Where the hell are you. Call me when you get this.'

'She doesn't sound happy,' Tyrone laughed.

'No, she does not.' Messaris smirked. 'As if I care what she thinks.'

'Do you think it is to do with the Melbourne blackout?'

'What do you reckon?' Messaris laughed, opening a bottle of water, taking a gulp before passing it to Tyrone, who took a mouthful, keeping his eyes on the road.

'Are you going to call her?'

'I might when we get to the airport.'

'She must be going ape-shit right now.'

Messaris stared out onto the passing landscape. 'When are the lights back on?'

'Power should be restored this afternoon. That's all I could manage, sorry.'

'No need to be sorry, young man.' Messaris glanced across at him and smiled. 'You did well. I'm very proud of you.'

'Thanks, but without Simone it might not have happened.'

'What have you got planned for her?'

'It depends — if she wants to come live the life of a fugitive then she's welcome, but if not, I suppose we end it. Don't get me wrong, I want her to come, but if she doesn't want the hassle then so be it.'

'Money more important than love, is it?' Messaris chided.

Tyrone kept his eyes on the road but gave a wry smile. 'When you say it like that, then perhaps it does sound callous. She's been involved in this for a few weeks, and comes from good stock — she may choose to stay in the life she knows.'

'Not sure her association with Millergoorra would help her, the bitch.'

'Why are you so riled by her?'

'It goes back a long way; I should have ended it with her when I had the chance.'

'If you did, you wouldn't be in the position you are in now.'

Messaris smiled at his protégé. 'You're a smart kid, aren't you?'

'I learnt everything from you, old man.'

The phone rang, interrupting them, and Messaris checked the number. 'Ah, good news, this is Macca.' He stabbed the answer button. 'Hey Macca, how are you? Enjoying your holiday?'

'No holiday here. The natives are getting restless and want to go back to civilisation. How did it go?'

'Excellent, you are now a rich man,' Messaris smiled, 'I'm thinking you can begin to bring them back to the mainland, just let me check a few things first and I'll confirm it with you. Get to Darwin as quick as you can we then can plan our next move.'

'How much?'

Messaris's tone changed. 'Why are you always about the money? I just said we'll know further once we're back in Darwin — just give me a chance to finalise a few things.'

'I don't trust the kaffirs, and I'm not convinced Tyrone was able to get you in.'

'Oh, Tyrone got me in all right, and the job is done. Just relax, will you?'

There was an extended pause before McGuiness replied. 'Sorry sir, I'm just a little crazy dealing with these women. Get me out of here as soon as you can, will you?'

'Will do, I'll be in touch soon — see you.'

Messaris slipped his phone into his jacket and rested his head on his hand as he gazed out onto the coast as they began their descent into the city. Fifty minutes later they parked their hire car, returned the keys and settled into a café in the terminal. Tyrone opened his laptop and clicked his way to the bank account to establish if the program was working. Nothing was registered, sending an anxious jolt through him. Messaris joined him after visiting the restrooms just as their order was delivered, taking a generous hungry bite into the ham and cheese toasty.

'What are you looking so worried about?'

Tyrone hesitated, reluctant to share his news. 'It's early days.'

'What is?'

'The money transfer.'

'How much do we have?' Tyrone was mute. 'Come on, spill the beans.' Messaris took another bite and reached for his coffee.

'We have nothing — so far. As I said, we will know more after the overnight clearance.'

Messaris stopped chewing and gawked at him. 'You said the money would begin today.'

'I know what I said.' Tyrone snapped at him.

'You said we would begin clearing the money and there would be little trace of what was happening.' Tyrone stared at his computer screen. 'You said, it was easy money and we just needed a switch in the system to open the gate for us.'

'It's slow, that's all. I'll check further when we're back to Darwin. Until then, let's just calm down and wait.'

'Are you serious?' Messaris barked, attracting attention from other patrons.

'I won't know for sure until I can check the system, and I can't do it here.'

'Son, you had better give me good news in Darwin, otherwise I will skin your arse — literally.'

Tyrone snapped his laptop shut and sat back, head bowed, arms crossed, avoiding his glare. The food now seemed inedible and Messaris didn't appreciate being disturbed by a call. 'What the hell do you want, bitch?'

'It's me, Neesham. What's going on?'

Messaris eyed Tyrone as he moved to a quiet corner of the café. 'Everything's fine, Jimmy, we're all on board.'

'How come the power is off in Melbourne? That wasn't the plan.'

'It wasn't your plan — it was always my plan.'

'I don't know what the hell you're talking about, but I told you the government agreed to our requests and wanted the blackouts to stop.'

'Well, good for you, Jimmy, but I told you, I wanted a reward and Melbourne needed to close.'

'This is not about money.'

'What's it about then, Jimmy? Tell me.'

'It's about the treaty — that was the plan, to get the treaty signed.'

'Where are you with all of that?'

'I have agreement to block Koning for at least ten years, and the government will sign the treaty with that condition.'

'That means nothing to me.'

'I was under the impression you wanted Koning stopped?'

'Sure, that was part of it — I want what you have, Jimmy.'

'Which is?'

'Money.'

'I don't have any money.'

'I suspect someone is paying you, they always do. I want a piece of the cake.'

'You closed Melbourne, so I should pay you? I'm confused.'

'No dickhead. I closed Melbourne, so I could get access to my money.'

'Have you got it?'

'Yes, and now I will enlighten Melbourne again.' Messaris smiled at his joke.

'When can we expect the grid to reactivate?'

'We said two days. Why the rush?' Messaris was curious to know why Neesham was so desperate.

'We also said we would not do Melbourne, and I don't want Sydney going down.'

'I never said I would not do Melbourne, and you can relax about Sydney.'

'How long before you can get it back on?'

'Today.'

'When today?'

Messaris glanced across at Tyrone who was watching him. 'Expect it back on before midnight.'

'Can you guarantee me?'

'No.'

'I need this, Conan.'

'How much is it worth to you?' There was no response and Messaris smiled. 'You see, Jimmy, it's only ever about the money.'

'Just get it done.'

'I'll speak to my people and then perhaps you can speak to your people.' Messaris ended the call, moseying back to the table. 'I don't trust that little prick. He's in this for himself, I would bet my last dollar on it — are you talking yet?'

'I did my best Conan, it's not my fault.'

'Let's not talk about it until we get to Darwin.'

❡

The flight to Darwin was uneventful, full of backpackers seeking to find the hidden soul of Australia and a spiritual connection with traditional lands. Making a profit was Messaris' spiritual necessity and couldn't understand the need for Europeans to come in search of fulfilment.

The mood between the men did not improve by the time they returned to their rental, the last house in East Point Road, and as they drove into the garage, automatic doors welcoming them, Messaris was more forgiving to Tyrone. 'Mate, grab a shower and have something to eat, then let me know what the true position of the account might be.'

Tyrone didn't respond; he suspected the news hadn't changed and he would have to deal with an angry man later. He got out of the Range Rover, trudging into the house and straight upstairs to put silence and distance between himself and Conan. Messaris followed him into the house, ambling to the lounge with uninterrupted views of Fanny Bay. He dropped his bag and stretched. He'd had little sleep since his mission in Melbourne and now wanted to rest before thinking about the future. He moved to the bar in the corner, pouring himself a large whisky, plonking in three ice cubes from the bar fridge freezer, then flopped into the expansive leather lounge, taking a generous mouthful.

It wasn't long before Tyrone could hear snoring. He ventured downstairs for food and a drink before scooting back to his room. It did cross his mind to leave but he knew Messaris would find him and consequences would be worse, so he began to rehearse an explanation, although he was unsure if he would be able to provide one. He was frightened.

Messaris began to stir many hours later, picked up his glass of diluted whisky and finished it off. He struggled to get up from the couch before crossing to the bar pouring another, then sitting at one of the stools. 'Tyrone! Are you ready?' he yelled to the ceiling. 'Tyrone!'

'Coming.' Tyrone was on the stairs.

'What's the news, son?'

'There isn't any, I'm afraid.' Tyrone stood at the foot of the stairs. 'There has been no transfer of funds.'

'Does that mean there never will be, or is it just a timing issue?'

'I don't know.'

'What do you mean, you don't know.'

'Just that, I don't know.' Tyrone hadn't moved, anxious not to get too close to Messaris. 'There is nothing in the accounts, and I haven't been able to get into the bank's system, my algoes don't seem to work anymore.'

'What does that mean?'

'I don't know,' Tyrone almost pleaded.

Messaris scratched his head roughly behind his ear then wiped his neck before running his hand across his face. 'You don't know if we wasted time getting into the place? You don't know if the hack worked? You don't know if we will get any money? Which is it?'

'I don't know.'

Messaris rolled his glass in his hand, squeezing and then rolling it again. 'You promised me a pay day and now we have nothing?'

'I tried, but maybe it wasn't uploaded correctly.'

'My fault? You're blaming me?'

'I don't know. Did you log out correctly?'

'You little prick, how dare you blame me.'

'I'm not, it's just the algoes should have worked, so they may not have been uploaded properly.'

'These algorithms, which you set up, haven't worked?'

'I think so.'

'You think so?' Messaris screeched, pitching his glass across the room, stalking toward Tyrone. 'You say we will be rich and now you tell me we have nothing?'

'It's not my fault.'

'Then whose is it?' Messaris screamed. 'We need to do it again — but this time properly and we both go in.' He began to pace.

'I can't get us back in, they've locked us out of the energy grid.'

Messaris clenched his fists, stretching his fingers then clenching again. 'I can't believe this. This has stuffed me around too much, and now I have nothing.'

'We gave it a good shot,' Tyrone smiled, stepping backward toward the stairs.

Messaris charged Tyrone, driving him onto the stairs, then sitting on him as he slammed into him — not slaps, but hard punches to the head, to his ears, face and neck. Tyrone freed his hands trying to protect himself. 'Stop it — stop!' he screamed.

'We gave it a good shot? Well, how's that one? And this one? Good enough for you?'

The unrelenting beating continued until Tyrone stopped screaming, flopping like a rag doll. Messaris, panting hard, lifted himself off the young man, standing above him like a champion gladiator, then staggered off the steps, watching as Tyrone curled into a foetal ball and lay still.

'I don't know what you have to do,' Messaris panted, 'but make this better for me, otherwise what we have is over — do you understand?' There was no response so Messaris kicked him. 'Do you?'

'Yes.' It was a whimper.

Messaris checked his bloodied hands and walked through to the kitchen to wash them. The cold water washed away the blood and he checked his knuckles for any damage, there was none. When he returned to the stairs Tyrone was gone, the only evidence of the beating, pools of blood on the tiled stairs. He walked through to the lounge and sat at the bar with a generous slug of whisky over ice in a new glass. He sipped it, ran his fingers through his hair, then drained the glass and poured another. As he put the bottle down he picked up the glass, raised it to his lips, but then smashed it against the wall. His phone startled him, snatching at it, tempted to let it go the way of the glass, but he controlled himself and answered.

'The power is back on, thank you.' It was Miller.

'What do you want, bitch?' Messaris growled.

'Ease up will you. I'm just letting you know the government will be making announcements tomorrow morning. We did it.'

'Tell someone who cares.'

'What's up with you?'

'You and your fucking mates.'

'What's wrong?'

'I'll tell you what's wrong, lady,' Messaris began to pace in front of the floor to ceiling windows, 'I took the risks and you get the glory.'

'Hey, I'm the one who's in danger, not you.'

'Well, you'd better run, princess, because within the hour Grobbelaar's daughter will call him and you will be tossed into jail for ever more.'

'It's too early.'

'Like I said — tell someone who cares.'

'You can't let her go yet, the deal isn't done.'

'And right there is the reason it will happen.'

'We've come too far to end this now — we are close to the finish, Conan, you can't — it will threaten Jimmy, as well as me.'

'Put him on,' Messaris said.

Miller passed the phone to Neesham and he thanked Messaris for ending the blackout.

'Jimmy, remember when I said it's only ever about the money?'

'Something like that, yes.'

'Well, I don't have any.'

'I thought you said you had an arrangement in Melbourne.'

Messaris stretched and rested his hand high above him on the window. 'Yes, well — shoulda, coulda, woulda.'

'What do you want?'

'I want double what I was offered.'

'No can do — it's the original deal or nothing.'

'Listen here, you kaffir,' Messaris hissed. 'You pay me my money, or I end this charade in Sydney, and you and your butch mate can go fuck yourselves in jail.'

'Now how do you propose to do that,' Neesham said.

'I've just given the order to release Grobbelaar's daughter. She'll be phoning Daddy within the hour I would reckon.'

'You can't do that.'

'I will unless I get my money — you have thirty minutes to make up your mind, otherwise, the girl is released.'

'I have no money to give you.'

'Then get it,' Messaris ended the call, gazing out across the bay. 'Bastards.' He tracked back to the bar, grabbed another glass, tossed ice into it and covered the cubes with whisky. Then flicked through his contacts, prodding the call button, waiting a few moments before McGuiness answered. 'Macca, let them go.'

'What's happened?'

'Get back to Darwin as quick as you can.'

'What's happened?'

'We need to rethink our plans.'

'Tell me, what has happened.'

'We didn't get it.'

'Nothing?'

'Not a cent.'

'Damn you, Messaris, you and your fancy ideas.'

'Get back to Darwin as quick as you can.'

20

Neesham dropped the phone and laid back on the couch, his mind flicking through scenarios, considering the consequences of Messaris's call.

Miller watched anxiety creep across his face. 'What's wrong?'

'You've got to go.'

'Go where?'

'I don't care — if you stay here you'll be in a lockup before the end of the day.'

'Are you threatening me?'

'No, just warning you. Messaris is releasing the girl within the hour which means your guaranteed security will be gone.'

Miller swallowed. She began pacing around the room trying to figure out what had just happened. 'Why has he done this?'

'He told me he hasn't got his money.' Neesham glimpsed over to Miller. 'You'd better go.'

'What are you going to do?'

'I think the government will go ahead with the deal — it would cause them too much political pain if they reneged now. I'll stay and drive it through. You, on the other hand, are considered an enemy of government and I reckon once you lose your security they'll come for you.'

'I need a car — and money.'

'What'll you do?'

'Watch you take the credit for the agreement, and no doubt the accolades lavished upon you from a far distant place.'

'Don't be like that — we've achieved what we wanted.'

'What we wanted? You and your Congress of do-nothings?'

'We've been fighting for recognition for years and now we've got it, and you're worried about who gets the credit?'

'You don't deserve the credit — you just wanted the mining stopped, not a homeland. Now we have it — well almost — and already you take credit: the father of sovereignty,' Miller laughed.

'Success has many fathers,' Neesham smiled thinly at the thought, trying to hide his true feelings. 'You'll be rewarded.'

'This is the problem with you fucking politicians, you always think you have to give out rewards,' Miller snapped. 'Just keep them off my back for a few days until I find Messaris.'

'Why, what will you do?'

'Once I find where he is, I'll let the feds know.'

'He's in Darwin.'

'It'll take me two days to drive there so I may go to Brisbane or further north and catch a plane. Get me a car and money.'

'Where do you think I can get a car from?'

'I'll take one of those outside.'

'A minister's car?' Neesham chortled.

'Tell them I need to run an errand.'

Neesham checked his watch; it was ten minutes since Messaris's warning. 'All right, I'll get you your car, but you're running out of time. Maybe you should just stay here and let's negotiate a deal for you.'

'I'm not going back to prison,' Miller said. 'So, you'd better get moving.'

¶

Ten minutes later Miller was driving through the gates of Kirribilli House after Neesham advised Whittington she needed to pick up an elder for the official signing of documents the following morning. It was a flimsy excuse, but the attorney general was pleased to get Miller out of the house leaving behind her weapon and equipment; she was displaying signs of anxiety and Whittington was worried about her unpredictability. A convicted terrorist with volatile tendencies and a gun, might lead to a violent incident no one wanted.

As she drove the hill through the small, winding streets Miller considered her options. Her initial plan was to head to Brisbane and grab a flight to Darwin. She wondered if Newcastle would be quicker — it was less of a drive — but dismissed the idea. There would not be flights to Darwin by the time she got there. An option was to drive, but there was no certainty they would not begin chasing her once they knew she was heading north. Melbourne was an option, but she was playing with the idea of getting caught, so decided on the risky move of getting on the next plane out of Sydney. If she was quick she would be out of Sydney before the prime minister took a call from his daughter. When she saw a sign indicating an on-ramp to the bridge she took it and was off to the airport almost thirty minutes away.

Miller left the car, keys in the ignition, in the departure drop-off zone twenty-five minutes later, hurrying to the Qantas sales desk. There was no queue and she asked the male attendant where the next departing flight was going, and if seats were available. He advised a flight was just about to take off, bound for Melbourne, and a seat was available.

'I'll take it. When is the next flight to Darwin from Melbourne?'

'There is none with seats available, but if you wanted to get to Darwin today you could either wait three hours here, or you could get a connection from Melbourne to Adelaide. It means you will be in Melbourne for ten minutes and if you have no baggage then you'll be able to have a good connection once you are in Adelaide. Do you have baggage?'

'Nope. Okay let's do it.'

'You'll need to get your skates on and scoot to Gate 13 as quick as you can — they are boarding now,' the attendant said, collecting boarding passes for the three flights and finalised the sale by swiping a credit card.

Miller thanked him and dashed off to security, jumping past the folks dragging computers from bags and taking off jewellery to clear security scanners. A security officer interested in her fatigues asked her to step aside so he could pass a wand over her, but there was no reaction, so she was waved off and began running to Gate 13.

'Ah, Miss Neesham, you're the lucky last. We're now ready for take-off,' the purser said as she entered the plane.

¶

Jimmy Neesham strolled into the dining room to ask about progress on drawing up of documents, fifty minutes after his warning call from Messaris. The prime minister lounged at the head of the table, his feet resting on it, tapping a thick cigar into a saucer, a fug of smoke floating above him. The attorney general was studying documents with the justice minister, conferring over the same papers. The general, who sat at the other end of the table drumming his fingers, acknowledged Neesham with a small nod as he entered.

Neesham sat at his allocated chair and surveyed the activity. The two ministers were correcting documents before them, but there were fewer red markings than on previous versions a few hours earlier. 'Prime Minister, I see we are nearing completion and the plan for the announcement tomorrow is progressing as agreed.' Neesham glanced at the prime minister. 'To show good faith, we will release your daughter and her friends.'

Grobbelaar kicked his feet from the table, sat up and glared to the general, who straightened up on hearing the news.

'You're prepared to toss in your bargaining chip?' Grobbelaar queried, perplexed.

'She wasn't a bargaining chip — she was just out of communication range for a few days.'

'I got the impression her life was at risk.'

'When she soon rings, she will tell you no such thing happened, and no doubt confirm she and her friends had a magnificent few days diving on remote reefs off Bali.'

'You expect us to take no action?' the general queried.

'What you do with Millergoorra is up to you.'

The attorney general glanced up from her editing, 'She's no longer here, but will be back within the hour.'

'You let her go?' The prime minister was baffled.

Whittington straightened. 'She seemed agitated, and I thought it best she go pick up a Congress elder from western Sydney for tomorrow's formal signing.'

'You didn't bother to check with me?' the general asked.

'Why would I do that, General? You report to me,' Whittington snapped.

'I could call off the entire negotiation right now because you have nothing forcing me to continue,' the prime minister declared, climbing to his feet.

'Only your word, Prime Minister,' Neesham replied.

'Could you give us a moment please, Jimmy. I need to talk to my team.' Grobbelaar ushered him from the room, then sat in the chair vacated by Neesham, slapping the table, smiling. 'What a bunch of kaffir fuckwits. We can drop this whole charade once Marli calls me and I know she's safe.' The others said nothing, letting the offensive words fade away. Grobbelaar considered his ministers. 'Anyone?' he asked.

The ministers couldn't respond before the general said, 'Let's pick up Millergoorra as the first priority.'

'Prime Minister, can I just caution restraint at this time,' Whittington said.

'Restraint?' Grobbelaar raised his voice. 'Are you serious?'

'This is already playing out in the community.'

'It was happening because I was being blackmailed.'

'It was happening because the country was under threat and we negotiated a peaceful solution,' Whittington said.

'We negotiated under duress. We are no longer under duress, therefore we don't need a solution that favours the kaffirs.'

'They are First Nation peoples,' Marilyn Hodge chided. 'That word is offensive.'

No one spoke.

'We owe it to them,' Whittington said.

'What do we owe? They have contributed nothing to this country and we continue to pay them to do nothing.'

'A little harsh I would have thought, Rene,' the general said.

'They have recognition in the constitution, they have the Karrakatta, which reports straight to the government, which in turn reports to the parliament; they have their Elders Council — what more do they want? We spend billions on them — we've given too much already.'

'Prime Minister, let us be pragmatic about this,' Whittington said. 'You will have a spike in the polling once this is announced, I guarantee it, the people will think you're a hero. Now is the time to do this; everything aligns, and we will be in power for at least two more terms because of what we announce tomorrow.'

'That's rubbish, the great unwashed will forget about this hiccup in history before Christmas.'

'What we need are casualties,' the general offered. The others turned to him in surprise. He explained further, 'Let's arrest folks who caused the blackouts and throw them in jail on terrorism charges. Once we have secured a few casualties, waiting for their day in court, then let's go forward with the UN treaty and perhaps we can manipulate the referendum to fail — win-win.'

The prime minister glanced across to Whittington. 'Where's Millergoorra?'

'She said she would be back within the hour,' Whittington replied.

The prime minister's phone buzzed at the end of the table and Grobbelaar hurried to answer. 'Hello?'

'Dad?'

'Marli, how are you — nice to hear your voice, hon.' Grobbelaar glimpsed up at his colleagues, smiled and fist pumped.

'What's the problem, I have about six missed calls from you, are you okay?'

'I'm fine — I just wanted to hear that you were safe.' Grobbelaar glanced to the ceiling trying to keep his voice calm. 'Where have you been?'

'Oh Dad, the last few days have been magnificent. We've been diving and camping out on a small remote island off Lombok. It's an hour trip by launch and we left all our technology with the operator. They told us bad weather was coming so we arrived back here about thirty minutes ago.'

'What's the operator's name?'

'It's just a local, but he employed international dive instructors and guides and a South African security chap who seemed to know his stuff. We met him in a bar in Kuta, that's how we found out about the trip, and the cost was too good to refuse.'

'Are you okay — are you safe?'

'Yes, of course, Dad — stop worrying, I'll be home in about two weeks.'

'What're your plans now?'

'We are off to Seminyak — we want to go to Potato Head, we hear it's great. Hey, I've got to go.'

'Okay, gorgeous, nice to hear from you. Keep in touch, please.'

'Sure Dad — and stop worrying. Love you.'

'I love you too, gorgeous, talk soon.' Grobbelaar dropped the phone and plunged his head into his hands. Hodge stood and went to him, rubbing his back, patting his shoulder. 'What a relief. I can't tell you how bad I've felt.'

Hodge said, 'Rene, it's good to know she's safe — a great result.'

'She's been out diving on a remote reef — laughing and having a great time. No threats, nothing.'

'I'll call off the operations team if you like, unless you want them to search for her captors,' the general suggested.

'What are we going to do with them — charge them with providing university students a good time? No, I think the folks we need are in Australia. Millergoorra is the one head I'd like to put on a stake.'

'What about the treaty?'

Grobbelaar ignored Whittington as he walked from the room.

'Now what do we do?' she asked the others.

'We don't need a legal solution to this, we need a political response,' Hodge advised.

'We can have both.' The general stood, stretching his back. 'As I said earlier, we need battlefield casualties from the other side — that means we need Millergoorra and her merry men — even the anarchists who were in the streets, especially those who did all the damage in Brisbane.'

'We have little evidence of who they are,' Hodge sighed.

'If we get Millergoorra we may be able to link the others.' The general walked to the door. 'You can still do the treaty and promise the referendum, but it doesn't mean you keep your promises.'

Whittington stared into the papers before her and said, 'The treaty will give us kudos in the eyes of most of the public.'

The general glimpsed back at the ministers. 'The real operational benefit to this energy chaos has been our ability to secure the grid — it could have been way more serious if a more violent group was involved, so that's a good thing.'

Hodge smiled. 'That means, we are walking out winners and screw the Aborigines?'

'They get their treaty, which is what Neesham is fighting for, and a promise of a referendum for sovereignty, which Australians will never vote yes, not with so many racists running around. I'd say we've come out even.' The general opened the door and walked out, leaving the ministers peering at each other.

'Let's get this done and we can get home,' Hodge said.

Whittington smiled, 'That would be rather nice. I miss my kids.'

⁋

Tyrone was aching and bruised, his eyes puffy and discoloured, welts from the choke hold marking his neck, displaying Messaris's gripping fingers. It hurt to walk but he needed to talk with Conan. He grimaced as he stepped over his blood then shuffled to the lounge, where he was laying on the leather couch, a glass of whisky in his hand.

'I have news for you.'

'What the hell do you want?' Messaris responded without lifting his head. 'I would have thought you'd left by now.'

'I did think about it.'

'Well then, why didn't you? You and I have nothing to say to each other.'

'Are you sure? I have news you might like.'

'Nothing you could say could ever interest me.' Messaris wouldn't face him.

'Nine million.'

Messaris, his eyes closed, said nothing,.

Tyrone stepped closer but keeping a safe distance. 'Would nine million dollars change your mind?' Still Messaris didn't respond, but he did raise the glass, tilt it to his lips, sipping whisky before easing it down. 'I may have discovered Jimmy Neesham has more than nine million dollars in his bank account.'

Messaris's eyes flicked open, focusing on the ceiling before he sat up, turning to Tyrone. 'You look dreadful.'

'Yeah, I may have fallen off a bus.'

'Best you buy yourself a new ticket and get back on.'

'Neesham has more than nine million dollars in one of his accounts, five has been deposited over the last month.'

'How do you know?'

'I hacked his computer and played around with his files and found pass codes for various bank accounts.'

Messaris drained his glass. 'Why?'

'To see if he had the money to pay us.'

'It seems he has more than enough to pay us.' Messaris stood, a little unsteady, staggering to the bar.

Tyrone backed away. 'It seems he may have been paid off.'

'Are you sure? He claims he has no money.'

'Obviously, he has,' said Tyrone, circling away.

'Can you get access?'

Tyrone snorted. 'Is the Pope a catholic?'

'We take our money and perhaps a little more to cover expenses?'

'You can take all of it.'

'No, I think we should take our share — just the five million, plus expenses.'

'How much?'

'A mill for Macca and a mill for you.'

'What about Miller and Simone?'

'Fuck 'em,' Messaris snarled, then smirked. 'That's right, you already have.'

Tyrone winced as his face reddened, 'When do you want it done?'

'When can you get access?'

'Tomorrow morning would be the best time.'

'Then let's rob the bank tomorrow morning.'

¶

The plane to Adelaide was delayed twenty minutes, allowing Miller to think through options and consider if the government would be tracking her. It would not be difficult to identify where she was once they established she was travelling under Neesham's name. CCTV cameras were everywhere, and she worried they would find her before she got on her flight to Darwin. Her options were limited — she could only confuse them — she stressed about the federal police waiting for her in Darwin, or even Adelaide. What if they were watching her now? She decided it time to alter her travel plans and hide as best as she could.

She flicked open her phone and called Qantas, asking for a seat to Brisbane under the name of Simone O'Donohue. She paid for it, again using Neesham's card, and her flight was confirmed for take-off in thirty minutes. After finalising the call, she then reconnected with

Qantas and purchased a ticket to Darwin under the name of Mary Whittington, with a ninety-minute wait in Brisbane.

There was just five minutes before the gate closed for departure to Adelaide; as Miller scampered toward the gate she sidestepped into a sports store purchasing a wind breaker jacket and hat, discarding the plastic carry bag she was given, shoving them under her shirt as she continued her stroll to the gate. There were around twenty people still queuing for the flight and she joined them, with other passengers falling in behind her. She handed her boarding pass to the flight attendant for scanning then queued onto the flight bridge, where she stopped, allowing others to pass her. She dragged on the oversized jacket, tugged an elastic hair tie from her pocket tying her hair back tight, putting on the cap. A flight attendant stepped into the flight bridge. Miller explaining, she thought she was going to vomit. 'I'll get a later flight,' she insisted. She waited as the attendant went back to his computer to cancel the ticket, and by the time he had reappeared Miller was squatting, feigning too ill to stand.

'All fine, Miss Neesham,' the attendant said. 'I've requested airport staff come and take you to the medical rooms. You can wait in the gate lounge for them — would you like a hand?'

Miller feigned difficult breathing. 'No, I'll be fine — you go. Thank you so much.'

The attendant left her once Miller struggled to her feet and was making her way back to the gate lounge. She waited, checking until the attendant boarded, then with head bowed, walking smaller, she stepped out into the lounge, passing behind a wall of restrooms. Out of line of sight from cameras she reversed her jacket, fluffed out her hair, frizzing it, tossing the cap onto a seat, stepping out into the terminal corridor, marching like any other traveller. She headed back to the sports store for a further change of clothes and another hat.

She chose a Brisbane Broncos themed, two-piece leisure suit with hat and scarf ridding herself of camos in the change room. She credited the four hundred dollars to Neesham's card, stepping out into the causeway, heading for the exit. She would then check-in electronically in the departure lounge before re-entering through security.

She made sure to keep close to fellow travellers, not providing too much space, happy she could be fooling any searching eyes.

Thirty minutes later her flight to Brisbane was climbing to its cruising altitude. Four gin and tonics later, Miller was taxiing across the tarmac to the Brisbane terminal. Although feeling weary she remembered to keep her head down, staying close to milling travellers as she walked to the main terminal. Like Melbourne she checked in using a self-service kiosk. Once through security, she settled for a burger and fries for dinner, sharing a table with a young family, joking with the youngsters and engaging the parents in polite conversation. Luckily, the family was travelling to Darwin, so Miller stayed close without being too pushy.

When the flight departed for Darwin she relaxed for the first time since leaving Kirribilli House, some nine hours earlier. The flight was expected into Darwin just after midnight, she figured she could be at Messaris's safe house before one. Maybe Simone knew where it was. Her anxiety level increased as she thought through various scenarios, deciding to wait until daylight before confronting him. She didn't know what to expect or how he would respond to her, so daylight seemed a better idea and gave her a chance to pack her gear.

She ordered another gin and tonic.

21

--

Grobbelaar was slumped in his favourite lounge chair by a window when Whittington found him. A cup of tea sat untouched on a wooden pedestal beside him and he seemed lost in thought, gazing out the big window to the harbour where a new day was dawning, his head resting in one hand, legs propped on a cushioned foot stool.

The attorney general sauntered over, not wanting to disturb the prime minister if asleep, but he heard her approach, dropped his hand and peeped up at her. 'Come and sit, what have you got for me?'

'I want to discuss your plans for this agreement — are you set on not going through with it?'

Grobbelaar didn't respond, still gazing out onto the brightening harbour. 'I never get tired of that view — stunning at this time of the morning.'

Whittington distracted for a moment, following the prime minister's gaze. 'One of the world's best.'

'I've been giving these last few weeks some further thought.'

'What have you decided?'

'I want jail time for the morons who held us to ransom.'

'Neesham?'

'Not so much him, but Millergoorra and her pals, the ones who threatened us. I think it's important to be tough on this, otherwise we are inviting copycats and the media will be tough on us if we don't respond.'

'We'll pick up Millergoorra and try to identify the hackers. We still don't know if it was done in Australia.'

'What about the street agitators? They've caused angst, especially in Brisbane and Melbourne.'

'That's a local police issue. We will help them round up the leaders.'
Grobbelaar didn't respond.

'What charges would you recommend be laid?' Whittington asked.

'The DPP can decide, but throw the book at them as far as I'm concerned.'

'Millergoorra could face extortion, possible kidnapping, coercion, terrorism, and no doubt breaching national security protocols. Her hacker mates could be charged with terrorism-related crimes.'

Grobbelaar nodded approval, watching as the Manly ferry steamed past. 'What do you think about this treaty and the referendum?'

Whittington shifted in her chair, thinking through responses. 'I thought we resolved this yesterday.' Grobbelaar didn't respond. 'I think the treaty abolishing mining is sound policy. It will provide you with political goodwill to argue for the projects we have planned in WA and leverage against any potential protests — to be honest, it's the right thing for the government to do.'

'Koning didn't seem fussed by it,' Grobbelaar said.

'He thinks he can get access to the deposits in ten years — he'll be long dead by then.'

Grobbelaar smiled at the comment. 'He thinks he's going to live for ever.'

'His company will, and his children may be easier to deal with,' she replied.

'I had dinner with his sons a few weeks back — they displayed similar arrogance as their father. Just the Boer way, I suppose.'

'Your family is Afrikaans, is it not?'

'Not that you would notice. They immigrated at the start of apartheid — they hated what was happening. They saw no future and relocated here. We are long past being South African, although my parents still salute the republic every year.'

'Which, the new one?'

'Christ, no — they still salute the republic, which was the Transvaal.'

'Surely, that ended before the twentieth century — the Boer wars ended it, didn't it?'

'Yes, but Afrikaners still dream of the homeland. My family has always celebrated significant events of Boer history. I remember my great-grandma instilling it into all of us kids: to acknowledge our roots and always be proud of who we are. When the Proteas come here for cricket they all support them, and they give me hell if they win.' Grobbelaar chuckled as he reflected on his memories.

Whittington licked her bottom lip, then gnawing it, said, 'A bit like Aborigines and their connection to country.'

Grobbelaar turned and smiled at his attorney general. 'Maybe.'

'Rene, these announcements will be huge. This may help to heal the angst and guilt we have endured for decades.'

'Nothing much happened after the apology — what makes you think this will be different?'

'This is very different because we are partitioning and delivering sovereignty.'

'The punters won't go for it.'

'They don't have to — just going through the policy development and preparing for the referendum will at least deliver two terms for us.'

'I may retire before then.'

'Your legacy will remain.'

'What happens if it gets up?'

'Then we'll establish a partitioned homeland and a separate, internationally recognised state.'

'Who pays for it?'

Whittington hesitated. 'These questions can be resolved, the point is, we will be the first to talk about it and we'll have the kudos.'

'It's about the politics for you, not the policy?'

'Rene, it's both — the left will never let us forget this bullshit, and if this is successful we can end it.'

'We can't ship them all to the Northern Territory, that's a ridiculous notion.'

'Not every Jew lives in Israel.'

Grobbelaar turned away, gazing out to the harbour and the yellow and pink sky. 'We just give it to them to do with as they will?'

'Yes, just like New Guinea.'

'Somewhat different, I would suggest,' Grobbelaar shifted in his chair.

'Yes, but similar, just like Israel, Singapore, India, and even Timor.'

'And, if they want the rest?'

'They won't.'

Grobbelaar eyed her with doubt and suspicion.

'Trust me, Rene, I'm from the government,' Whittington said.

He smiled and turned his attention to the increasing amounts of harbour traffic. 'Just get me some arrests.'

¶

Tyrone was up wanting to beat the sun to hack Neesham's account before the east coast monitors were focused on unusual money transfers. It would be difficult to launder transactions, but he was confident he could move it between various accounts five or six times before Messaris had access to the windfall. He would use the accounts he'd set up for the transfer of the Reserve Bank funds. The channels were open, and he would close them once the money had transferred through. He listened for Messaris hearing the snores of an old man afflicted with too much alcohol.

For a skilled hacker like Tyrone security walls surrounding most personal computers were not difficult to break. He deciphered Neesham's access code and password, allowing him into his everyday access accounts. From this entry point he found access into the trading accounts for the Congress, then translating various primary accounts to ascertain identity numbers and passwords for Neesham's very private accounts. He admired Jimmy's attempts to prevent hackers and anyone curious, but they were never enough; now, as well as Jimmy and his bank manager, Tyrone had access. It took an hour to figure out the transfer limitations to the accounts as the sun brightened his room.

He paused, thinking through how to take the funds, deciding to make seven withdrawals, transferring the cash into different accounts, passing it initially through the Congress's account, then into Jimmy's more practical trading accounts, before sharing it amongst the various international accounts he established. Twenty more minutes and it was done. He then re-entered Neesham's account to identify where the initial payment came from, but after a frustrating thirty minutes to break account numbers he gave up, accepting that it was too hard to crack for a reason.

'Must be a government.'

His fingers worked fast as he transferred seven million through various accounts before closing them, erasing any evidence of movement to another account. Anyone searching would find the money was withdrawn from an ATM and he used his favourites without security cameras in Indonesia, Spain and Japan, providing codes and algorithms to any interested investigator with evidence money had been transferred to other accounts using the ATMs in ten thousand dollar lots — when in fact it hadn't.

Tyrone walked down stairs a little after eight o'clock to prepare breakfast and organise a no doubt grateful Messaris a strong coffee.

¶

Kirribilli House was a hive of activity, with staff and media buzzing about preparing for a major announcement from the prime minister at eleven o'clock. Grobbelaar had refreshed and changed into a tailored blue suit, white shirt and bright orange and grey tie and was sitting at his kitchen bench with tea and toast prepared by his chef. He hadn't bothered with the papers feeling less anxious than he did twenty-four hours earlier.

Mary Whittington joined him. 'We found her and then lost her, I'm afraid.'

Grobbelaar sipped his tea. 'Take me through it.'

'She left my car at the airport and we confirmed she purchased three connecting flights to get to Darwin. We have her arriving in Melbourne, then boarding a flight to Adelaide; we had a team of police waiting for her in Adelaide, but when she didn't disembark on arrival the feds checked the passenger manifest and found she was a late withdrawal from the flight. We then checked camera footage in Melbourne and identified her boarding, then observed a figure we now believe is Millergoorra leaving the aircraft entry point ten minutes later. She didn't get on.'

'Is she still in Melbourne?'

'We don't know — we have a team searching the airport, but we are yet to identify her. We have nothing on cameras once she re-entered the terminal from the gate, but we continue to check. We believe she may have changed her appearance.'

'You think?' Grobbelaar snapped.

'We are considering options on how this may have happened, but it takes time.'

'What does Neesham have to say?'

'He disavowed her and denies any knowledge of what she was up to.'

'I need to point a finger at someone and have them taken into custody, and she's one we know. The shock-jocks will kill us if we don't.'

'Prime Minister, we are doing our best — it will just take time. We'll find her, we have good people working on it.'

'You had better find her — if you don't, it will cost you your job.'

Whittington paused, examining Grobbelaar's face for any empathy but was disappointed. 'Do you want my resignation now?'

'No, of course not. I want someone in custody for this crap that's had us running around like chooks with heads cut off.'

'We'll get her — trust me.'

'You're from the government, right?' Grobbelaar chuckled.

Whittington laughed with him before saying, 'Are you set for the announcement?'

'Yes — I've asked Lewe Koning to join us. I'm not expecting anything untoward, but it sends a positive political message if we have a corporate victim to answer questions about UN treaty sanctions impacting the future of mining. There won't be much sympathy for him.'

'It could be problematic. Are you sure you want to do that?'

Grobbelaar paused, tugging his nose before turning to Whittington. 'He's a trusted friend and he's doing us a favour ...'

'He's getting a deal.'

'... and it will be good for us in the electorate — mining getting slammed and the environment winning always win votes. We just need to hold our base.'

'What about the referendum?'

'I know the politics, but I think it could become a negative issue for us.'

'How so?'

'It could get up.' Grobbelaar grimaced at the thought. 'Then what would we do?'

'You make it happen and become the greatest leader in Australian history.'

'Even though I don't want it.'

'Referendums are the people's opportunity to give us their preferred decision — let them make the choice.'

'Fucking democracy.'

§

Jimmy Neesham stood before the bathroom mirror readying himself for the official ceremony. The single-breasted black suit sat easily on him and he tightened his green tie, staring back at his image. On the bench before him were takeaway tubs of ochre pastes ready for application. He took a red headband and tied it tight at his hairline, then flicked white powder into his hair, greying it further, brushing away any spills from his jacket. He dunked two fingers of each hand into a white paste and dragged them from the bridge of his nose across his cheeks to his ears. Dipping a finger back in the tub he then wiped it across his forehead, repeating the process to leave a thick white crescent line. He washed his hands and filled a plate with yellow ochre, rolling it around into a thick puddle the size of his hand. He pressed his hand into the mixture, moving it back and forth, then without hesitation pressed it to his face, for a few moments, leaving a vivid yellow handprint across his nose, mouth and jaw. He was ready.

After washing his hands, Neesham swung a full kangaroo-skin cape over himself, tying it across his chest. It was tailored for him, lined and made from more than one skin. If he was to represent five hundred nations he wanted to appear presidential, regal and traditional. He had thought about it for many weeks and saw no irony in the fact a Chinese tailor in Darwin stitched the cloak together for him. He was a probable new leader of a First Nation homeland and this was a new time — a new future. It was his time.

As he repacked makeup into his overnight bag, his telephone buzzed a message advising him to call his bank manager. Neesham left his bag at the top of the stairs and began to descend but Grobbelaar met him coming the other way.

'What the hell are you doing, Jimmy?' Grobbelaar laughed as he stopped to take in the entire ensemble. 'Are you going to a fancy-dress event or something?'

'No, I thought I would dress for the official signing.'

'Nice touch, the media will go crazy — see you soon.' Grobbelaar stepped past him.

As Neesham got to the bottom of the stairs he turned and called back to the prime minister, 'I'd like you to use my tribal name from now on, if you don't mind.'

Grobbelaar was on the landing and glanced over the balustrade. 'Whatever you say, Jimmy.' He guffawed as he moved off to his suite.

The exchange drove a dagger of anxiety into Neesham. He began to hesitate about his use of the formal regalia. As he entered the lounge, milling guests fell silent. Mary Whittington approached extending her hand.

'Mr Neesham, please come in, can I get you a drink?' Neesham didn't take her hand and she was embarrassed.

'I would prefer you use my tribal name.'

'Of course, what is it?' Whittington squeezed a polite smile.

'Yaarabyth Binagarrie.'

'Yaara . . .'

'. . . byth Binagarrie.'

'Yaarabyth Bin . . .'

'Binagarrie.'

'Yaarabyth Binagarrie. Nice one — what does it mean?'

Neesham gawked at Whittington. 'What does Mary mean?'

Whittington didn't respond seeming perplexed.

'Why do you expect Aborigines to know the meaning of their names when you don't know yours?'

'Ah yes, I see your point. Would you like a drink?' Whittington waved a steward over and Neesham took a glass of water from the laden tray.

'I must say you look fabulous and in keeping with the theme of the media conference.'

'This is the start of a new era for my people and I thought I would treat the occasion with respect — I hope you will.'

'You got us to the table with dubious strategies coercing violence toward the government and the community — I wouldn't be taking the high moral ground if I were you,' Whittington retorted as she swept away.

Neesham took the time to slip his phone from his jacket to call his bank, hoping guests would see he was busy and not accost him with patronising questions.

'Jimmy, thanks for calling,' the bank manager was quick to business. 'We've had significant funds transferred through your account today and we are required to report it to the federal agency, but I wanted to check with you first.'

'What funds?' Neesham was taken aback. 'Are you talking about the Congress's accounts?'

'Yes, and no. Money came through to Congress accounts from an investment account, and then immediately transferred into your personal accounts. Then, and this is what concerns us, almost as swiftly, amounts were transferred to various international accounts.'

'You are kidding?'

'No, I'm not. This is a very serious issue for us and we are under a legal obligation to report the movement.'

'I have no idea what you're talking about — what money?'

'Seven million dollars in seven separate transactions.'

Neesham needed water and slugging a large gulp. 'This must be a mistake. I don't have that sort of money and I don't have any accounts overseas.'

'What is rather damning is that the money came into the Congress accounts first, then transferred to yours, then you transferred the money out to places so far unknown.'

'Any idea who might have done this? Any details?'

'The markings related to the transactions are quite strange.'

'What are they?'

'Three of them are marked with capital cities, a fourth is marked Tasmania and the other entries are marked bonus.'

'Let me guess,' Neesham recognised a link, screwing his face. 'They were marked Perth, Brisbane and Melbourne.'

'Yes — any idea what it might be?'

Neesham didn't respond. 'What do you need from me?'

'I'm required to report this to AUSTRAC. I'm sure they will be in touch with you later today. As you know it's illegal to transfer large sums without formal notification or forewarning.'

'This wasn't me.'

'I suspect not, and we will try to confirm that by identifying how this was done and by whom, but I have to report it anyway.

It will be up to the government to respond — I just wanted to let you know.'

Neesham ended the call, switching on his private banking account app. He needed to check his nest egg for the balance. He tapped in his password, but it was rejected. He tried again, this time to ensure he made no mistake, and again it was rejected. 'Those pricks.' He tried once more with the same result. Then he tried again and used the word Messaris as the password, and he was in. He clicked his way to the balance of the account to find it seven million dollars less than the day before.

'Fuck,' he yelled, then realised others were staring at him. 'Sorry,' he waved his phone, 'bad news.'

¶

'Ladies and gentlemen, thank you for coming to this historic announcement.' Grobbelaar was standing at a lectern emblazoned with the Australian coat-of-arms on the lawns of Kirribilli, with Sydney Harbour in the background. Before him government ministers, local members of parliament, plus various dignitaries sitting in the morning sun on covered chairs. Journalists stood at the back taking notes, cameras positioned recording the announcement. 'We are here today to provide a better future for our Indigenous brothers and sisters, and I pay respect to the Cammeraygal people on whose land we meet today, and I pay respect to their elders past, present and emerging, some of whom are here today.

'I'm also honoured to welcome and acknowledge the Governor-General Sir William Cohen and Lady Cohen who have stepped across from Admiralty House for the occasion. I acknowledge the Attorney General the Honourable Mary Whittington and other cabinet colleagues. I also welcome community and business leaders and recognise Lewe Koning for attending this announcement. Lewe has been an integral part of this agreement and I thank him for his input. I would also like to acknowledge the attendance of Northern

Territory elder Yaarabyth Binagarrie.' Grobbelaar indicated to Neesham, setting off a frenzy of cameras. 'Yaarabyth will join us soon at the table to my left for an official signing of historic documents.'

❡

Miller was yet to contact Messaris and snuggled up on the couch in her apartment with a mug of herbal tea to watch the announcement in Sydney. She laughed when she saw Neesham in his skin cloak and painted face. 'Always the opportunist politician, Jimmy.'

❡

'Today my government will be announcing significant policy changes affecting all of Australia and more importantly the First Nation peoples, in particular their future generations.' Grobbelaar read the speech prepared, but paused, glanced up and going off script said, 'it's been a terrible time for our community, with the terrorist attacks on our power grid. The government was held to ransom to respond to the demands of terrorists determined to achieve their political ends by sabotaging the national energy grid. These terrorist attacks brought out the dregs of society and they waged war against the community, the police, and in the end the defence force. This was unacceptable, and we expect arrests and charges for those few Australians we have identified as ringleaders, and as we speak we are close to making arrests.'

Miller laughed.

'Ladies and gentlemen, the United Nations has little sovereignty upon the Australian people, yet it deemed it imperative we sign a treaty that would ban mining within Arnhem Land. We had already issued mining licenses and I want to acknowledge the graciousness of Lewe Koning in allowing the government to negotiate an outcome.'

❡

Messaris laughed when he heard the prime minister mention Koning's name. 'That prick has been shafting Australia and stealing its riches for years.'

'Just like we did with Neesham,' Tyrone smiled.

'Yeah — we should go pick up Macca.'

'Wait, let's go after this. What did Grobbelaar mean when he said they were close to arrests?'

'I suspect they almost have Millergoorra and your dropkick girlfriend.'

'Hey, ease up on the abuse, will you?'

'Don't worry, son, I'm joking; they have no idea who we are and I'm sure Millergoorra won't give us up. She better not.'

¶

'My government considered all options available to achieve a positive outcome and we determined a treaty be signed today.'

Grobbelaar smiled, nodding ever so slightly to Koning who knew what the prime minister meant, and it wasn't the words he was hearing.

'I am pleased to announce today my government will recognise the United Nations declaration of protection for northern Australia, in particular, Arnhem Land, and sign a treaty giving protection to these lands of our First Nations under the international recognition of culture and the continuance of the spiritual ownership of country suspending all future mining activity in the Arnhem Land region.'

A sudden burst of applause interrupted the prime minister, he smiled as he waited for the clapping to trail off.

'It is my government's intention to work with traditional owners to ensure their needs are met and we will do whatever we can to ensure their rights are protected. This treaty is a new era in the relationship between First Nations and the community of Australia. I call upon the Attorney General and His Excellency the Governor-General to step forward to sign and witness the documents.'

Neesham's phone buzzed a text delivery and he stealthily withdrew it from his jacket pocket, keeping it under his cloak. He peered at the screen: Congratulations, Mr Jimmy.

Grobbelaar sat at the table alongside the governor-general as photographers recorded the signing of documents. The Cabinet ministers gathered behind them smiling at the right moment before the signing of the three formal documents. Grobbelaar lifted one of the leather folders to show the signatures, prompting another burst of applause and whirring shutters.

Grobbelaar then returned to the lectern and waited until his colleagues were seated.

'Ladies and gentlemen, this is a day that will be etched in Australian history, for we are also making a second historic announcement, one that will recognise the culture and claims of our First Nation peoples.'

There was a sudden mood change within the audience as they paid closer attention to the prime minister.

'As the dominant culture in Australia for well over two hundred years, western civilisation has ignored the rights of the people who were here when Europeans first came ashore at Botany Bay. As a new country we did not recognise the sovereignty of those nations who were here before us and we ignored their rights and their culture. We enacted into law the fiction of terra nullius, thus ensuring the decisions made by governments for over two hundred years, the policies we introduced and the programs we established ignored the rights of the first peoples. We ignored their culture, their ancient history, and diminished their worth in our society. Governments and institutions tried to assimilate our first peoples; we signalled that unless you join us, there will be no future for you. We were ignorant, and we have failed them.'

Neesham listened, trying to contain his excitement.

'Our first peoples are more likely than any other group in Australia to have the poorest health outcomes, the poorest education outcomes, the poorest housing, and we continue to incarcerate them in greater numbers than ever before.

'The Keating government, last century, promised things would change with the introduction of native title after the High Court abolished the ridiculous notion of terra nullius. It was a fiction, yet the goodwill associated with native title has not born fruit as expected.

'The Rudd government apologised to the Stolen Generations, but many in the broader Australian community believed he was apologising for every poor outcome, when indeed he was not. On any measure, there were no improved outcomes after the apology and we have failed in our duty to deliver on expectations.'

The audience listened to the prime minister with a number of television channels interrupting normal programming by switching to live broadcast.

'There remains too much hate, too much distrust, too much disrespect, and too much talk with not enough action.' Some in the audience clapped but stopped when others did not join them. 'We have to do something that will provide a future and allow the great nations of our first people to reclaim their history, reclaim their heritage and reclaim their culture. It is time Australia provided them with a future that is theirs, not ours, and allow them to be masters of their own destiny.

'I have come to realise this cannot be achieved with recognition in the constitution, as it has not provided any improvement in outcomes since the referendum. Improvement cannot be achieved by throwing more and more money into programs without first addressing culture and heritage. We continue to refuse to address what Aboriginal people truly need, and I have learnt, and now believe, that what they crave is sovereignty over their own country.'

The audience appeared stunned by the statement, glancing about to others to confirm if feelings were shared. Heads were shaking while others nodded.

'World history shows us we can provide a future for the oppressed by giving them independence from the dominant culture.'

Grobbelaar paused for a moment to ensure everyone was paying attention and focused on him.

'Recognising we must act; today, I announce the establishment of a partitioned sovereign state that will become the sole autonomous responsibility of Aboriginal nations. This homeland will allow Aborigines to live in a state governed by Aboriginal people for Aboriginal people, with Aboriginal laws, Aboriginal economy, and Aboriginal culture. An Aboriginal society with full independence from Australia. It is proposed the Northern Territory will be partitioned to create a sovereign independent state, a homeland for the first peoples. My government will engage with Aboriginal leaders and the broader Australian community to fully debate the issues seeking approval from the Australian people by referendum of this partitioning.

'Our initial strategy is to offer advice and support during the transition leading to partitioning, and establishing a new nation, with the establishment of a representative parliament. We then anticipate this new elected body will set about building the government bureaucracy needed to assist in the construction of community infrastructure for the new nation.

'We will stand ready to support this new nation whenever they ask for assistance. The timing of transition will be negotiated with the Karrakatta and the Elders' Council once the Act of Parliament allowing the partitioning referendum is enacted. There will be much discussion and engagement for the parliament with the community using various parliamentary committees and public hearings. In goodwill, we will work in partnership with all Aboriginal leaders to ensure we deliver this historic change.

'Fellow Australians, it is time for us to recognise and accept our past with all its faults and provide a better future of which we can proud. It is time to stop the talk and the guilt of the past, and take pride in the future. It is time for us to do the right thing. It is time for us to establish an independent Aboriginal nation.'

The audience as one jumped to their feet and cheered. The prime minister smiled and after several moments waved them down.

'I plan to introduce government legislation for the referendum in the parliament within a week, seeking to conduct the referendum within twelve months, allowing a transfer of power within two maybe three years. I now call upon the executive director of the Karrakatta, Yaarabyth Binagarrie, to say a few words.'

Neesham rose then stepped to the lectern, welcomed with a hearty handshake from the prime minister, Grobbelaar using the moment to smile at the cameras and ensure the audience knew who was leading the decision. Neesham stood, head bowed, hands gripping the lectern as he waited to control his nerves.

'My people have worked long and hard to achieve this decision and with immense pride I represent them today as we enter a new era of our history.' Neesham paused and turned to the cameras. 'We are going home.'

22

Two hours after the announcement, when the celebrations had quietened, Neesham moved away from the dignitaries to a place where he could make a number of phone calls. He advised the attorney general he needed to speak to a few people and she understood that he might need to speak to elders of the Karrakatta, but he had more urgent business to attend to. His first call was to Messaris.

'You slimy bastard, how dare you take what's mine.'

'You told me you had no money, so when we found out you did, we were very surprised. We decided to take what you owe us, and you can continue to tell your truth.'

'I want it back.'

'Doubtful. You will never see us again.'

'This doesn't end here.'

'Don't promise something you can't deliver. You had your chance to provide for us, but you didn't. We did what we were asked to do and even more by organising the street armies. You, on the other hand, took a secret commission from we know not who, and decided not to share it with us. We took what we thought was fair. You have no evidence implicating us, and you've got what you want, but we can change all that if you force us to take action against you.'

'I want my money back.'

'You're dreaming, Jimmy. Enjoy the accolades, you've worked hard for them.'

'You will be hearing from me and the cops.'

'Yeah right — fuck off.'

The call ended.

Neesham considered his options and swiped his way to the bank manager to find out if the money was recoverable — it wasn't, at least not for a few weeks until they tracked it. He dodged the manager's questions about the origin of the funds, but he would be ready for any questions when the authorities decided to question him. International donations was the response he decided to use when the questions came.

He now craved massive retribution on Messaris but was hampered in what he could do, so he called Miller.

'What the hell are you dressed in cuz? Was it fancy dress?'

'I thought it would be appropriate for a historic event like announcing a homeland. Are you pleased?'

'I'm ecstatic and looking forward to working with you to get the right outcomes before the referendum.'

'That may not be possible.'

'What do you mean?'

'They want someone to punish and it seems it's either you, or the others.'

'Why not give up Messaris's mob?'

'You're the voice they want to shame and silence.'

'I got what we wanted,' Miller smiled.

'Yes, but they think you stepped over the line.'

'What are you going to do to protect me?'

'There's not much I can do — my hands are tied.'

'Tied around what — a bag of silver, you Judas?'

'They need someone — they've settled on you.'

'That's crap. Give up Messaris.'

'He got his money and he's long gone.' Neesham ran a finger along his jaw.

'Where did he get his money from?'

'I don't know, but I suspect it had something to do with the Melbourne blackout.'

'I knew there was something fishy about him.'

Neesham paused for a moment, choosing his words with care. 'You know he's closer to you than you think?'

'How so?'

'He was security at the mine you blew.'

Miller didn't respond.

'His mate Terry was the shooter who took you down.'

Miller couldn't speak. She felt a clenching ache in her stomach. 'You knew this?'

'I wanted to protect you, I always have.'

'You brought us together knowing they almost killed me?'

Neesham smiled, enjoying the intensity in Miller's voice. 'It's of no consequence now, he's gone.'

'I'll fucking kill him,' Miller snarled.

'Just remember the police are after you. Go bush, you won't find him.'

Miller tossed the phone aside, stood up from the couch and paced about her apartment considering what she could do. She picked up the phone, keying in a number, waiting for a response. 'Hello, is that you sweetie?'

'Nellie? Oh my gosh I have been so worried — where are you?'

'All's good, I'm in Darwin and about to come out to the house — are you okay? Do we need anything?'

'No, the larder is full and the wine rack is waiting for you.'

'You're so gorgeous, thank you for doing that.'

'Has everything been done — did we get it?'

'The treaty has been signed and even better than that.' Miller paused, enjoying Simone's anticipation.

'What? Tell me — don't tease me.'

'The government has agreed to a homeland and will hold a referendum within twelve months.'

Simone shrieked and Miller laughed as she held the handset away from her ear. 'I just have a few things to clear up and should be out there around one in the morning.'

'That is fantastic news — oh Nellie, what a win for you — for your people. This is amazing.'

'Yeah, it's not bad I suppose.'

'Not bad? You are kidding me — it's historic. Oh, I can't wait to see you.'

'I'll be there as soon as I can, I have the truck packed with supplies and I'm ready to go, I just need to do something. Have you heard from Tyrone?'

'The last I heard he was going to the safe house the boys used in Darwin.'

'Do you know where that is?'

'On the coast somewhere, let me think. It's a big place near East Point in Fanny Bay. I think the road is called East Point, oddly enough. Big white house on the corner — the last one.'

'Thanks, sweetie. Relax and I'll be there before you wake in the morning.'

'I won't sleep — I'm too excited. We have much to celebrate.'

¶

Messaris wasn't expecting a knock at the door and he wasn't expecting Miller. 'Millergoorra. Welcome — what can I do for you?' He stepped aside allowing her to enter the house.

'I believe you're cashed up and ready to do a runner?'

'Who's been telling you stories?' Messaris smiled, circling away from her — cagey.

'I want to know why you set me up?'

'I didn't set you up.'

'You let the PM's daughter go early — I call that a set-up.'

'You were getting what you wanted, and we needed to end the charade — you're here aren't you?'

'With little help from you.'

'What do you want?'

'I want transport out of Australia and money and that can't be traced to me.'

'How much?'

'I'm told you have enough.'

Messaris eyed her before responding. 'Do you want a drink? I'm just on my way to the airport, but we've got time for a drink.'

'I don't want to drink with you.'

'Don't be like that — we're friends.'

Miller stepped closer as he backed away to the bar.

'You don't mind if I have one?'

'Help yourself,' Miller said, as she considered what she needed to weaken her opponent. 'Terry about?'

'That's the reason I need to go to the airport,' Messaris poured a whisky, 'are you sure you don't want one?'

'I'm fine, thanks.'

'I just need ice, won't be a moment.' Messaris took his glass to the kitchen, 'have a seat.'

Miller sat at the bar, thoughts rushing through her mind as she considered various scenarios. She wiped her hands on her camo pants, repositioning herself on the stool, placing a boot on the floor. Messaris was swiftly back, rattling ice as he strolled back behind the bar, leaning on it, facing Miller.

'What do you really want?'

Miller didn't respond, avoiding his gaze, scratching for a plan. 'I want redemption.'

'Oh, come on Nellie — redemption for what, letting the girl go?'

'No, not really.'

'You want more money?'

Miller was silent, glancing about her, wiping her hands. 'No.'

'Then for what?'

'For you almost killing me.' The words had just got to Messaris when Miller grabbed the whisky bottle and smashed it into the side of his head. It didn't break, the thud was impressive, the force drawing blood from the battered flesh. Reeling, Messaris staggered and collapsed. Miller leapt off the stool kicking him in the side so hard he grunted as air was forced out. She raised the whisky bottle high above her head like a club and brought it down toward his head.

Messaris was stunned, but raised his arm, blocking the blow, sending the bottle flying. It smashed on the marble floor as he swept his leg across the back of Miller's feet, bringing her down. Before she was able to recover he was on her, punching her in the face and splitting her nose and lip. He gripped her hair and punched, and punched again, as hard as he could, hoping to break her jaw. Miller groaned trying to resist but one solid punch following another, Messaris's signet ring splitting her eyebrow spurting blood to the floor.

'Stop.' The cry came from behind. Messaris glanced up mid thump to identify the source. Tyrone was at the bar, a 9 mm in both hands aimed at Messaris.

'What the hell do you want?'

'I want you to stop.'

'Why — do you want her?'

'Stop, or I'll shoot.'

'I'm going to screw this bitch before I kill her. Let's do it together. It'll be fun.'

'I want you to leave her alone — get off her.'

Messaris summed up the threat and slid off stumbling away from the bar into the lounge. He wiped his face — blood masked much of it, his white eyeballs in stark contrast. His hand was covered in blood and he wiped it over his shirt. 'See what you've done to my clean shirt, you bitch.'

Miller struggled to a sitting position. She touched her eye to assess the damage. Blood was flowing from her nose and she spat more blood as she staggered to her feet.

'Get out of here,' Tyrone said, still pointing the gun at Messaris. When she didn't move, he added, 'Now.'

Miller shuffled from the room, holding one arm out in front and the other across her bruised chest. She got to the front door fumbling to open it. As she stepped out Messaris yelled after her, 'It ain't over princess.' He spat blood as he hobbled to the bar, 'What do you plan to do with that?'

'Oh, don't worry, it's not loaded — I couldn't find the ammo.'

'Bastard,' Messaris smirked. 'Just for that I am going to penalise you a hundred big ones from your bonus.'

'I don't want any money from you — I've had enough.'

'What the hell? What are you saying?'

'I've learnt a lot from you, but I think it best we part ways.'

'Why, because I clipped you around a bit?'

'It's not that.'

'What is it then? I thought we were good.'

Tyrone paused and placed the gun on the bar. 'I don't want to end up like you.'

Messaris smirked at him, wiped the blood from his mouth and picked up the untouched whisky, pausing before he took a mouthful. 'Fair enough.' It hurt to swallow.

'When you go to the airport I won't be here when you get back.'

'I shouldn't think you'd want to see Macca. He'd want to finish what I started.'

'That's my point — I'd rather go and do something else.'

'Let me stake you.'

'I don't want any money.' Tyrone stepped back and then turned to head upstairs, away from Messaris.

9

Miller struggled into the cabin of her Ford. When she managed to sit behind the wheel she gunned the engine into action and the heavy throaty roar could be heard streets away. Slowly, wearily, she clipped on the seat belt and as she waited for the pain to subside she dragged the phone from the console and punching in a number she knew off by heart.

'I believe you're hunting for me,' Miller croaked, glancing at her face in the rear-view mirror, turning away from what she saw.

'I wasn't expecting to hear from you again.'

'I'm sorry to hear that, I've always enjoyed our conversations,' she said as she juiced the engine. It roared, ready for action. 'I have some news for you.'

The prime minister clicked his fingers toward the attorney general and waved her over. 'This'll be interesting, go on.' Grobbelaar then put the phone on speaker, so Whittington could hear.

'I'm told you want someone for the power outages? I can give you a name and an address.'

'Why?'

'I want you to leave me alone.'

'You caused all of this.'

'It was Messaris, Conan Messaris — his idea and his people.' Miller coughed and spat blood through the window.

'Who is he?'

'He's a South African, just like you. He worked for Koning and that's why he planned this — he wanted to block Koning.'

'What's his name again?'

'Conan Messaris. He's the guy who shot me all those years ago at the diamond mine.'

Whittington glanced at the prime minister and shook her head, then said, 'That wasn't Messaris. According to your file the shooter was a chap called Terry McGuinness.'

'Yes, well that says a lot — he was the one who grabbed your daughter.'

'Where are they?'

'In Darwin — one is at the airport coming in from Asia, and the other is in hospital.'

'Which hospital?' Whittington asked, scribbling.

'I don't know.'

'Then how do you know he's in hospital?'

'Because I'm about to put him there.' Miller gunned the engine and engaged the gears, squealing the tires as it took off toward the white Range Rover reversing from the driveway of the white house on the corner. Messaris didn't notice it until it was upon him and the bull bars of the F650 Ford smashed into the side of the car.

23

Miller sat on the beach watching Simone enjoy the water. It was four weeks since her confrontation and she was still very sore. The eyebrow had been stitched but her eyes were still bruised. The warmth of the sun, the peace, the water revitalised her. Simone was fishing the way Miller had taught her, but she was yet to spear any of the small coral trout abundant in the cove.

'Come on girl, what's taking you so long?' Miller shouted.

'There's a whole bunch here but they're slippery little suckers.'

'Do you want me to do it?'

'If you want to eat you may have to.'

Miller stood, discarding her white cotton frock before striding into the water and grabbing the spear. 'Let me do it.' She dived under the water and disappeared. Simone was always impressed by the lung capacity of her friend. When she failed to appear after a minute, Simone began to search for any movement, but found none. Then behind her there was a splash. Miller staggered to her feet and plunged the spear into the water then withdrew it with a wriggling fish on the end. 'Let's eat.'

'That's impressive.'

'You have much to learn about nature and being able to feed yourself,' Miller laughed as she splashed ashore. She picked up her frock and walked back to the house. 'Do you want to do it?'

'I'm obliged to now.'

'Grab some leaves from over there,' Miller pointed to an evergreen plant with broad leaves, 'and take some trailers from the climber and I'll show you how to do it.' Simone ran, picking two leaves from the plant and snapping off a few creeper suckers before joining Miller in the kitchen. 'I'm going to have a shower first. Do you want to wait or join me?'

'Let's get washed off and then I can get dinner started.'

The water was refreshing and warm and they showered off the salt and sand from their day on the beach. Miller left the shower first and threw a towel to Simone as she turned off the water.

'Does life get any better than this?'

Miller smiled. 'I love this place — my soul is here.'

'I love that we are able to share it.'

'You don't miss Sydney and your man?'

'I will, but not right now.'

'Have you heard from him?' Miller asked as she vigorously dried her hair.

'Nope — although I was sent a text a week ago asking me to call.'

'Did you?' Miller came toward her with a pump bottle of moisturiser in her hand. 'Could you rub some of this into my back please?'

'Sure.'

Miller turned, cupping her hair, holding it above her shoulders.

'Have you ever been sunburnt?'

Miller laughed. 'Of course. Just because I'm brown doesn't mean the sun doesn't burn.'

'My tan is coming along.'

'No matter how hard you try, sweetie, you'll never be my colour.'

'Your skin is great.'

'For a woman my age, you mean — you cheeky possum.'

'No, I meant it's soft and supple.' Simone slapped Miller's bottom. 'Done.'

'Do you want me to do you?'

Simone blushed, Miller, embarrassed, added. 'I mean your back?'

'Yes, please.'

♀

The meal was sumptuous, and they laughed their way through a second bottle of wine, climbed under the mosquito net and collapsed. Nothing disturbed them until Miller shook Simone's shoulder, startling her. Miller placed a finger on her lips.

'We have company,' she whispered.

'Where — who?' Simone grumbled, trying to sit up and see what Miller could see.

'There's a boat in the bay. Could be fishermen, but we should be careful.'

'What do you want to do?'

'I want you to go to the high ground and stay there, no matter what happens.'

'What are you going to do?'

'Not sure who they are or what they want, so I'll decide when I know a bit more.'

'Why don't we go and see them together?'

'They could be coming for me — they don't know you, so, stay hidden. There's supplies up there, and a gun.'

'A gun? What am I going to do with a gun?'

'Try not to kill yourself — now get dressed and get going.'

Miller pulled on her camo trousers, a black singlet and boots.

Simone slipped out of bed, dressing in jeans, t-shirt and sneakers. She grabbed a bag, shoving a water bottle and food into it, preparing to leave. Miller hugged her hard, kissed her cheek and she left, following an overgrown path they had trodden together when they were setting up their safe place.

Miller watched her go in the predawn light, then trotted back to the kitchen, dragging a locker from under a bench. She clipped it open, removed the top layer of utensils to expose a false bottom, which she lifted out to reach a small arsenal of lethal weapons. She clipped on a belt, slipped a knife into the sheath, attached two grenades and checked her pistol before replacing it in the holster. The final weapon she chose was an AK47, which she checked, setting the safety before striding out toward the beach.

She kept to the thick foliage and watched the boat, almost one hundred metres from shore. There was no movement nor mooring lights. In the increasing clarity of dawn, she saw that it was a similar shape to a fishing vessel, but she still couldn't be sure. Miller waited, noticing what seemed like a large fish, perhaps a dolphin, in the water off to her right near the shoreline. The light was playing tricks with her eyesight and she strained to make out what it was. As it came closer to shore she could see there were two parts to it, then realised it was two people crawling toward the shore in what she first assumed to be wet suits. On closer inspection she realised they were dressed in water fatigues and heavily armed. Both had masks and small snorkels, which they discarded as they crawled over the sand toward the vegetation line.

Miller watched as they checked semi-automatic handguns. These folks were armed and dangerous, and Miller moved deeper into the foliage. She didn't recognise them and as the light increased she made out a third and fourth figure on the boat. She could hear muffled speech from the people along the beach, then they began creeping toward the house. She guessed this wasn't a friendly visit and trailed them using paths she'd known since childhood, watching the dark figures advance through the undergrowth.

The rainforest was wakening, the noise of a new day increasing from an isolated squawk to a chorus of twitters and calls. Hidden by the foliage, Miller watched as the visitors stepped stealthily up onto the verandah, weapons at the ready. They searched the building and, realising no one was home, straightened and seemed to relax. Miller moved closer to listen.

'She was here.' The accent was South African. 'I can smell her.'

The second man walked to the bed, placing his now ungloved hand in the centre. 'The bed is still warm, so she's nearby. Go and check for her truck. If it's still there, try and disable it, just in case.'

The first man hurried from the house, stumbling up the main path to check on nearby vehicles. The second man tugged at his rubber balaclava, freeing his head and face from the tight fit. Miller gasped when she recognised Messaris. He crept about the house picking up items and replacing them. He picked up the white cotton dress Miller had worn the previous day, studied it, then rubbed it into his face, before draping it over the back of a chair. He walked into the kitchen picking at the food left on a plate and finishing the small amount of wine left in a glass.

Various options flooded through Miller's head as she watched Messaris rummage through her house. She decided the best option was to sneak away and join Simone at the safe place on the high ground overlooking the bay. She moved back into the foliage and began to circle the house toward the obscure track leading away from the house. As she stepped through undergrowth a blunt forceful tap to her head stopped in her tracks.

'Where are you going, missy?' McGuiness shoved his handgun into her head. 'You'd better let me have that.' He reached in front and grabbed her weapon slinging it over his shoulder before stepping around to face her, his pistol still close to her head, finger on the trigger. 'Get moving.'

Miller stepped back toward the house and when she appeared on the verandah Messaris rushed out to greet her, punching her in the stomach. She collapsed to the floor, sucking in breath. 'How charming to see you again. I bet you're surprised to see us.'

Miller struggled to breathe, gasping for air as McGuiness lifted her and threw her into a chair by the kitchen table. As she raised her head he slapped her, knocking her from the chair. He dragged her back to the seat then stepped behind her, grabbing her hair, dragging up her face so she could see Messaris.

'I reckon you know this is not going to end well,' Messaris smiled as he dragged up a chair and sitting in front of her. 'I could have forgiven you for the scar on my head.' He touched it with a finger. 'I could have forgiven you for getting the better of me with your truck. You know, you almost killed me.' Messaris smiled as he glimpsed up at McGuiness. 'Thankfully, Macca here, landed early and saw the carnage. He got me out of that mess and saved my life,' he stared at Miller, 'but Nellie, what I can never forgive is you telling the government who I am and where I could be found. For this you will be punished, and if you see the end of this day alive, you'll wish you hadn't.'

Messaris reached behind him and withdrew a large hunting knife, held it in front of her face and then pressed the point on her right knee. 'It's time for you to make a decision, right now. Do you want to live or do you not?' Miller flicked her eyes to his face and he smiled. 'I need an answer, because Macca here will slit your throat right now and leave you to die a horrible death, or you can live. What's it to be?'

Miller tried to speak but could only make a strained noise as she fought against McGuiness' the tight grip.

'You see, if you chose life you will live until sunset and then we'll kill you. But before we do that, we'll have fun with you — the type of fun we're used to and we haven't had for a long . . .' Messaris dragged the knife along her thigh, swapped legs and dragged it back, with enough pressure to guarantee it hurt, '. . . long time. I know Macca here is keen to have his wicked way with you, and I can assure you he is not gentle like me.' Messaris leered at her, waiting for a response, wanting fear to wash over her. 'What's it to be — death with dignity or a short life like a dog?'

'I vote for the dog,' McGuiness said, in a strangled voice, excitement building.

Miller was ready. End it now, she thought. She stopped resisting and McGuiness snapped her head back, her throat now exposed and ready for the blade.

'You see, he wants you — just like he wanted your family all those years ago.'

Miller registered the comment and ran a scenario through her head. Not only were these pricks the security detail at the diamond mine, but they'd slaughtered her mob at East Alligator River. These were the men she hated all those years. She dragged her head forward and said: 'Live.'

Messaris sat back and laughed. 'Man, that is a surprise. I was sure you'd have chosen death with dignity. Well, fuck me.' He peered up at McGuiness and shrugged his shoulders. 'Let her breathe so she can speak.' McGuiness loosened his grip and the tension left her.

'You're a stupid woman, but I'm ready to have fun with you, you old hag — what about you Macca?'

'So long as I get to finish her, I don't care when.'

'Okay, then bring her up to the table.'

McGuiness gripped her hair, swung an arm around her neck and lifted her struggling from the chair, dragging her to the nearby table, leaning her against it, slapping her so hard she fell back onto it. He then grabbed her wrists and dragged her the length of the table and held her down. She resisted as best she could, but her head and face ached, and she felt numb. Still, she remained alert, waiting for the right moment.

Messaris stood beside her gazing down, like a surgeon preparing for the first incision. He unclipped her belt and yanked it from her. 'You certainly were packing. Grenades? What were you thinking?' He smiled as he dropped the equipment. He then gripped her between the legs, as if he were picking up a heavy bag, and squeezed. 'I bet it's been a while since you've had a man . . . hey, here's a thought — have you ever had a man?' His grip was tight, and his face leering in front of hers, hoping to see fear.

Miller spat, hitting him under his eye and he reeled back, wiping spittle from his face with the back of his hand. He leered down at her, licked his hand and then smashed his fist into her nose.

¶

Miller opened her eyes.

The nightmare was continuing but she might have missed some of it because her singlet was now shredded and Messaris was biting her breast. She screamed.

'Ah, good, you're back.'

Miller ran her tongue across her lips tasting blood. She just needed a moment and wondered if it would ever come. Messaris was now rubbing his hands over her breasts, squeezing hard, as if he was wringing out a wet shirt. He placed his knife tip below her nipple and pushed in. The skin resisted but then gave way to the pressure. Blood welled and he withdrew the knife. 'Oh good, we now have breast blood — you like breast blood don't you, Macca?'

McGuiness released a wrist, wiped up the blood with a finger and rolled it into his mouth. 'Yum.'

Messaris glanced at him in surprise. 'You like that, don't you?'

'It's been a while.'

Miller seized the moment, kicked and twisted herself off the table, breaking the hold on her wrist. Messaris clutched for her but she slid under the table, grabbing her belt as she crashed past his legs. McGuiness shoved Messaris aside trying to grab her, giving her precious seconds as she scrambled to the living room and dived over the lounge. McGuiness was not far behind and Messaris clambered after him. She rolled onto the floor, whipped her gun from its holster, and in one movement released the safety firing off five rounds, as McGuiness came flying at her, hitting him in the head and body. He landed with a thump on her, dead.

Messaris paused to assess what had happened. He couldn't see Miller until she struggled out from under his dead mate with the pistol pointed at him.

'Back off!' Miller growled, teeth bared.

'Wait, just a minute — relax.'

Miller fired a round into his knee and he collapsed, shrieking, trying to hold together the busted joint. She straightened and edged toward Messaris, still squirming and whimpering in pain. 'Oh, shut up, arsehole.'

'Why did you have to go and do that?'

'You killed my family.' Miller cocked her weapon.

Messaris gritted his teeth, gazing up at her. 'What?'

'Which one of you shot me?'

Messaris said nothing and Miller brought her boot down on his shattered knee. He screamed, and she released the pressure. 'Which one?'

'He did.' Messaris flicked his head toward his dead colleague.

Miller walked over to the corpse and struggled to flick him over, so she could study him. She gazed down, then emptied the magazine. As she walked back to Messaris she released the magazine and it slid out, dropping to the floor. She found her belt and reloaded her pistol, priming the breach, then stood above Messaris with the weapon pointed at his head.

'Please don't kill me,' he pleaded.

Miller studied him. 'You are pathetic. Tough when you have the upper hand, but now look at you — a snivelling coward.'

'I'll pay you.' Messaris was desperate.

'You haven't got enough money.'

'Two million — I'll give you two million, just don't kill me.'

'You make me sick.'

'Let's talk about it.'

'Nothing to talk about — I'm not sure how you evaded the police, but I suspect you'll enjoy prison.' Miller lowered the gun.

'You're not going to kill me?' Messaris began to sob.

'I wouldn't waste a slug on a dog like you.'

'That's a shame.' Messaris lunged at her, plunging his knife into her thigh then preparing for another lunge. As she raised her gun he whacked her wrist away, and the pistol flew across the room, out onto the verandah. Miller took a step, stumbled and fell. Messaris grabbed at her and she kicked his shattered knee. He yelped, absorbing the pain, trying to straddle her. She fought and punched but it was useless. He kept coming.

Messaris slumped on top of her. His weight and strength clamped her to the floor. He lifted his knife but Miller blocked it, holding it from her. Bloodied spittle dripped from Messaris as he tried to drive the knife into her. She jammed her forearm across his arm, raised her other hand and drove her thumb into his eye. He shook his head free of her but never released the pressure of on the knife.

'Wait — wait.' Miller said, panting. 'Let's talk about this.'

'Sssh, sssh, sssh, sssh, sssh,' Messaris hissed in reassurance as she brought her free hand in to resist his pressure.

'All right, you win — I'm sorry,' Miller gasped. 'I said you win.'

Messaris slithered forward, adding more weight through his shoulders. The tip of the knife touching the skin above her heart.

'Come on Conan, you're better than this,' she said now holding her breath, resistance fading.

'Sssh, sssh sssh,' Messaris whispered, as the knife entered her. 'Everything'll be okay.'

Miller watched the perspiration drip from his nose, defeated, and within moments her heart stopped.

24

Six months after the successful referendum approving the partitioning of the Northern Territory, re-elected Prime Minister Grobbelaar was concluding his Second Reading speech. He was introducing the enabling legislation for the establishment of an independent Aboriginal homeland state. He stood before the dispatch box in the House of Representatives, the galleries packed with national and international dignitaries to witness the historic event.

'Madam Speaker, let me finish by referring honourable members to the history of this parliament and the intent of many of its legislators to provide for our first people. I don't believe there was ever malice in the decisions of previous administrations, but there is an ongoing difference of opinion about outcomes achieved, which we must take responsibility.

'Since I entered the parliament, I have been a strong advocate for our Indigenous family, and over the years I have developed the idea of sovereignty and the establishment of a homeland.'

Mary Whittington, sitting behind the prime minister, glanced down, never surprised by politics.

'In recent years, I initiated the idea of the establishment of a homeland state for First Nations through my discussions with the United Aboriginal Congress, and although there was initial reluctance, we began working together to achieve the result we have today.

'We have in the galleries today many of the Karrakatta tribal leaders and elders, and I thank them for attending on this historic day. This is not the end of their fight for sovereignty, for there is much we need to do. We will work together to ensure the newest nation in the world develops and prospers. It is my pledge that this new country will offer all of the existing government services and we will ensure those who live in this new nation will not be disadvantaged and retain their citizenship of Australia.

'I also assure First Nation people who do not relocate to their homeland that they will retain full access to all government services and will not be disadvantaged if they choose to remain in Australia. In other words, our commitment to our First Nation people will not falter — we will do what we need to do to improve health and education outcomes, because we value our First Nations.

'Speaker as we move forward, I recognise the Secretary General of the United Nations in the gallery today who has guided us in the development of the legislation we have introduced today. I also recognise the Commonwealth Secretary General who presented an invitation for the new nation to join the commonwealth. The recognition and support for our newest nation is strong and is the realisation of the dream I had when I first entered the parliament.

'Let me assure all Australians this historic legislation will pave the way for Aboriginal people to once again determine their own future. The Australian government will not intervene, nor will we speak in any manner that undermines this new nation. We will provide support when called upon, provide resources when asked, as we do with every nation in our region. We wish you well and we look forward to Independence Day in two years. I move the legislation be read a second time.'

The members of parliament rose as one to acclaim the prime minister, which prompted the packed galleries to also rise. Cameras fired off as applause developed to cheers with a rousing three cheers for the prime minister. Grobbelaar beamed, waving, knowing these photographic moments would immortalise him and his legacy;

history would record him as the father of the new nation. His ministers surrounded him full of congratulations, wanting to share the photographic opportunity, apart from two ministers who stood to the side and were yet to join the exuberance: Mary Whittington and Marilyn Hodge.

¶

Neesham watched the parliament from the function room at the Northern Territory parliament building in Mitchell Street. The idea of partitioning the Territory was welcomed by most of the population, keen to rid themselves of Australian taxes and laws, and over regulation. The Indigenous peoples supported the idea, although they remained concerned about their own rights if cousins from the southern states flooded the new nation. They wanted protection from any possible invasion of Aboriginal nations, wanting their rights as traditional owners to stand, and their voices heard. Neesham laughed at the irony when he first spoke at the Karrakatta, addressing their concerns.

He strolled into Herbert Street and wondered if the settler lawyer would keep his street name. No doubt there would be a discussion about place names and he concluded this could be a contentious issue amongst the working group assigned to establish the new nation. As he crossed the street toward the Esplanade he pondered the name of the new nation and smiled as he considered the debates that would happen about a name and a flag. Statehood would be no easy task and he made a mental note to examine the process in Timor Leste when they had to deal with these crazy, but important issues.

The Karrakatta members were excited about sovereignty. Although they would have preferred the entire continent handed over, they recognised that would never happen and accepted the concept of a homeland. Speaker after speaker claimed they had raised the issue before and their mob had been supporting the idea for decades. Neesham claimed the idea, and recorded within historic minutes, that he had proposed the idea prior to Millergoorra being sentenced for terrorism. He claimed at the time that her actions were not terrorism, and that she should be recognised as a freedom fighter.

There was no further evidence of the idea being discussed until Miller had been released, but Neesham insisted he was the head negotiator in convincing the government it was time to address the concept of sovereignty. In hindsight, he was pleased to have dressed in traditional garb for the announcement; it gave him a national profile and he had been nominated as the first president of the nation. There wasn't overwhelming support for this idea, but Neesham knew what he needed to do politically to end up living in government house, which had been identified as the new presidential residence.

As he strode up the stairs to his office he smiled, recollecting the agreement he secured with Grobbelaar. The prime minister was to claim authorship of the idea in return for his support for Neesham's appointment as president. He just needed to get fifty per cent plus one support in the Karrakatta and his dream would be fulfilled.

He entered his office tossing his keys on the desk, walking to the sideboard, pouring himself a chilled water from the fountain. He turned back to his desk and jolted back. 'Don't you ever wait outside?' Neesham said, collecting himself. 'You almost gave me a heart attack.'

'Mr Jimmy, we are your friends, we do not wait outside.' Teo and another envoy sat in the high-backed leather chairs appearing like characters from a Bogart movie: white linen suits, bow ties and plastered-back hair.

'What do you want?'

'We wish to congratulate you. You have done what we asked in the past and we now wish to support your campaign as president of the new nation.'

'As I said, what do you want?'

'We want you to provide the Chinese government with mining and exploration rights for your new country, and we want you to overrule any veto by the Australian government.'

'I can't do that.'

'Not yet. We expect as president you are able to make such an executive order in our favour.'

'What do we get in return?'

'You get generous royalty, much more than the South Africans and Australian mining companies pay.'

'What else?'

'We are prepared to guarantee your anticipated tax receipts for ten years to ensure you have enough money and capital to build the government infrastructure you will require to service your people.'

'That's very generous of you, but what do you want?' Neesham asked with suspicion.

'We ask that there be no restrictions on what and how we mine.'

'We will not approve that.'

'Of course, but let me reassure you, we will allow Indigenous considerations and if we must meet environmental demands then we will. But as the Arabs have shown, this arrangement will provide significant economic growth for the population, raising them from long-term poverty, and unless your new government takes the Venezuelan route, your new economy will be a world leader.' Teo crossed his thin legs, picking at the crease on his knee.

'I don't have the authority to promise you anything.'

'You will, when you are president.'

Neesham sat back and considered the proposition for a moment. 'You can guarantee me the presidency?'

'Nothing in politics is certain, you must know that, but, if we know we can count on you when it comes to mining licences, then we have ways of ensuing you will get the numbers for your candidacy.'

Neesham rocked back in his chair, then sat up to the desk. 'What's in it for me?'

'President not enough for you, Mr Jimmy?'

'I have invested too much in getting the South African agreement annulled.'

'We invested five million — is that not enough?'

'That was used in getting the result you wanted — this new deal is different.'

'It seems you want more money, Mr Jimmy — is that it?'

Neesham stopped himself, then said, 'I have my needs.'

'You always have your needs, and we are happy to reward you.'

'How much?'

'We will pass ten million to you, and another ten when the deal is proclaimed.'

'Done.'

'But you will have to sign this document.' Teo extracted a large folded paper from inside his jacket. 'You will allow my colleague, Mr Teo, to photograph you and me as you do.'

'His name is Teo?' Neesham chuckled.

'We are all Teo.'

'Why this now?' Neesham reached for the paper and waited for his visitors to position themselves as he scanned it, stunned to see the payment amounts already within the agreement. 'You've never asked me to do this in the past.'

'You were not in a position of such power before, and we need reassurance you are with us.'

'You don't trust me?' Neesham smiled for the camera.

'Of course, we do, Mr President. We are your friends.'

¶

The fire crackled and embers flew when Tyrone tossed on a log of driftwood. It was developing into a huge beach bonfire and Simone sat and watched as the flames leapt higher. She had brought Tyrone to the bay, insisting on him lighting a fire. Nellie had often talked about fire and what it meant to her. Now, Simone wanted to come to the beach and let the fire release her from her grief and despair.

Tyrone supported her when she wanted to hire a boat and visit the bay, and they had shipped off from Darwin two days earlier, reaching Nellie's country late in the afternoon. He collected wood and built a small fire, but Simone insisted he build it as a totem. The fire now roared, sending flames high and embers floating away in the slight breeze.

'Are you okay?'

'Yeah, I'm fine,' Simone whispered as she watched the flames, wrapped up in an enormous woollen cardigan over her light clothes. She tugged her knees close. 'We can go soon.'

'Take all the time you need.'

Simone smiled and nodded, thankful for his understanding but knowing he could never understand why they were there or what she needed to do.

The sky was beginning to glow with the luxuriant pinks and oranges of sunset as she gazed out across the headland and recollected her safe place where she hid during the confrontation. She heard the gunfire and the voices and watched the boat move closer to shore. Two men had helped another on board then loaded what appeared to be a body. She waited as Nellie told her to do long into the day before considering it safe to venture to the house. She used the bushcraft skills she had been taught to stay low, blend in and become one with the land. It had taken her time but eventually she came to the house, wishing she hadn't.

Simone found Miller already under attack from the bush — insects helping themselves, flies feeding and a curious bird pecking at her thigh. She stepped into the house stiff with fear for what she would find and when she did find it, she collapsed, wailing the torment from her. Soon she found enough courage to go to Nellie. She was turning grey and her beautiful skin was cold as Simone stroked her face closing her eyelids. Buzzing flies drummed about her as she cradled Miller's head, weeping distress and sadness.

It took some time for her to recover and plan what she should do. She struggled to lift her friend, but managed to drag Miller to the bed, laying her in the centre with her hands crossed over her chest. Simone then cut the remaining clothes from her, discarding her boots, carefully bathing her body, cleaning insects from her wounds, wiping away any trace of blood. She brushed her hair and then caressed her favourite oil over her body — she deserved to look nice when they came for her.

Simone then covered Miller with a sheet and hauled the mosquito netting around to keep insects out. She lit all the candles in the house after circling them around the bed. As nightfall came the only bright light was from the mausoleum she created for Nellie.

The authorities arrived soon after eight next morning. Simone spent the night keeping vigil beside her friend's body, playing her favourite music, drinking her favourite wine. She didn't watch the paramedics take her away and could only provide the police with scant information, but she told them all she knew.

The government announced they had found the terrorist who had caused the community so much grief. They said she had acted alone, and came to a gruesome end by her own hand when confronted by authorities with arrest imminent. No one objected, no one cared — except Simone. She could do nothing to change the government narrative and when she heard Jimmy Neesham dismiss her influence on Indigenous policy she stopped caring. But now one last task needed to done.

She stood and walked over to Tyrone. He embraced her, sharing the love she needed. She stepped back, shook off her cardigan, slipping out of her singlet and shorts. 'Take these aboard, I'll be with you soon.'

Tyrone didn't speak. He collected the glasses, the wine and remaining food, shoved her clothes into a waterproof bag and waded back to the cruiser anchored just off shore. Simone stood before the fire, raised her hands to the sky as shown by her friend.

'Nellie,' she cried, 'I call upon you to tell me what I should do.'

She stood, hands held high, Tyrone watching as he backed out to the boat, wondering if he needed to do anything.

After a few moments, she reached down into the fire's edge and withdraw a blazing log the size of a torch and ran to the house. She thrust the burning torch against the cotton drapes that hung throughout the house, igniting them in an instant. Flames crawled up the walls and then into the roof. She opened the gas jets on the stove, tossing oil on the floor then ignited it. She smashed a vodka bottle on another section of the floor, torching it. She shoved the torch into the soft furnishings and anything else that would feed the flames. Then she went into the bedroom, gazed at the bed still clad in the decaying sheets from long ago. Struck by sadness, she tossed the torch into the centre of the bed where it smouldered before igniting, kicking flames high into the netting. She gazed at the burning bed then escaped through the shower recess before running back to the beach.

As she reached the water's edge she turned to watch the house now engulfed in flames, the dry wooden construction succumbing to the intensity of fire. She turned with an enormous satisfied smile to see if Tyrone was watching and waved, before turning back.

'Nellie Millergoorra, last of the Umbakarta people of the Yolgnu nation,' Simone yelled to the sky, her hands stretching to the sunset. 'I call upon you to rest safe in your spirit and be done with sorry business. I call upon you to take pride in your strength and your will to fight for your people, and be pleased that I, Simone O'Donohue, now acknowledged as Millergoorra in my heart, will honour and respect you for evermore. I declare that your country is my country, and together we will not allow others to enjoy what was once ours, and your elders.' She began sobbing, fighting back emotion as she dropped to her knees with head bowed. 'I miss you Nellie,' she glanced up, 'you'll be with me forever, here in my heart,' she touched her chest, 'and deep in my soul.'

Tyrone sat on the bow of the boat observing the fire, which now seemed out of control, careering toward the headland. He watched as Simone swam back to the boat, like a mermaid, glad to be alive. 'All good?' he called to her as she climbed the ladder, boarding the boat.

'Yep,' Simone smiled. 'It's done. Let's go home.'

FIRST NATION ACKNOWLEDGEMENTS

This is a work of fiction and respectfully used the names of various nations and clans within Australia, which are listed below as they appeared in the story for notation from internet research. Other names and meaning are listed.

Umbakarta   A fictional name. However, it is a homage to the Umbugarla language of Arnhem land, which is now, unfortunately, extinct.

Warrane   The Aboriginal name for Sydney Cove as recorded in a number of First Fleet journals, maps and vocabularies, was Warrane, also spelt as War-ran, Warrang and Wee-rong.

Karrakatta   The name is a concatenation of two Aboriginal words, katta meaning hill and karra perhaps meaning a bird, an edible root, or an orchid. It is the name of the Perth Cemetery where the authors' parents are buried.

Gadigal   The Gadigal are a clan of the Eora Nation. The territory of the Gadi (gal) people stretched along the southern side of Port Jackson (Sydney Harbour) from South Head to around what is now known as Petersham.

Tahuni Lingah   Tasmanian clan from the Huon River region.

Eora	There are about 29 clan groups of the Sydney metropolitan area referred to collectively as the Eora Nation. The 'Eora people' was the name given to the coastal Indigenous peoples around Sydney.
Kuku Yalanji	The Kuku Yalanji, also known as Gugu-Yalanji, Kuku Yalandji or Kokojelandji, are an Aboriginal Australian people originating from the rainforest regions of Far North Queensland.
Noongar	Peoples who live in the south-west corner of Western Australia, from Geraldton on the west coast to Esperance on the south coast. Noongar country is the land occupied by 14 different groups: Amangu, Ballardong, Yued, Kaneang, Koreng, Mineng, Njakinjaki, Njung, Pibelmen, Pindjarup, Wardandi, Whadju, Wiilman and Wudjari.
Kulin	The Kulin nation is an alliance of five Indigenous Australian nations in south central Victoria, Australia. Their collective territory extends around Port Phillip and Western Port, up into the Great Dividing Range and the Loddon and Goulburn River valleys.
Yorta Yorta	The Yorta Yorta, also known as Jotijota, are an Indigenous people who have traditionally inhabited the area surrounding the junction of the Goulburn and Murray Rivers in present-day north-eastern Victoria and southern New South Wales.

Kombumerri	The Kombumerri clan are one of nine distinct named clan estate groups of the Yugambeh people and the name refers to the Indigenous people of the Nerang area on the Gold Coast, Queensland.
Yugambeh	The Yugambeh are a group of Indigenous clans whose ancestors all spoke one or more dialects of the Yugambeh language. Their traditional lands are located in what is now south-east Queensland and the Northern Rivers of New South Wales, situated in the Logan City, Gold Coast, Scenic Rim, and Tweed City regions.
Tulgi-gin	The Tulgi-gin clan are one of nine distinct named clan estate groups of the Yugambeh people and the name refers to the Indigenous people of the Tweed area in the Tweed Shire, New South Wales.
Cudgenburra	The Cudgenburra clan are one of nine distinct named clan estate groups of the Yugambeh people and the name refers to the Indigenous people centered along the Logan, Albert, Coomera, Nerang, and Tweed rivers, Queensland.
Mooburra	The Mooburra nation is one of the traditional custodians of the land surrounding the Tweed River.
Turrbal	The Turrbal nation are people from the region of Brisbane, Queensland.

Jagera	Jagera nation are the Indigenous people who are the traditional owners of the territories from Moreton Bay to the base of the Toowoomba ranges.
Kirribilli	The name Kirribilli is derived from an Aboriginal word *Kiarabilli*, which means 'good fishing spot'.
Yaarabyth	Fictional name
Binagarrie	Fictional name
Cammeraygal	The traditional lands of the Cammeraygal people are now contained within much of the North Sydney, Willoughby, Mosman, Manly and Warringah local government areas.
Yolgnu	The Yolngu nation or Yolŋu are an aggregation of Aboriginal Australian people inhabiting north-eastern Arnhem Land in the Northern Territory.

AUTHOR'S NOTE

The history of Australia has many versions that require respect and understanding for the voices who claim to be historians. Like the history of the developing world, what happened in the past is often recorded by the dominate culture, without much acknowledgement for those who deal with loss of culture, language and land.

There are many examples within modern history where the conquering culture has either been defeated, retreated or given sovereignty back to the original peoples. In Australia we have taken a different perspective; perhaps driven by since proven legal fiction of terra nullius — the concept of *'no-one was here first'* — accepted as wrong by the High Court. This notion has pervaded government policy for centuries and disavows the need to correct previous government decisions. Native Title was seen as an instrument to right the wrong, but legal requirement does not provide reparation for loss of culture, language nor recognise history. In other words, the vanquisher remains the dominant culture for ever more.

Australia now drives toward a multicultural society, deemed by many to be a highly successful policy — where many immigrants have come from all over the globe to make this land their home bringing their culture, colouring Australia. Yet a gap remains; Australian history did not commence in 1788. We continue to ignore the sovereignty needs of the First Nations. Many would argue government policy has attempted to assimilate and prosper the lives of the First Nation peoples and, yes, there are many examples of success — but a cultural gap remains.

Culture, in particular indigenous First Nation culture, in my view, is worth fighting for.

ACKNOWLEDGEMENTS

This project is special and there have been many who have provided advice, opinion and perhaps wisdom about the text and the issue. Having a willingness to listen and seeking advice is never a bad thing.

I want to acknowledge the many young indigenous interns who worked within my office as a federal politician. It could not have been easy working for a conservative, but they played a vital role in the work they did for the community, and I especially recognise Millie Rundell.

Professor, Dr Brad Murphy and his lovely bride (sic), Jackie Beer have been very supportive, and I thank them for their advice.

Patty Kavadias, Trish Stewart, and Anne and Michael Keaney have provided valuable feedback as has Phil and Cate Barresi, Deborah Daly and Michael Tate. Greg and Anthea Pelgrave as always add much humour to my writing and my brother Peter continues to provide solid support as does Ashleigh Summers, a future politician. Denise and Paul Tyrrell provide great support and I am grateful for their promotional efforts.

I thank my colleagues at Yarraville writer's group for their willingness to provide suggestions and support. I also acknowledge the great work the Australian Society of Authors do to support novelists needing a kindly word. I encourage you to join your local writers' group and even join your representative body to increase the voice of authors.

I referenced the Steam Packet Hotel in the story, which is one of the oldest and best pubs in Melbourne, and acknowledge all the good folk lending an ear to stories extolled over a few cold frothies.

I also acknowledge the good folk of Williamstown who make the village the best kept secret in Melbourne.

I thank the many folks who contact me to discuss my work and I appreciate their feedback.

I want to thank 852 Press for the effort in providing support to an author wanting get the story onto bookshelves. The great Nan McNab used her editing skills to assist with development and I remain extremely appreciative.

The support I receive from my extended family and friends is terrific and I look forward to discussing politics with you all whenever we meet.

Finally, Julia, Anthony, Kaitlyn and Taylor provide many laughs, good times and support my writing, thank you.

ABOUT THE AUTHOR

As a political insider, Richard Evans served as a federal member of parliament for Cowan in Western Australia during the turbulent 1990s. He now specialises in writing political thrillers, writing about the exotic characters in the mysterious world of the Australian Parliament. He lives above a pub, opposite a church in the historic bayside village of Williamstown, overlooking the grand international city of Melbourne.

For more information about his other books, visit:

www.richardevans-author.com

BOOK 1 DEMOCRACY TRILOGY

DECEIT

A plane crash begins a sequence of events which leads corrupt Prime Minister Andrew Gerrard, after a long political career, to rush through legislation designed to secure his ill-gotten gains for his retirement. Stalwart — and soon retired — Clerk of the Parliament, Gordon O'Brien, sets out to foil the Prime Minister's plan with the help of investigative journalist, Anita Devlin.

O'Brien, a stickler for correct parliamentary process is concerned by the rush to legislation and becomes aware of various incidents, which by themselves would mean little but collectively shape a conspiracy to defraud the government.

The Clerk anticipates there is a potential fraud upon the government being enacted, he has run out of time and now must act. He forces the Speaker to resign and O'Brien takes her place, causing the parliament to prorogue, imposing a general election, preventing the fraud.

BOOK 2 DEMOCRACY TRILOGY

DUPLICITY

The Mercantiles, a long-established, clandestine group of high-taxpaying business owners have grown frustrated by Prime Minister Andrew Gerrard's failure to meet promises, and decide the nation needs a change of government at the upcoming election. They call upon experienced and ruthless political operative Jonathan Wolff to organise their election campaign, and defeat the prime minister.

Realising he cannot win the election his way, Wolff initiates an explosive campaign designed to remove the prime minister by defeating him in his own electorate using an independent candidate. Tapping into the communities' latent anxiety over immigration policy, the community is subjected to violent demonstrations, triggering increased racist attacks. Ironically, the candidate Wolff supports — and manipulates to drive the campaign against the prime minister — is Indian immigrant and university professor, Jaya Rukhmani.

Investigative journalist Anita Devlin is appointed by her editor to promote the Stanley campaign as the publishing owner, unknown to her, is a member of the Mercantiles. She discovers the nefarious Wolff strategically working the campaign, and endeavours to expose his influence and manipulation.

DOOMED

Three years after the change of government, the nation is facing huge social, policy, and environmental-related disasters yet the Australian government seems paralyzed on how to proceed. Two senior ministers resolve that a change of prime minister is essential for Australia's future, and begin to lay the foundations for his dismissal.

Meanwhile, the parliament is held in a balance of power by the independent, Jaya Rukhmani, who can decide at any time if government legislation will be approved. Upon hearing the news that former prime minister Andrew Gerrard wishes to re-enter parliament, Jaya turns to Barton Messenger as an ally.

Doomed takes us behind the scenes of a parliament unaware of how their ambitions and political manipulations affect the everyday Australian. When the environment and economy are brought into the mix, which will be the one to flourish, and which one is doomed?

Coming Soon